Dayko's Rime

Dayko's Rime

The Twith Logue Chronicles
Adventures with the Little People

Kenneth G. Old

and

Patty Old West

Volume Eight
Second Edition

Dayko's Rime
Copyright © 2018 by *Kenneth G. Old and Patty Old West* .

ISBN: 978-1-948282-91-8

All rights reserved.

No part of this publication may be reproduced, distributed, or transmitted in any form or by any means, including photocopying, recording, or other electronic or mechanical methods, without the prior written permission of the publisher, except in the case of brief quotations embodied in critical reviews and certain other noncommercial uses permitted by copyright law.

For permission requests, write to the publisher at the address below.

Poetry excerpts from Footprints in the Dust by Kenneth G. Old
Map of Lyminge and Gyminge by Rich and Lisa Ballou

The Twith Logue Chronicles
Volume 1   *The Wizard of Wozzle*
Volume 2   *Squidgy on the Brook*
Volume 3   *Gibbins Brook Farm*
Volume 4   *The Wizard Strikes Twice*
Volume 5   *Beyonders in Gyminge*
Volume 6   *The SnuggleWump Roars*
Volume 7   *The Secret Quest*
Volume 8   *Dayko's Rime*

Other books by Kenneth G. Old
A Boy and His Lunch
Footprints in the Dust
So Great a Cloud
Walking the Way

Yorkshire Publishing
3207 South Norwood Avenue
Tulsa, Oklahoma 74135
www.YorkshirePublishing.com
918.394.2665

*Ken spinning tales of the Little People
to children gathered on Sandes Hill*

Dedicated to the children who first heard these stories
at the boarding school in Murree, Pakistan.

Eagle's Flight

Better grasp at a flying star
Than seize the sweet fruit on the bough.
Better than walking tall, by far,
Is to soar with the eagles now.
When there is a chance to choose
There are things only birds can see.
Better by far wings than shoes.
Alas, earthbound mortals are we.
Better a child's mind set alight
With fantasy's call to be free
Than a hundred facts put right
To maintain its captivity.

Acknowledgements

Special thanks go to Margaret Spoelman, Patrick Wilburn, and Kim Dang for kindly making copies of the first chapters Ken sent by e-mail. Ken's creative genius generated more than would fit into one book. It was split and the second one also became too large and had to be divided. Eventually the story became twelve volumes known as *The Twith Logue Chronicles*. They chronicle the adventures of the Little People who are only half-a-thumb-high, from the time they are exiled from their homeland until they are able to return many centuries later.

It is with deep appreciation that I acknowledge the proof-reading skills of my three precious daughters, Sandy Gaudette, Becky Shupe, and Karin Spanner. They have spent endless hours reading and re-reading the manuscript to ensure there are no stray errors.

Finally, I must give credit to my dear, kind, considerate, thoughtful, and wonderful husband, Roy. His patient, loving, support has allowed me to continue the process of sharing these delightful stories with others.

Lyminge, Gyminge, and the Brook or Common

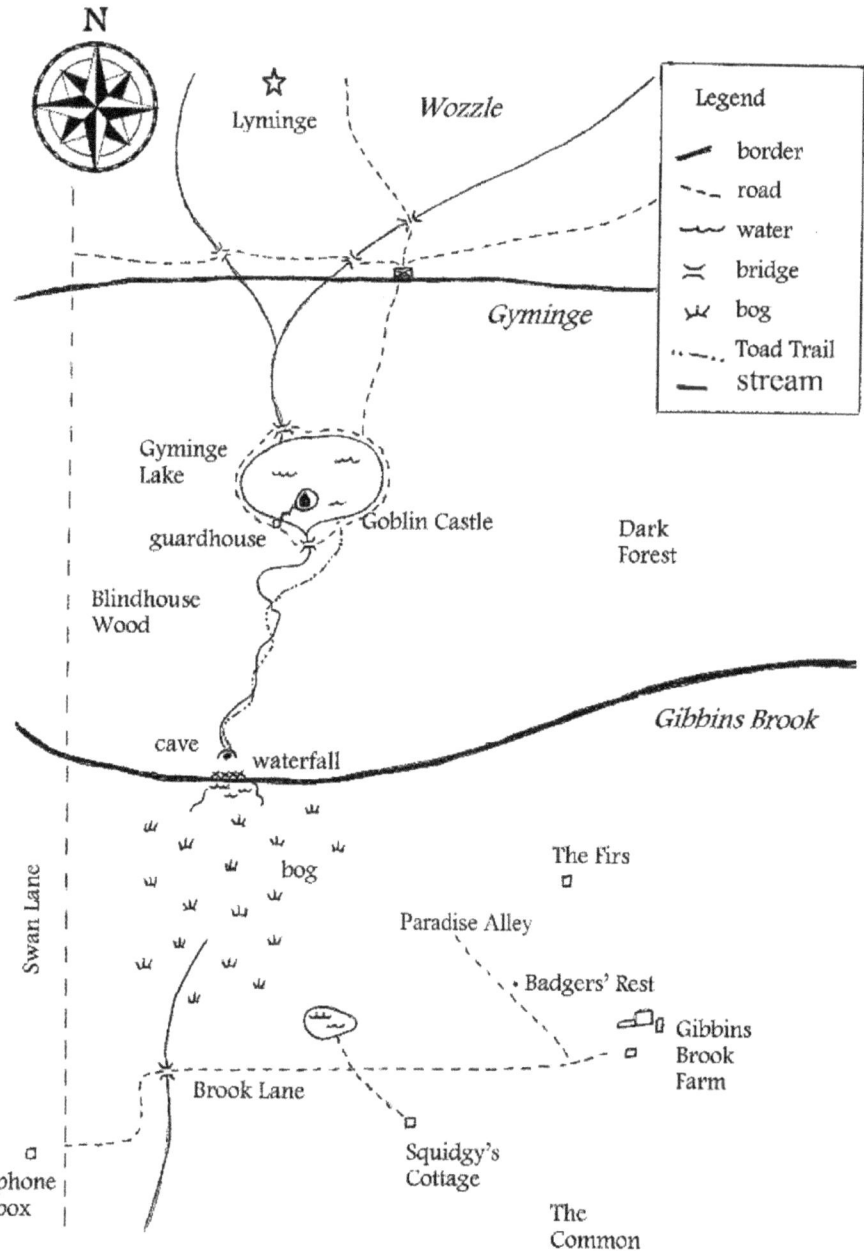

The Brook

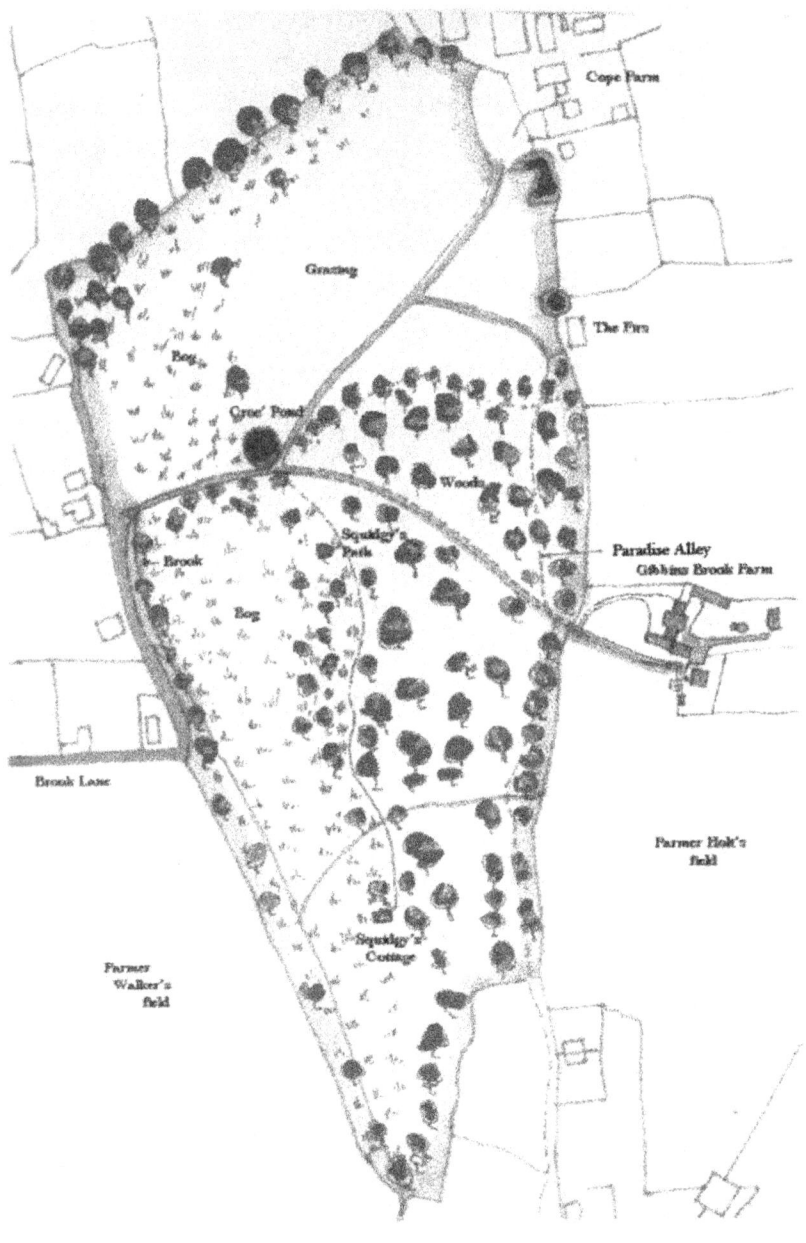

Preface

Gumpa loved to tell stories to children. It gave him a chance to be a child again himself. The Twith Logue Chronicles, which just means "Little People Stories," are fanciful, imaginative fairy tales that he told over a period of more than fifty years to children from ages five to fifteen. He just made them up as he went along, and the children always wanted to hear more. They would ask, "Will you please read some more out of your head?" The heroes of these stories are the Little People, only half-a-thumb high, known as the Twith Logue or just plain Twith.

When Gumpa retired, there weren't so many children around; so he began writing the stories to send to children. The stories are a mixture of reality and fantasy, and sometimes it is hard to tell where one leaves off and the other begins. I think that sometimes he didn't even know himself. The reality part is the old Tudor farmhouse and the surrounding area known as Gibbins Brook in Kent, England. The fantasy part is the Little People — Jock and Jordy; Taymar and Gerald; Cymbeline, her brother Barney, and her uncle, Stumpy. The adventures they have with Gumpa are where reality fades into fantasy.

In the first book, a boy named Griswold who lives in Cornwall learns how to do magic and becomes a Wizard. But he uses magic for wicked purposes and develops a twitch. It could have been a finger or a toe, but the Wizard has a twitchy right eye. He can change himself into almost anything as long as it moves and has an eye that can twitch. And that's his real problem because no disguise he uses can conceal the fact of who he really is. He delights in causing all kinds of chaos and confusion, but the twitch foils many devious plans conceived by his brilliant mind.

The Little People have their origins in myth and are far older than we are. They may be tiny folk, only half-a-thumb high, but they are very wise and know many things we don't. They can talk to animals and birds. They do not use magic, and they always tell the truth. Even though they're so small, they've managed to survive for many centuries. They live in the kingdoms of Gyminge and Wozzle, just north of Gibbins Brook.

The wicked Wizard decides to invade these countries and become their ruler. By the magic he learned a thousand years ago, he makes himself half-a-thumb high and conquers first Wozzle and then Gyminge. Many of the Little People refuse to be his subjects, so he seals them up in bottles. Those who agree to be his subjects are turned into goblins. The Wizard begins to weave an invisible curtain around Wozzle and Gyminge. Before he gets it completed, seven of the Little People manage to escape to the Beyond with their valuable Book of Lore and the Shadow Book, which contains the shadows of children who have helped in the past. They settle on Gibbins Brook.

The Little People have an ongoing battle with the Wizard of Wozzle. It was more than a thousand years ago that the Wizard invaded and captured their land. Now he lives in the castle in the center of Gyminge Lake with his raven, Rasputin. The invisible curtain around both Wozzle and Gyminge is to protect against invasion and prevent any more of the Little People from escaping.

For several centuries, the seven who escaped lived in Smiler's cottage in the woods at the south end of the Brook. Thirty years ago, they had to leave in a hurry. One stormy day, an old woman from Cornwall, Mrs. Squidge, flew in on a broomstick with her midnight black cat, Cajjer, and a strange beast she calls a SnuggleWump. She moved into the cottage and it's now called Squidgy's cottage. She met two of the Little People and told the Wizard about them. Until then, he didn't know where to find those who had escaped. Now he makes frequent trips from Gyminge into the Beyond attempting to capture them, and they have an ongoing battle with him and his allies.

The Rime of the ancient Seer, Dayko, has foretold that a Child will lead the Twith to victory. So the Twith send for children to help them.

The first four to arrive are Stormy and Bajjer from America, and Specs and Ginger from England. When it becomes apparent that the Wizard is planning a full-scale attack on the farmhouse at Gibbins Brook, other children are sent for. The first attack fails, but then the Wizard captures gran'ma and takes her to Gyminge Castle. As soon as the new children arrive, Jock, the Twith leader, takes half with him on an expedition to rescue her. The other half stay to guard the farmhouse under the command of Taymar, Jock's right-hand man.

The rescue team meets a woodcutter whose daughter has also been captured and taken to the castle. Together, they manage to rescue both gran'ma and his daughter, but he gets seriously wounded and Gumpa is also injured. The woodcutter is sent back to the Brook on Crusty, the golden eagle who managed to find his way into Gyminge through the hole in the curtain that the Wizard uses.

Having succeeded in dividing the Twith forces, the Wizard made an all-out attack on the farmhouse using all his goblin forces, Rasputin, Squidgy and her SnuggleWump. The foxes and the ferret joined in. All the other animals and birds on the brook helped the Twith. The children were ready for him, and he was soundly defeated. No longer is the Wizard clearly winning. At long last, the tide of struggle is changing.

The rescue team returned and there was a big celebration honoring Gran'ma. In the last book, the Shadow brothers, Bimbo and Bollin were sent to Gyminge on a Secret Quest. They were captured, but escaped with another prisoner nicknamed Scayper.

Just one more thing before we continue the adventures of the Little People. The Twith only have the weapon of Truth to use and will have nothing whatever to do with deceit. The children who want to help battle the Wizard must also always tell the truth themselves, no matter how hard that might be. Otherwise, they will put the Little People in real danger.

Now picture yourself sitting on Gumpa's knee or gathered with other children at his feet and listen as he puts you into the world of the Little People, challenging you to tell the truth and taking you into strange and exciting adventures. Enjoy the fun of Gumpa's overactive imagination.

The Brilliant Wizard

It's the second day after the Wizard's defeat at the farmhouse. Squidgy has brought him afternoon tea. The Wizard isn't happy. His head droops in despair, and he puts his hand against his forehead to support it. He laments, "The entire battle was a fiasco. My main weapon, the SnuggleWump, failed miserably. The coward ran away before the battle ever began. The goblin king is a mass of welts from hiding in the stinging nettles. All my crack forces turned tail and ran. Worst of all, my faithful companion, Rasputin, is missing."

He glances at Mrs. Squidge and silently moans, 'That incompetent woman failed to show up at all, and her batch of titchy teros was worthless. Fortunately, she's a reasonably good cook, but because her yeast buns have strange properties, I avoid them like the plague. Those are what caused such disastrous effects turning a lizard into a SnuggleWump and the chickens into titchy teros. I'll continue to be cautious. I don't know what might happen if I ate one! I could end up as a cockroach with two heads!' Instead, he clears the full plate of anchovy paste sandwiches and mince pies. 'I know these are safe even though they are out of season. It's certainly not the best food I've ever eaten.' Nevertheless, lies cost nothing, so he compliments her. "My dear lady, you are surely the master chef of your time. The meal was absolutely superb. There's no doubt about it. Your talent is unmatched."

Mrs. Squidge is eager to believe all that the Wizard says. She smiles with satisfaction. "Thank you, Griswold. I'm glad you enjoyed your meal."

When he's on the Brook, the Wizard is Beyonder-size. This is his original size. He was born an ordinary boy except some of his features are considerably larger than an ordinary boy would hope, or hope not, to possess. His ears are large, and his nose, in proportion to the size of his face, is even larger. He has a high forehead, and his piercing dark brown eyes are spaced well apart.

Griswold was once a scullery boy in a Cornish castle on a cliff facing the sea to the west. He is the fourteenth son of his father and, like most fourteenth sons, is immensely ambitious. While on the beach, he discovered a tiny man in a bottle. The wee fellow was only half-a-thumb high and was on his way to America to become the coach of a famous basketball team. Although neither America nor basketball exist yet, the Little People can see into the future. That inspired Griswold with the thought, 'Anything is possible if you have vision, courage, and determination.' His first motto becomes "I can. I will!" Later he discards it for others. He worked his way up through the staff at the castle so he could be the chief librarian and read all the books on magic.

The lad realized he would need an assistant and trained a fledgling raven to do his bidding. It was a good choice. These bruising birds, bigger than a mallard and largest of the crow family, are aggressive and love a fight, even with birds larger than themselves. There would be much fighting for Rasputin in the years ahead.

Griswold's studies and experiments in magic resulted in King Druthan banishing him from Cornwall for a thousand years, but that has long since expired. He immediately invaded Wozzle and then Gyminge, easily conquering King Rufus and his valiant troops. He smiles with satisfaction as he recalls it. 'I have built my life and reputation on that success. Once one or two of my current minor problems are sorted out, I'll be ready to move on to greater things and apply my gifts to the problems of Beyonders as well as Twith.

The Wizard was a little past middle-age when he discovered how to manage time and control aging the way the Twith do. He has chosen to remain at that age. Although he was a little above medium height, over the years his shoulders have become stooped. Thin in build, his fingers are long and bony. He's clean shaven, and while shaving each morning, he practices a twisted sneer in the mirror. He finds it attractive. 'I think it makes me look charming, cynical, and rather cool.'

His favorite color is black — even his pajamas are black. When he's dressed for meeting people, his clothes are always elegant — black pointed shoes, a black suit and cloak, and a tall, black hat with a large brim. He does, however, occasionally sport a spotted red-and-white scarf.

The master magician is highly intelligent; his mind is keen, alert, never at rest, and always ranging far and wide. He considers he has a keen sense of humor although it's rarely observed. In recent years, he toured all over Cornwall giving lectures on magic. King Druthan seems forgotten. People aren't even sure he's still alive. Every lecture given by the Wizard has received rapturous applause. His demonstrations have left the audience gasping with amazement, even awe. He's the preeminent magician in the area of transformations.

Other magicians and Wizards worldwide write to him with their questions, seeking answers. The Wizard knows — there's no doubt in his mind — that he's the most superior magician of all time. As he thinks of other famous magicians, he's puffed up with his own importance. 'Merlin? He's a bungling amateur long past his best. Arabian and Persian magicians? Bah, just a bunch of foreigners. Simon of Samaria? A religious dreamer. There isn't one that can switch size and species as I can. This is my specialty. My role changes are instantaneous and are spoken of by the fraternity with admiration. I'm the expert, and authorities on magic are on the edge of their chairs as they listen to me. I'm the supreme authority.' He straightens up again at these thoughts and gives himself an imaginary pat on the back.

Unfortunately, he twitches. All those who practice magic twitch somewhere. Even Mrs. Squidge, who would hardly qualify as even a low level magician, has a minor twitch, a twitchy finger. The twitchy right eye of the superb, preeminent, stand-alone Master Magician is an immediate giveaway. Brilliant plan after brilliant plan is foiled as his disguise is penetrated, and the danger signals are sounded by those he's about to attack.

His long-term goal is to transform himself into the largest land animal there is, an elephant. He has a vast range of transformations to his credit. He's changed himself instantaneously into a wide range of birds, a bee, a spider, and a small pony, but he hasn't yet attempted an elephant. 'Before I attempt the peak of my transformation career, I need to eliminate this irritating eye twitch. It betrays that, whatever I become, it is actually me, the Wizard of Wozzle. I have good reason to believe that the Twith Book of Lore contains the secret of how to cure the Magician's Twitch. To achieve my destiny — the ultimate goal of progression to the top — I need that information. It was almost within my grasp, but it slipped away. The Twith themselves are but a minor nuisance standing in my way. I would long ago have left them to stew in their own juice on the Brook and secured my boundaries except for one thing. I need to get their Book of Lore. And I am determined, by hook or by crook, that I will get it!'

It's his fierce determination to cure the twitch that has led him into his present series of problems. There are other factors involved, but he doesn't yet admit that it's his own mistakes that are to blame. The Wizard never admits that he has failed. He's like the spider that Robert Bruce watched. Time and time again, it tried to swing its thin thread from one beam to the next. Six times it tried. Six times it failed. The seventh time, it succeeded in fastening the silver thread to the distant beam and could begin weaving its web. The Wizard too has a web to weave. He won't give up. 'If at first I don't succeed, I'll try and try again!' He smirks to himself. "That can be my new motto."

Griswold constantly surprises himself with his brilliant ideas and clarity of thought in times of difficulty. 'There's no one else who is capable of thinking in circles the way I can, let alone straight lines. Lesser men crumble, but I flourish. I'm a giant among pygmies even though I think it myself. Mentally, I have a Beyonder brain in a world of Twith.'

This thought leads him to plans for his future. 'Being half-a-thumb high has given me control over Wozzle and then over Gyminge as well. Now to the future!' His ambitions lead him to consider resuming Beyonder-size permanently in the not too distant future. He enjoys wealth and power and is amassing as much of each as he can.

He's a man of immense vision for himself and maintains a world view which he enthusiastically shares with Mrs. Squidge. "The world will be a better place and will run more smoothly when I control it, and I get it properly organized. These Twith who presently oppose me are a mere hiccup in my journey to complete power that I'm embarked on. I

Dayko's Rime

may now be engaged in dealing with the Twith, but world leadership in the future beckons large and broad. I'm called to rule over Beyonders in the same way as I do now with the Little People. Simple people need smart people to do their thinking for them. And smart people need even smarter people to do their thinking for them. That leaves me alone at the top. It's a simple matter of logic and clearly the best solution." He briefly allows himself the thought of marble statues labeled *"Griswold the Benefactor"* erected all around the land by grateful future generations.

The Wizard recently completed another brilliant idea; he's full of them. He flashes his cynical smile and allows himself another pat on the back as he recalls it. "I have closed off access into Gyminge through the curtain while I'm away on the Brook. I need to protect things back home so that the incompetent men I left in charge there can't excel in their foolishness."

He isn't aware that this has locked Rasputin inside Gyminge.

Squidgy's Unique Creatures

Mrs. Squidge is a woman of late middle age, plump, and friendly as Cornish women usually are. She was deserted by her husband in favor of the girl working in the sweetshop opposite his butcher shop. Since that time, Squidgy has studied hard and now looks forward to graduating with a diploma in magic. In the back of her mind, she has things she would like to do to Mr. Squidge once she qualifies. Thirty years ago, she flew to Gyminge on her broomstick to see the Wizard. She never got there because of the curtain that was in the way. Instead, she crashed onto the roof of a cottage in the middle of the Brook known as Smiler's cottage. She made it her home, and now it's called Squidgy's cottage. She had two companions with her — a bad-tempered, midnight black cat, Cajjer, and a strange animal called a SnuggleWump. He is huge!

Squidgy appears to have a strange gift which may or may not be connected with magic. It may be just a natural gift she has. Maybe all Cornish people have it; they do seem to possess certain distinctly different, very special qualities. In Squidgy's case though, the oddity is in her cooking. When she makes yeast buns, the mix sometimes gets out of hand. The buns that result have strange effect on the creatures that eat them. So far six hens have been transformed into blackbird-sized pterodactyls. They have been nicknamed titchy teros. They perch on the ridge of the roof until the mistress of the cottage calls them. They are there right now, waiting patiently for a summons.

The oddest creature is the one that lies across Squidgy's path as her WatchGuard. The SnuggleWump began life as a lizard. He made the mistake of wandering into a goldfish pond where Squidgy scattered yeast bun crumbs. The goldfish sensibly died and saved themselves a lot of trouble. The lizard grew and grew and grew and partially split himself in two. He now has two heads on long sinuous necks. Each head has only one eye. The eyes are red when the animal is angry and green when he's contented.

Although it has nothing to do with the yeast buns, he only has one ear on each head. Originally, there were two on each head. He lost the first one when Jacko, the ferret, stole the Shadow Book belonging to the Twith. There was a big fight at the cottage with three Twith and their owl friend, Tuwhit. Jacko ended up on the SnuggleWump. As he clawed into an ear, the SnuggleWump shrieked in pain. His open jaws missed the ferret and bit off the ear instead. Then before the fight at the farmhouse ever began, an ear was lost on the other head. The goblin driver on the head already missing an ear, swung his sword just as the other head was on the way up.

All the yeast bun creatures have an interesting trait to their characters. They just love Mrs. Squidge and are completely loyal to her. They always try their best to do whatever their mistress asks of them.

The evening before yesterday, while the others were out fighting at the farmhouse, the king of the moles discovered the stash of yeast buns that changed the chickens into teros. Squidgy hadn't gotten around to disposing of them. Unaware of their unique properties and feeling very hungry, he gobbled down several. MoleKing suffers from more than just a stomach ache. Squidgy now has acquired another admirer. When he heard the voices upstairs of those returning from the battle at the farmhouse, he bolted the door of his basement bedroom so no one could come in and see him.

The first voice Moley recognized was Squidgy's as she talked to Cajjer. He could hear her rocking chair creaking all night as she waited for the Wizard to return. It was no lullaby for the uncomfortable mole. He would gladly have welcomed sleep to blot out the thought of what happened to him. He isn't quite sure what happened, but he fears the worst. He hasn't dared to turn on the light to look in the mirror. He checked his neck and is relieved to find that there's only one. At least, he isn't a baby brother to the SnuggleWump. However, what he feels as he touches himself is frightening. He's hungry but is afraid to look for anything to eat lest something more happen.

The goblin king was the next one back from the fighting at the farmhouse. He must have hurt himself, for he was groaning all that first night in the next bedroom. Moley wondered what on earth the Twith could have done to him.

The Wizard came back after dawn yesterday. Just as daylight began to creep into the room, Moley pulled the curtain across the small basement window. He didn't want anyone peering in. The Wizard wasn't in a good mood from the moment he arrived back home with a distinct limp, and it — the mood, not the limp — steadily got worse throughout the day. Today has been no better. It hasn't helped that Moley is able to follow the conversations upstairs from his own room. Noise in the cottage carries easily from room to room and through the floors.

MoleKing dreads a summons from above. Apart from everything else, Moley's stomach still hurts. It's not just hunger, although he hasn't eaten anything for two days. He has never experienced such pain. He hasn't dared to groan since Mrs. Squidge returned. He's been chewing the edge of the floor mat to relieve his agony. Something happened to his mouth. It's gone strangely hard. When the Wizard began laying into King Haymun, every word seemed as though it was directed at him and cut through him like a knife.

The mole begins to wonder what to do. "I will eventually be discovered. There's no basement exit where I can slip away onto the Brook. Besides, I need advice. There must be a remedy for my problem somewhere, and either the Wizard or Mrs. Squidge will know. I dread going upstairs right now. I'll just wait until I feel a little better."

The door slams. From that noise and the previous conversation, it sounds as though King Haymun has left for Gyminge at last. Only the Wizard, Mrs. Squidge, and Moley are now in the cottage. There's quiet conversation, and the two rocking chairs creak with their own individual noises.

Squidgy is concerned about the Wizard. 'After his recent defeat at the farmhouse, dear Griswold seems discouraged, almost depressed. He keeps muttering to himself. I'm afraid he might throw a spell or two, and one of them might hit me. Somehow, I want to make him feel better and look on the brighter side of things.' She makes cocoa and prepares some refreshments. She doesn't put any of her yeast buns on the plate. Instead, she just puts some buns, blackberry jam, and apple tarts on the plate.

Good-bye, MoleKing

Downstairs, MoleKing summons up all his courage to venture upstairs. He has to decide what to wear. He slips on his silk dressing gown. It isn't comfortable. "This is far too small. I wish it had a different pattern or at least different colors. The black-and-white stripes make me look like a zebra. I'll have to go barefoot. My feet won't fit in my slippers at all."

He pulls back the door bolt. Slowly and painfully, he climbs up the stairs. It's as difficult as always trying to walk on two hind legs. At the top of the stairs, he drops to a four-legged walk. Whatever creature he's become must also be naturally four-legged. Although a mole's eyes are weak, even at the best of times, he now sees much better than he used to. Having been in the dark basement for so long, he puts up his paw to shade his eyes as he enters the bright sitting room.

The Wizard flings out a casual, "Hi, Moley, you've been... Liminy, jiminy wineskins and leather bottles! What on earth happened to you?" He jumps to his feet and retreats three steps back towards the front door. There are some things that surprise even a Wizard.

Mrs. Squidge takes one look, screams loudly, and kicks her feet up into the air and faints. Fortunately, the rocking chair rotates backward away from the fire. Unfortunately, it ends up on top of Squidgy.

The Wizard can't absorb what he sees. His mind, going into retreat mode, gives him flashbacks of a visit to a zoo when he was a child. 'I don't think that I ever saw a creature like this in the zoo! The zebras I remember were the size of horses.' He's never been to Australia, or he would know that Moley is now a duckmole, also called a duck-billed platypus. These unique creatures are duck-billed, beaver-tailed, otter-footed mammals that lay eggs.

His mind now goes into overdrive on a different track. This double-track thinking is a gift that he's proud of even though he doesn't say so. 'Squidgy has done it again! How does she do it? She has to be prevented from doing it! She could do it to anybody! Just anybody! She doesn't know how to reverse it! It's like starting an avalanche with a pebble and then standing in front of it. But this gift, properly directed and channeled, could have a multitude of uses.'

The Wizard gulps, looks around for the glass of water, and gulps again. So far the ex-mole has said nothing. He just stands there. Then he waddles over and tries to pull the chair off of Mrs. Squidge. When he offers to help her up, she screams and faints again.

The Wizard motions the creature before him to back off and says, "Now, now, Mrs. Squidge." That's not a particularly helpful thing to say to a woman about to go into hysterics. It's no more helpful than saying "There, there." But for the moment, he isn't finding it easy to express himself with that crisp alertness for which he's so well known. Eventually, he manages to splutter, "Wha-wha-what happened to you, Moley?"

"I-I-I don't know. It happened all of a sudden. Do you know what's happened to me? I need help. I feel all kinds of funny. It happened after I had a snack for supper while you were out. What am I? Can you put me back like I was?"

The remark about a snack breaks into Mrs. Squidge's wandering senses and galvanizes her into action. She struggles to her feet, sets the rocker upright, and scuttles into the pantry to check for the yeast buns she stashed away behind the potatoes. They look just as she left them. MoleKing, rather ex-MoleKing, had attempted to cover his tracks. It isn't until she counts them that she knows for sure. She moans, "Yes, someone took several of my yeast buns!"

Racing back from the pantry into the sitting room, she confronts Moley. "You took some of my yeast buns. That's what you did. Serves you right, you greedy old, old… whatever you are!"

Moley bursts into uncontrollable weeping. 'There's no one I respect more than this dear, gracious, gentle lady who has so generously been my hostess over the last few days. How can one whom I admire so devotedly speak to me so harshly?' It's just too much. He sobs as though his heart will break.

The Wizard passes him a cloth table napkin from the sideboard to wipe away his tears, wipes his own brow with another, and speaks gently to him. "Here, Moley. Why don't you sit down?" He offers the ex-mole Squidgy's chair.

Squidgy isn't having that! She pulls it away and sits in it herself.

What both the Wizard and Mrs. Squidge are looking at is a creature such as they have never imagined. It bears some resemblance to a mole, but it's only superficial and very slight. It is nearly three times the size of a mole and comes up almost to the Wizard's knee. Its feet are webbed, like those of a duck. They will be of little use for digging mole tunnels anymore. They look more as though they are intended for swimming. Creating molehills is no longer an option for this creature.

MoleKing is getting used to the strong light and isn't blinking as much as he did at first. At least that's an improvement, but it's the only one. He knows his tail has lengthened from a short stump to a length half as long as his body, resembling a beaver's tail. His paws have long strong nails and by no means as suitable for digging earth as the short claws he once had.

It isn't just Moley's dressing gown that makes him look like a zebra. The animal he's become is strangely white-and-black striped like a zebra. The stripes encircle his body and legs in successive rings. On the head, they run up and down his face to where his mouth should be. The most surprising characteristic of this creature is a beak that runs from just below his eyes for a length the width of the Wizard's hand. It resembles a duck's bill except that it's grey-black in color and not orange-yellow. His fur is no longer the short, soft, black fur of a mole, but more like that of an otter or other water mammal.

The Wizard draws in a large breath. He realizes, 'There needs to be some clear thinking here. I am obviously the one to do it.' He tells the creature, "Lie down on the hearth while we figure out what to do." He wonders, 'Does he bark like a dog, or does he quack like a duck? The creature will have to resign as king of the moles. It's a pity. MoleKing has been a useful ally. I may have to help the moles select another ruler.

I probably should find a different name for him than Moley. He is certainly no longer a mole! Although what he is, I have no idea.'

He asks Mrs. Squidge, "Have you discovered any antidote to your yeast buns?"

Squidgy is fearful. She is also defensive, so replies with a sharp, "No!"

Griswold turns back to Moley and suggests, "You should probably decide whether you are a four-legged bird without feathers or a deformed duck. Considering your tail and new fur, maybe you should be called a beater — a mix between a beaver and an otter. Even better, with that beak, you can be a duck-beater— a mix between a duck, a beaver, and an otter. Since ducks lay eggs, you could be considered to be a half-brother to an eggbeater." The Wizard gives a little chuckle of delight. He enjoys his twisted sense of humor. "If you don't like any of those, we can invent a name for you. Or maybe you have some ideas yourself. It's fortunate that you don't have two heads."

The odd and very confused animal hasn't yet reached the point where he's grateful for what has not happened to him.

The Wizard has a suggestion. "Perhaps tomorrow you might like to take a stroll up to the pond and try swimming. You look as though you were designed to swim. Would you like a sardine sandwich? That would test whether your natural diet is fish."

"No, I don't want anything. My stomach hurts."

'Just as well,' thinks Squidgy. 'I don't have any sardines in my pantry anyway.'

The Wizard is still trying to be helpful. "How about calling yourself a Zebrotter, a zebra marked otter for the time being?"

Moley has no comment. 'I just want to get fixed back to what I was before this happened.' Never before have the very limited physical qualities of a common, ordinary, farm garden mole seemed so desirable and attractive as they do now.

Mrs. Squidge sighs. 'When is life ever going to settle down?'

Surprisingly for the Wizard, he asks rather tenderly, "Are you feeling alright, my dear lady?"

Gibbins Brook and the Farmhouse

The farm on the Brook is located in the little village of Sellindge in Kent, England. The Brook is a large uncultivated and partially wooded land used by the villagers for walking their dogs. These open spaces are becoming thicker and thicker each year with the bracken that spreads everywhere. The woods are a variety of trees — silver birch, oak, ash, hawthorn, elder, and elm. Badgers live in the woods, and the foxes live in their dens in more open areas in the bracken.

Part of the area of the Brook is a bog. The southwest corner of the Brook is one of only three bogs in Kent. It is only by crossing the bog that the Little People can get into their homeland. The opening in the Wizard's curtain that allows the annual migration of the toads to the lake in Gyminge is at the far end of the bog.

Gibbins Brook Farm is on the eastern boundary of the Brook. It has a farmhouse, a barn, a stable, and a cowshed. It isn't used as a farm, any longer although the fields around the farm and pasture are cultivated by Farmer Holt. Between the farmhouse and the woods on the Brook is a barley field. Not too far into the depth of the woods and before the bog is reached is the only home actually built on the Brook itself. Squidgy's cottage was built by Smiler long before the land was designated as common land, so it was allowed to stay.

Gumpa and gran'ma live in the farmhouse. Gumpa hasn't always lived at Gibbins Brook Farm. His family was looking for a place to live after returning from abroad. In a mysterious way, they were led to the Brook. When Gumpa found out that the Little People were already settled there, his mind was made up. Fortunately, the farmhouse has enough room for the hosts of children staying there for the summer. They have come to help the Little People in their battle against the Wizard. The farmhouse is almost five and a half centuries old. It was built before Columbus discovered America! The doors are narrow, and the low ceilings have beams that were salvaged from an old shipwreck on the Atlantic coast. The large Inglenook fireplace served as a cook fire and oven. The six bedrooms and the attic all have a lot of hiding places for playing hide-and-seek.

The four families who live on the farm are all related. Gumpa told the children "You can call my brother *Uncle* Andy." He and his wife live in the building once used as a stable. Andy's oldest daughter and her husband live in the converted barn with their three children. The cowshed is now comfortable living quarters for Uncle Andy's youngest daughter, Julie, and her family. She and her husband, Max, have two children.

On the opposite side of the Brook is Brook Lane which leads to Swan Lane and the village where the general store, post office, and Mucky Duck Pub are located.

The only Twith in the farmhouse until recently were Stumpy and his family. Stumpy is the oldest of the Twith and is custodian of Cymbeline and Barney. When his brother and his wife both died in the great plague,

Stumpy took over the care of their two children. He loves them more than he can ever find words to say. They are his life.

When he first came to the Brook, he enjoyed walking down by the pond. One day he accidentally stepped on the nose of a crocodile, and it snapped his foot off. He whacked it with his stick before it could swallow it. He now carries his foot in a little red bag waiting to find someone who can sew it back on. The loss of his foot makes him feel that he can no longer take as good care of his two young charges. In fact, they have been taking care of him. The three of them live together in a special apartment built for them by Uncle Andy above the fireplace in the farmhouse. The apartment even has a special workshop for the old man to do his woodcarving.

Cymbeline, a pretty girl with long brown hair, is about sixteen years old and performs happily all the various activities required in caring for five Twith men and her brother, Barney. He has chosen to stay just ten years old, and he provides most of the dirty clothes his sister has to wash.

Elisheba, one of the new arrivals from Gyminge, now shares Cymbeline's room. The two girls enjoy each other's company very much. The rest of the Twith live in Twith Mansion, which was especially built for them underground when they had to move from Smiler's cottage thirty years ago. Jock and Jordy share a room, Taymar and Gerald share a room next to his office and the records room, and Cydlo is making good use of one of the guest rooms. The entrance to the mansion is through a hollow log that lies flat on the near side of the sycamore tree. That entrance is guarded by Buffo, the toad. There is another passage from the mansion that curves towards the farmhouse. Steps lead up to the hearth of the fireplace.

Upon gran'ma's return from captivity, it was decided the main meal would be in Twith Mansion for a while. She and Gumpa and all the Beyonder children have been shrunk to half-a-thumb high. When the busy evening meal is over, gran'ma and Cymbeline organize the wash-up and dish-drying crews. The others, still gathered at the table, are busy chatting.

Jock feels the time has arrived for a full meeting in the long room in the farmhouse. "Everyone will share the adventures of the last few days. We need to catch up with each other. The conference will also decide what we need to do next. We'll meet just as soon as everyone can get upstairs. Perhaps in half an hour."

Crusty the eagle swings in towards the farmhouse and lands on the top of the well.

He is welcomed by Buffo. The toad has almost recovered from being shrunk by the Wizard when he went to Gyminge. He begins to feel more like himself. Grabbing the bell rope, he tugs on it once to signal that there is a visitor waiting at the door.

Jock leaves to find out who it is. Swinging the door open, he sees his eagle friend back from his errand. "What did you find, Crusty?"

"After I delivered the two Shadow brothers, Bimbo and Bollin, and the goblin doctor to the waterfall, I went searching for the hole in the curtain like you asked. I found it two days ago, but now it has completely disappeared. I haven't been all around the curtain, but at least on the south side of it, there's no way through. Any new journeys into Gyminge are out of the question for me or any other bird unless a further opening in the curtain can be found or made. Do you want me to try and follow Bimbo and Bollin through the waterfall?"

"No, I have something else for you to do. I want you to be present when we have our meeting. Tuwhit should stay on duty at Squidgy's cottage, but you can tell him the news from our meeting. That way both of you will be kept well informed."

Crusty shakes his wise old head. "It will be better, and I'll be more comfortable, if I keep watch at the cottage while the Wizard's inside. I'll tell Blackie, the leader of the rabbits, to be especially alert as well. I noticed that Stormy, the American girl, is quick to sort out what's most important. I can easily understand what she says. She can keep notes of what happens in your meeting and share with me later."

Jock agrees. "You are right, my wise old friend. You keep watch for us. Stormy can report everything to you later."

Farmhouse Get-Together

Returning to the others, Jock asks Vickie, "Will you invite your grandfather to come across and join us?" At the door, he touches her back to Beyonder-size, and she skips off across the yard. She and her brother, Mike, really enjoy having so many other children around. Vickie is the same age as Ginger, who is nine, and the two have become special friends.

She reflects on the exciting adventures they've been sharing. "If it hadn't been so frantic, I would have quite enjoyed the first part of the battle at the farmhouse. At the end though, Ollie got hurt and didn't recover. I miss him so much! It feels like there's a hole in my heart that won't go away. Ah, there's Granddad. It looks like he's cleaning his car. Granddad, Jock wants you to come listen to what's been happening lately. Do you have time to join us?"

Uncle Andy nods. "Yes, I'll be across. I'll come right now if you'll wait for me to get rid of this bucket." He's relieved that his short toothbrush mustache from his adventure as Signor Antonio Toferetto has finally come off. His upper lip is raw with the steady tugging at it. He needed to be disguised so Squidgy wouldn't recognize him when he went to her cottage to retrieve the Twith treasures buried under the hearth. The ring that got stuck on his finger finally worked its way off too. He thinks, 'Strange how you can wear a ring for a month and pay no attention to it. But if you want it off and it won't come off, then it seems as though the most important thing in the world is to get it off. I'm glad it's gone!"

He takes hold of his granddaughter's hand, and they walk across together. He's curious. "Where are all the children finding a place to sleep?"

Vickie explains what she knows. "The three Shadow girls are using one of the spare rooms in Twith Mansion. Two of Gumpa's granddaughters, Titch and Crickett, are in the small room at the top of the stairs in the farmhouse and the sisters from Michigan, Katie and Gretchen, are in the small room next to it. Stormy and Ginger shifted things around to make space for Rachael and Jenn in the large end room. AJ has the tiny middle room to himself. Austin, Lucas, and Jared are in the guest bedroom next to Gumpa and gran'ma. They have to stay extra quiet after nine o'clock bedtime, which is hardest for Jared. Specs and Bajjer tidied up the attic room so Micah and Nick can sleep up there with them."

She shares the most recent news. "Bimbo and Bollin went back to Gyminge on a secret quest. The goblin king was seen following them, but I reckon the boys should be able to take care of themselves."

When they arrive at the farmhouse, Gumpa and gran'ma aren't in their separate easy chairs. They're snuggled close together on the settee, holding hands. Now that she's home after being captured by the Wizard, Gumpa wants to keep her as close to him as possible. Several children sit or lie on the carpets before the fireplace. Others use the various easy chairs or hard-backed chairs. Stormy gives Uncle Andy her easy chair and slides down onto the carpet. Only Bollin and Bimbo are missing.

These days, it's very different when Uncle Andy goes over to the farmhouse. He can now see the Little People. It makes his visits so much more enjoyable! When those who have returned from rescuing gran'ma realize that Uncle Andy can now see the Little People, they break into excited clapping and chattering. Good things have indeed happened while they were away.

This evening he sees for the first time, the woodcutter, Cydlo, and his daughter, Elisheba. Cydlo has slowly climbed the steps from Twith Mansion up to the fireplace. He had to lay his hand on Taymar's shoulder for support. He's still recovering from the injury he received when rescuing his daughter from the castle and he limps as he moves across the hearth.

Andy studies the woodcutter. 'He's a big man for a Twith — taller than Taymar even though he's not yet walking to his full height. He has a fine face. His hair has the same short bob as the other Twith men. And his red beard is neatly trimmed.' He runs his fingers across his own beard, wondering if it could use a trim.

Gumpa has set two small tea tables in the middle of the fireplace hearth for the Twith to use. On the larger table are chairs brought up from below and plenty of cushions. Specs lifts Cydlo and Taymar and puts them with the other Twith. There are a dozen in all now — the original seven, the two new Twith, and the three Shadow girls. Cymbeline isn't sitting in her usual place next to gran'ma this time. She's with Elisheba, her new Twith friend, who wants to be near her father.

On the smaller table in front of them, in the charge of Gerald, are the treasures Uncle Andy brought from Squidgy's cottage. One is a little wooden chest with a curved lid. Next to it is a tiny gold gift box decorated with a gold-and-white ribbon and a white satin rose in the center. There is also a small gold crown. In addition, Gerald has brought the two Twith Books. Few of those present have ever seen all the items that are on display.

Jock opens the meeting. "Please make sure you're all comfortable. We're likely to be a long while, but please be patient. Now we're back together again, we need to share our separate adventures. Those on the rescue team need to be filled in on the Wizard's attack on the farmhouse. Those left behind to defend it need to hear about the rescue of gran'ma and Elisheba. It's my pleasure to introduce our new friends, Cydlo and his daughter, Elisheba.

"Cydlo was largely responsible for the safety and success of the Gyminge expedition to rescue gran'ma. Fortunately, in spite of the Wizard's success in dividing our forces, it didn't result in any permanent harm to us. However, time moves on. The Wizard is even at this moment next door on the Brook plotting his next move against us. We know he's a tireless enemy who will never accept defeat.

"Bimbo and Bollin are back in Gyminge on a secret quest that I'll describe later, although I expect Bollin back soon with news of their progress. Dr. Vyruss Tyfuss, the goblin king's personal physician, has gone with them. We decided to take a risk and ask him to help us."

The children who were on the rescue team are surprised to hear that the Twith have enlisted the help of a goblin, but don't say anything.

"Meanwhile, we can be confident that the Wizard knows that the birds who help us are one of the strongest weapons we have. During the battle at the farmhouse, they chased Rasputin as far as the castle. Crusty told me that the opening through the curtain is now closed so now we won't have the birds to help us in Gyminge."

"I doubt the Wizard will make any further attacks on us here on the Brook where we have so many friends to help us. The odds are too much against him. I expect him to return home soon. He will probably make it easy for us to reenter Gyminge where he has unlimited control. With all his forces available, he'll be confident that he can defeat us. It's up to us to prove him wrong even although there are surely great difficulties ahead. Once there, he may make it impossible for us to leave. But that's a challenge we're willing to accept.

"Because few of us know everything about all that's taken place in the past few days, we will now share those events. By sharing with each other, we can gain greater wisdom to guide us as we go forward. First, I'll ask Gerald to explain the treasures on the table."

Gerald and the Treasures

Centuries ago, Gerald was an apprentice seer to Dayko, the High Seer. When the seven Little People escaped from Gyminge, only he, Stumpy, Cymbeline, and Barney never left the Brook. Jock, Jordy, and Taymar became the Three Twithketeers traveling all over the world.

Gerald plays many roles in the little Twith community. As the scribe and historian, he's the Keeper of the Lore. Every event is carefully written with beautiful script in a variety of colors. His work is neat and tidy, and he enjoys getting the details just right. Because he has the best handwriting, he's usually the one who writes any letters or notes. He's also the doctor as well as the cobbler. When he makes footwear for Cymbeline, his skill is evident as he creates shoes, slippers, and sandals of superlative quality. Cymbeline knows that for her birthday she'll get new footwear from him fit for a queen to wear. It's his way of saying, "We love you, Cymbeline, and appreciate all that you do for us."

Gerald is about the same height as Jordy but of a slender build. He wears his fair hair gathered into a ponytail, and he's the only Twith that needs glasses. He rarely wears a cap, even in the rain. Gerald's rounded shoulders are due to bending over his books. However, it could partly be because he blames himself for making the mistake of showing himself to Squidgy. That resulted in the Wizard knowing where they are and gathering his forces against them.

Gerald is happy to tell about the treasures displayed on the table. "When we first arrived on the Brook, we met a kindly man named Smiler who gave us shelter. He prepared a hiding place for our treasures under his fireplace hearth. We had to leave them there when Squidgy moved into the cottage. There was no way we could ever retrieve them by ourselves. We needed a Beyonder to do it for us." The little scribe looks over at Uncle Andy and smiles.

Uncle Andy stirs uncomfortably. 'I hope I'm not going to be celebrated again. They have already done that!'

Gerald, sympathetic to Uncle Andy's desire to avoid attention, tries to be brief about the recovery of the treasures, but there are many questions from gran'ma's rescue team. Micah, ever curious, asks, "How was it possible for Uncle Andy to remove them from right under Squidgy's nose?"

Vickie asks, "May I tell what happened?"

Uncle Andy breathes a grateful sigh and nods happily.

The girl is excited and proud about this adventure of her grandfather. When she's excited, she talks rapidly and her words fall over themselves like a cascading waterfall.

Uncle Andy relaxes. He loves his oldest granddaughter, and she's so happy telling the story! There is absolute silence as she begins, then giggles as she talks about disguising her granddad as Signor Antonio and his operatic solo he sang for Squidgy. That's followed by *'ooohs'* of apprehension when the ferret entered Squidgy's cottage. Jacko has a keen sense of smell and could have penetrated Uncle Andy's disguise except that all he could smell was the garlic Uncle Andy was breathing out. There are great sighs of relief as the treasures are recovered from beneath the hearth. Next is laughter at Mrs. Squidge making yeast buns laced with cement mortar, and finally, eyes open wide with wonder as Vickie tells of the chickens belonging to her uncle Max being transformed into baby pterodactyls.

Gerald picks up the tiny gold box. He removes and sets on the table a crowned helmet, a broadsword, and two pieces of body armor — a breastplate and a backplate. He turns to Jock. "Will you explain about the armor and the sword?"

Jock picks up the king's helmet. It's obviously way too big for Jock. He holds it up for all to see. At the top is a crown. The Beyonders have only seen something like it in the Tower of London or in a museum. Next he picks up the breastplate, places it in front of his chest, and indicates how the backplate attaches to it providing front and back protection. He points out the hole in the breastplate where a javelin pierced it, wounding the king as he fought the goblin army invading

Gyminge. Finally, he picks up the broadsword, holds it high for everyone to see, and then puts it back on the table. "These four pieces belong to King Rufus. On the last day of free Gyminge, Jordy, Cymbeline and I were with him. He didn't want to escape with us. He wanted to stay with his people. We left him in a secret room behind the fireplace in his apartments at the castle with a little food and water. He was seriously injured. We have no way of knowing whether he was able to use the escape tunnel to the quarry, or was discovered, or whether he even survived.

"The king appointed me to be leader of the Twith in the Beyond, to serve with his authority until we return to Gyminge. I feel that events are moving fast and I won't need to be the leader much longer.

"When we escaped from Gyminge, I wore this armor and helmet and held the sword high as Crusty carried us away to freedom. The helmet is so big; I couldn't see anything at all. We hoped the Wizard would think the king had escaped to the Beyond and not search for him. Dr. Tyfuss told us that was indeed what happened."

The Treasure Chest

Gerald steps over to the table. "Besides what Jock has shown and explained to us, there is this treasure chest and its contents. The chest belonged to Queen Sheba since childhood and held some of her most precious treasures. The king gave it to Dayko to use for the treasures being sent to the Beyond."

All eyes turn to the small wooden chest. No bigger than a thimble, it's delicately fashioned. Five reinforcing straps of wood strengthen the curved, hinged lid. All corners and edges are reinforced with metal straps, and the exterior is decorated with artistic designs. At the sides are aged leather handles. A key intended to unlock the chest hangs by a loop from one of the handles.

Everyone is anxious to see what's inside, but Gerald doesn't move to open it just yet.

"Before the chest was hidden, I placed a seal over the keyhole and impressed the sign of the Royal Crest into it. We wanted to see whether everything was as it had been placed years ago. Taymar checked that the seal wasn't broken, and then Cymbeline and Barney opened the treasure box. Everything was there, and nothing had been removed. I'll show you what is in it and explain what they are, and then I'll put them back in the chest. Some of them are mentioned in Dayko's Rime and will be used for the Return." He unties the loop holding the key, unlocks the chest, and lifts the lid. Inside is a shallow tray divided into three sections, and he sets it to one side. From the bottom of the chest, he removes two small brown earthenware pots, each sealed with a wooden plug. They are different sizes.

He holds then up so everyone can see. "These pots are empty now, but they contained the powder that Dayko gave me so that both Crusty and Tuwhit will be able to live as long as we do. Without the powder, both of these close friends would have died long ago of old age. It's because of them and their help that we have reached the point of our Return." He sets the pots on the table.

Gerald lifts up a small pewter goblet. It isn't jeweled or ornate so it wouldn't have cost very much, but it's easy to see that it's of great importance to Gerald. He explains, "This is the Goblet of Consecration. It was used for the coronation of all the monarchs of Gyminge from the very first one. It's one of the historic treasures of the kingdom. Some future king, anointed with the oil of consecration, will one day make the promises to rule his kingdom in Truth to some new High Seer." Slowly he lowers it onto the table.

From the shallow tray Gerald takes a small vial of oil. "This is the oil of consecration that will be used. There's only a little left, and it's used very sparingly." He sets it carefully next to the goblet.

Gerald isn't finished showing the treasures in the chest. Nevertheless, he now turns to the books. "This is the Shadow Book. It's something like a photograph album but much more. Jock collected the shadows of children as they helped in the past, and I put them in the Shadow

Book. Bimbo, Bollin, Ellie, Margaret, and Ruthie all have shadows in the book. As you know, Jock can call them back off the page, and they are the same age as when they helped in the past. You can see that they are different than real children in that they come back half-a-thumb high and they are weightless. We lost possession of the Shadow Book when Jacko, Max's escaped ferret, got into the records room and stole it. We were fortunate to recover it, or else we wouldn't have the Shadow children here now to help us. Although it fell in the mud; it wasn't badly damaged. We keep the shadows of all the children who help us, whether they are far away or here on the Brook. Your shadows, children, will be in it before summer's end."

He lays down the Shadow Book and picks up the other book. "Recorded in this Book of Lore is the Wisdom of the Twith from the beginning of our history. Dayko entrusted me, although I was only an apprentice seer, to make the entries. I have continued to do so as you can see by my ink-stained fingers."

Gerald has tears in his eyes as he turns to the next item. The memories are as clear as though it happened yesterday. He lifts out a rolled woven belt. Holding the end of it, he unrolls the broad, decorated belt to its bronze buckle. Red, purple, and green colors are delicately worked into repeated patterns of circles among leaves and flowers. The belt has brown stains along its length. He doesn't comment on the stains and slowly rerolls the belt and puts it down beside the goblet. "The High Seer wears this belt as a sign of his office. To a seer, there's no greater honor. Dayko was wearing it when he was struck by the arrows that killed him. As he died in my arms, he said that I will know who to give it to when the time comes. Until now, I've had no indication who that might be, but from all that's happening, I think we may be close to that time."

Gerald picks up the little gold crown. "This isn't really one of our treasures. Rather, it's one of our trophies. Before many of you children arrived, Stumpy was captured by Rasputin and taken to Squidgy's cottage. During the rescue, the escaping goblin king threw his crown at Jock who caught it on his arm and brought it back here. Perhaps it's a trophy we may one-day exchange for something we want more."

He has one final treasure to remove from the chest.

The Last of the Treasures

Gerald opens the secret compartment in the lid and removes the final item from the treasure chest. He holds it up high for all to see. It's a wide gold ring made to fit a large finger. In the center is an artfully cut, huge ruby. Smaller stones are set on each side in the filigree band. It is strikingly beautiful and fit for a king.

Gerald explains, "This is the Ring of Accession. Dayko placed this on the middle finger of the right hand of King Rufus at the time of his coronation. As it was placed on the king's finger, it began to glow from within, as though needing no borrowed light. This is how we know

King Rufus is our rightful king. Should anyone else wear it, the ring glows with its natural ruby luster. However, when our king wears it, the ring takes on the vitality of the king. It shines with its own brighter light as though illuminated from within. One day we hope our king will wear it again, and this is the way we will prove that he is truly the king. There will be no mistaking." Gerald puts the ring inside the goblet and straightens himself. All the treasures in the chest have been displayed.

However, Gerald isn't done. "There's one last item for you to see. We are just now adding it to our store of treasures. Stormy will tell us how it came into our possession and Bajjer will explain what it is. First, Stormy."

Gran'ma loves this young American girl whose determination reminds her so much of her own childhood. She is eleven nearing twelve, briskly self-reliant, and charged with energy, and her brown eyes twinkle mischievously. As a young girl, gran'ma would have liked her brown hair to be long enough to wear in a ponytail, but her mother kept it cut short. Stormy has a sturdy build and is of average height. With a rosy outdoors complexion, wearing jeans and a patterned shirt, she looks and is a tomboy. Gran'ma never was.

Stormy was sitting on the carpet. She gets up and stands in front of the fireplace. She's composed and happy and makes a little bow before she speaks. "Only two days ago, early Monday morning, Bimbo and I left to go to Gyminge to catch up with Jock. We went through the curtain at the waterfall and climbed up the bank to the toad tunnel that leads into Gyminge. By accident, Bimbo found a shelf in the roof of the cave. He couldn't reach completely to the far back of it, but he could feel the edge of something. He climbed on his backpack and managed to drag it out. It was wrapped in soft leather and really dusty. It must have been untouched for hundreds of years. He put it in his backpack. Jock discovered it there when we caught up with the others on the edge of Blindhouse Wood. Bajjer, you can tell what happened next."

Bajjer, Stormy's brother, is just nine. His birthday was celebrated dramatically at the farmhouse shortly after he arrived. He seems older than his years because almost since he learned to walk, he's been trying to catch up with and then keep up with his sister. He has her attractive smile. Bajjer is highly active. If he isn't fiddling with something in his hands, he's jumping, skipping, or hopping, trying to get someone's attention. He's a bit skinny in build. His hair is light brown, but caught in certain light it shows gingery red tints. The tail of his shirt is outside his jeans and hangs below a purple sweater.

The youngster grins from ear to ear. He takes Stormy's place at the fireplace. "On the edge of Blindhouse Wood, Jock opened the pouch almost as though he knew what he would find in it. I think the gold emblem on the pouch gave him a clue." Enthusiastically, he pulls out a soft leather pouch from under his shirt. He holds it up for all to see. He doesn't intend to open it, just show it. He points out the faded gold insignia but it's difficult for the others to see clearly what it might be.

In the silence that grips everybody, Gerald realizes that this little boy has been carrying the precious treasure through thick and thin in Gyminge. He has been prepared to give his life to protect it. 'Jock didn't misplace his trust in one of the youngest members of his expedition. This is the boy's moment, not mine.' He changes his intention to take over. "Open it, Bajjer, and show us what's inside."

Bajjer unties the two straps that close the pouch tight. He knows what he'll find. Almost overcome by the occasion, he slowly withdraws a gold scabbard. Eyes widen in surprise. He shows it around, first to the Twith and Shadow children on the table and then to the others. Everyone is silent. They realize this is a special moment not to be interrupted by questions.

Showing little sign of wear or use, the scabbard is inscribed with seals and symbols. It's made from a beaten gold sheet shaped on a wooden pattern which was later withdrawn. It's decorated with flowers — roses and thistles — that are linked by trailing vines of ivy. The central line running up the scabbard glitters with alternate rubies and diamonds. Bajjer points to the upper end to bring attention to the insignia of a rearing horse, a crouching lion, and a crown. He pulls out a dirk and holds it up in one hand with the scabbard in the other.

There's indrawn breath from all the Twith who weren't on the expedition. All of the Twith have seen that symbol before and recognize it.

It's the Twith Royal Crest. Many are remembering Dayko's Rime and the line about a dirk. This means they are one step closer to the Return!

A dirk is a short, straight dagger, sharply pointed for stabbing. It's a small weapon used for fighting when locked in hand-to-hand combat. This dirk is no ordinary dirk, however. They can all see that. This is a ceremonial dirk, an indication of the office of the holder. The hilt is gold and the blade is bronze. Neither gold nor bronze tarnishes, and this dirk bears not a trace of rust.

The hilt is curiously fashioned. All parts of it are gold. The handle represents a twisted rope. At the top a blood-red ruby is set into a spherical knob. The large gem is similar to the one they just saw in the king's ring. Inset around the diameter of the sphere is a ring of smaller rubies. The cross guard twinkles in the light from two lines of small diamonds inset on both sides. The ends curve down and run parallel to the blade. The triangular knuckle guard once again shows the insignia of a rearing horse, a crouching lion, and a crown.

The blade is also unique in its design. It's narrow and long, about three times as long as the hilt. It's thick like a diamond shape that has been squeezed as it issues from the guard. There's a four-way taper to the point to give the blade strength right to its extreme end. Each of the four distinct sides has inscriptions, but the markings can hardly impair its deadly intent. The tip of the sharp-pointed blade shows brown stains.

There is a tiny secondary dirk halfway down the scabbard. Bajjer removes that and shows it around. It's a smaller replica of the larger original, but without a knuckle guard. Obviously, all the items were made by a very skillful craftsman.

Bajjer continues, "Jock asked me to be the Guardian of the Royal Dirk. He said this was the sign and symbol since ancient times of the royal house of Twith. I promised to guard it with my life until we returned to the Brook. We are here now, so I will pass the dirk back to Jock for safekeeping."

Everyone watching is silent. Bajjer replaces the dirks in the scabbard and places the scabbard on the smoothed out pouch. Lifting them flat on his hands, he extends his arms to Jock, bowing his head towards him as he does so. He's pleased, 'I've successfully completed my task as Guardian of the Dirk. I haven't let Jock down.'

Jock takes the offered treasure. "From all of us Twith, Bajjer, I thank you for guarding the dirk since it was recovered. Gerald, will you come forward? As custodian of our treasures, I now place this into your charge. Do you accept full responsibility?"

Gerald receives the dirk with a solemn nod, ties the pouch with its two straps, and places it softly, almost reverently, on the table with the other treasures. As he returns to his seat, he tells Jock, "I have finished displaying the Twith treasures. You may continue with the rest of the meeting."

Taymar's Story

Jock now takes over the meeting. "You have already heard from gran'ma and me about our journey to Gyminge. We just heard from Vickie about Uncle Andy's successful visit to the cottage. However, I understand something more than that occurred while we were away. It's time to hear what happened at the farmhouse since we left four days ago. Taymar, will you give us the details of those exciting events?"

Taymar stands up and moves over to the fireplace. He's the tallest of the seven Twith. His hair, like most of the Twith, is barbered by Stumpy and is bobbed at little less than shoulder length. He wears a leather vest, and beneath it is a dark green shirt that contrasts with his ginger hair. His full-length pants are narrow in the leg, and he wears moccasin type shoes of soft leather handcrafted by Gerald.

There's an air of mystery about Taymar. He escaped from Gyminge earlier than the others on the back of his owl, Tuwhit. The king ordered him to flee to the far west of Cornwall. Much later he joined up with Jock and Jordy for adventures in different parts of the world. Around his neck, he wears a small leather pouch that he frequently fingers, as though to remind himself of something or to draw courage from its contents. He's gentle and wise as well as courageous and resourceful.

Elisheba has seen little of him so far, but thinks to herself, 'I've rarely seen a young man with such natural courtesy and so instantly likeable. His blue eyes sparkle with fun. He's so unassuming yet so self-confident with deep inner reserves. He's relaxed and at ease. I wonder why he and Cymbeline haven't taken up with each other? He's very handsome, and she is such a pretty girl. The two of them are obviously fond of each other.'

Taymar begins his story. "I invite others who were also present to join in whenever there's something you'd like to add. We congratulate you, Jock, for your confidence in the courage of the young Beyonders. They have made sure that the Twith will live to fight another day. There isn't one I would wish to single out because all of them behaved admirably. There's no one else I would rather have had helping me in the battle at the farmhouse.

"When Gerald returned early from the expedition to rescue gran'ma, he told us that the Wizard was back here on the Brook. It was clear that the reason the Wizard kidnapped gran'ma was to divide us, and he succeeded in doing that. And now he knew that Jock was on his way towards Goblin Castle. It meant that he would soon attack the farmhouse. Although we couldn't find out where they were, we guessed that his goblin army was hidden somewhere on the Brook waiting for his order to attack. But we knew we could rely on our bird and animal friends on the Brook to help us defend the farmhouse."

The children know that Tuwhit and Sparky have always kept watch at Squidgy's cottage for the Twith. The badgers were the first animals to provide protection for the Twith when Squidgy first arrived on the Brook. They would be happy to help if needed. The rabbits too could be called on to help. And then there's always Buffo's kin, the toads. Yes, the Twith have many friends to help them battle the Wizard.

Taymar continues, "We were caught by surprise about two hours after sunset when Sparky brought us news that the attack was underway. It was dark, and we decided that the best way to defend the farmhouse was to have all the lights out and open all the doors and windows. The Beyonder children remained full-size to defend the farmhouse. The Shadow children and we Twith guarded Twith Mansion. Cydlo was seriously ill, and we also had two goblin prisoners to be concerned about because Crusty brought one that was drowning in the bog and Bimbo brought one he had captured."

Although Taymar had no way of knowing, the Wizard had asked Mrs. Squidge to make blinders for the SnuggleWump. They were intended to keep his flashing red eyes from signaling his approach. He had a goblin driver mounted on each head in order to lead a vast group of armed goblins through the barley field. The goblins disappeared into a mole tunnel that circled the farmhouse. Moles were stationed at intervals around the circle waiting for a signal to start digging upwards so the goblins could get to the surface and attack.

Also unknown to the Twith, Squidgy had been instructed by the Wizard to crash her broomstick through the kitchen window as the signal for the moles to start digging. However, the magpies didn't let her get even close to the farm. They chased her as far as the curtain where she had a collision. The broomstick without anyone on it, flew out over the Channel heading for the Eiffel Tower. She and Cajjer landed in the croc' pond and painfully made their way back to the cottage. They never participated in the attack at all.

The fighting at the farmhouse was started by the old farm dog. There were no yard lights on, so no one noticed Ollie wandering over to investigate whether there was any food in his bowl. He smelled a strange creature on *his* territory. The SnuggleWump had stationed himself in front of the farmhouse door. Immediately, the spaniel attacked the animal. Barking wildly, he tried to scare him off.

Ginger raises her hand. "Can I share what happened to me and Vickie?" Taymar nods. "We heard a deafening ROAR, and soon after that, Rasputin came in through the kitchen window. We slammed the door shut so he couldn't get beyond the kitchen and went after him. When I swung my mop at him, I broke the fluorescent ceiling light." She looks over at gran'ma. "I didn't mean to. Sorry."

Gran'ma smiles sympathetically. "It's alright. It can be replaced. You can't."

Vickie wants to share the rest. "I stepped into the pantry and turned on that light. Some of the smaller birds stationed around the house came in after Rasputin. He got out as soon as he could." The two girls smile at each other as they recall their success in fighting off the raven.

Barney breaks in. "Remember, I was the one who had the brilliant idea of inviting the toads to a Raisin-Fest." Stumpy and Cymbeline chuckle at the boy's enthusiasm.

He's right. The father toads had gathered on the Brook awaiting the return of their wives and newborn children. They were happy to accept the invitation. Toads really like raisins. Buffo had joined the mothers and babies streaming out of Gyminge and led the parade to the farmhouse. He and Bingo provided choir music as they marched up from the Brook. It had quite a beat to it, and the toads kept singing and dancing all the way to the farmhouse.

Immediately ahead of them, goblins were pouring out of tunnels all around the house. As the toads approached, the goblins had to inch closer and closer to the walls. They were squeezed tight against the walls by hundreds of toads surrounding the house waiting for the Raisin-Fest. The goblins had no place to move except up the ivy covering the walls. When they did, the birds picked them off like cherries on a tree and dropped them into the cow pond.

Tuwhit and Crusty joined in to help Ollie fight off the SnuggleWump. Tuwhit went for the eye on one head and Crusty went for the eye on the other head. There were more loud ROARS. The three attackers were too much for the SnuggleWump. He gave up the struggle and shuffled forlornly all the way back to Squidgy's cottage.

Nick raises his hand. "Can I tell about the bat?"

Taymar smiles and nods approval to the impetuous boy.

"A bat came in through the front door. We felt sure it was the Wizard. By that time, lights were on throughout the house. It was essential that the bat not be given time to change himself into something huge. A couple of the birds flew straight at him. His wing got badly torn. The bat escaped through the guest bedroom window. We never saw it again."

Titch adds, "I went after him with a rolling pin for what he did to gran'ma." She looks over at the couple on the settee who smile their approval.

Taymar is sobered as he explains further details of the battle. "All had gone well so far, but the foxes went after the teros that were now back at the chicken roost. Ollie smelled the foxes and went for them. Fluke pulled himself loose from his collar and joined in to help him. They ended up fighting six foxes in the cow pond. The foxes fled, but after fighting the SnuggleWump first and then the foxes, Ollie was seriously wounded. Some ribs were broken. Max waded into the pond and took Ollie back to his house. Uncle Andy and the others did what they could, but the spaniel was too badly injured and didn't recover. Fluke was hurt too, but not as badly."

All the Twith and many of the children swallow hard at the memory of their faithful friend.

"There was no one left to fight. Before we released the goblins, we took their weapons, their belts, their braces, and their boots."

By now, the American children know that braces aren't what they have on their teeth. They are suspenders.

"We took," — Taymar looks over towards the settee — "most of Gumpa's stock of raisins for the Raisin-Fest and shared them with the goblins, the toads, the rabbits, and the birds. We let the badgers finish off any that were left. We didn't think you would mind, Gumpa."

Gumpa gives a wry little grin and thinks, 'Well, I'll have to make a trip to the grocery store before I can make any more yeast buns. But that's alright.'

Dayko's Rime

Cydlo and Elisheba are thoughtful after hearing about the battle. Cydlo now has a better understanding of the seriousness of what was going on around him that first evening after he arrived. He is humbled. 'These Beyonder children risked everything just to help the Twith. I experienced that same kind of bravery when they rescued gran'ma, but this time, it wasn't even for one of their own. Their help will increase our chances for the Return. Things are looking up at last.'

Elisheba realizes, 'I've come into an unusual band of brothers and sisters that fully accept me. And it includes Beyonders willing to risk themselves for the good of the Twith. They have many differences but the same fierce determination. They are knitted together by the desire to achieve a common goal — our Return to Gyminge.'

Jock has a suggestion. "There are several matters yet to cover. I'd like Gerald to put what has happened into a time frame. Cydlo and Elisheba need an opportunity to tell their story. There's the special errand the two Shadow boys are on in Gyminge to discuss too. First, though, how about we take a break to stretch? Would you girls like to see whether there's any cocoa or biscuits left? You just stay put gran'ma."

Gran'ma grins and decides to relax just where she is. That isn't easy for gran'ma. She's one who likes to jump up and get things done herself. But she thinks, 'I don't need to stir myself this time. Everyone is so glad to have me back, they all want to help however they can. They are happy to do that, and I need to let them do it.'

Stormy and Vickie see to the drinks for the Beyonders. Micah volunteers to serve the cookies. He has his thumb on the chocolate-coated cookie to make sure he gets it himself. He grins. 'Gumpa's advice for saving the cookie I want works like a charm.' Cymbeline and Barney disappear down into Twith Mansion to bring up enough drinking mugs for the Twith.

Previously, Jock had asked gran'ma to make copies of Dayko's Rime for all the Beyonders. At Gerald's request, she has numbered the lines from one to thirty-six. As they stand and stretch or move about, each of the Beyonders is given a copy. Gumpa has shrunk enough copies of the Rime for each of the Twith and the Shadow children to have one. Specs has put a copy on cardboard that's folded so it stands upright for Gerald to use.

The empty cocoa cups and mugs are cleared away, and people settle down once again. Micah offers Nick another biscuit before he takes them back out to the kitchen. There he helps himself to one more before he puts the plate down, pauses a moment, and decides to pop another one into his pocket in case he gets hungry. Then he returns to his seat.

Gerald stands by the Rime. Before he begins, he asks, "Are all the windows securely closed?" They are. "This part of our conversation must be kept secret between ourselves. Anyone not present at this time, other than Bimbo and Bollin, Tuwhit and Crusty, will not be told about what's said, and no copy of the Rime is to be shared or shown to anyone else without permission from Jock or myself. If you children want to keep your copies after the meeting, you must make sure they're kept hidden safely away. The Wizard must not find out about it. At the same time, we hope to benefit from the shared wisdom of all present, and I hope everyone will speak up."

The Rime is new to Elisheba. As she reads it, she looks over at her father with amazement.

Gerald explains about the poem. "Dayko was the last High Seer of the Twith. Our seers could see into the future although what they saw was not always immediately understandable, even to them. Dayko was writing this before he visited the king at the castle the last time they met. He returned home, greatly troubled in his heart over the future of the Twith. It was then that he completed the Rime, even while the attack on the castle was going on."

Gerald bends over and opens up the cover of the Book of Lore. Inside it is a folded piece of vellum which is very thin leather prepared for writing on. He opens it and shows it around for all of them to see. The writing is altogether different from the fine artistic work in the Book of Lore. It's faded and indistinct. It has clearly been written in a hurry and the lines aren't straight and parallel. Several words have been crossed out and changed. It's easy to see that it's verses of a poem.

"This is Dayko's Rime. It's the last thing he wrote, and he left it for our guidance. I'll read the whole poem to you first, and then we'll go through it in more detail. It will take us some time to do that, so we probably won't complete it today." He reads the poem slowly and without pausing for comments. He has a pointer, and as he talks, he sometimes points to the line of the Rime he's reciting.

1. *Forget not the land that you leave*
2. *As you flee from the pain and grief.*
3. *Let Truth in your heart ever burn,*
4. *It alone can bring your Return.*
5. *The hour the Return shall begin,*
6. *The captive shall tug at her chain.*
7. *Two spheres of night only you stay,*
8. *You shall not have longer a day.*
9. *From the water the shield will come,*
10. *The sword will come forth from the stone,*
11. *The dirk from the dust will return,*
12. *And the cloth will give up the crown.*
13. *The open door's better to guard*
14. *Than one which is bolted and barred.*
15. *Though conspire the foe and his friend*
16. *Yet the dog shall win in the end.*
17. *You go through the heart of the log,*
18. *Though the way is hid in the bog.*
19. *Black and white the flag high will rise.*
20. *The Child shall lead on to the Prize.*
21. *The goblet holds no draught of wine*
22. *And yields but a drop at a time.*
23. *The King will arise in the wood.*

24. *The Rime is at last understood.*
25. *The armour the flame will withstand.*
26. *Salt wind shall blow over the land*
27. *For light in the heart of the ring*
28. *Shall end the restraint of the king.*
29. *The belt is restored from the fire.*
30. *Brides shall process to the byre.*
31. *The loss of the Lore gives grief,*
32. *Though what is that to a life?*
33. *The fall will lead straight to the wall.*
34. *Hope is restored last of all.*
35. *Two reds in the night shall be green.*
36. *All's done. I've told what I've seen.*

Each of the listeners recognizes lines that make sense. Even the new children are making sense of some of the lines. Other lines make no sense at all. The poem means more to some than to others.

"Now let's look more carefully. You can mark notes on your copies, if you want. Stormy has pencils. I'll try to explain what I understand. You should share any thoughts you might have."

Gerald Explains the Rime

"The first verse says that only Truth can bring our Return. This is why all of us, not just the Twith, must always tell the Truth. If we stray from it, or can be persuaded to do so, then the Wizard remains secure in Gyminge, and nothing we can do will defeat him. If the Wizard knew what Dayko wrote, he would be delighted if we would tell lies the way he does. That would mean that by our own choice and action, we are forever barred from our own country. There could be, like a hidden mousetrap in front of us, a trap to tempt us to lie. It might be only a little lie, maybe what some call a white lie, maybe a half-truth that isn't the whole truth. But just one such tiny slipup will be enough to bar our return home.

"Look now at verse two. This verse tells us when the Return will begin and how long we have left to our Return."

5. *The hour the Return shall begin,*
6. *The captive shall tug at her chain.*
7. *Two spheres of night only you stay,*
8. *You shall not have longer a day.*

"From line six, we know that the captive is a woman, we know that she's chained, and we know that she struggles to get free. We have to ask ourselves whether this has yet happened."

Rachael's hand shoots up.

"Yes, Rachael?"

"Gran'ma was chained up in the laundry at Goblin Castle. AJ used his axe and cut her loose near her ankle and also where the chain was fastened to the floor. Then gran'ma threw the chain at the goblins up on the wall."

Gran'ma and AJ are nodding. Yes, that's what happened.

Gerald continues. He had already reached this same conclusion. "Then let's put a tick against line six. Now what do these first two lines of the verse mean for us? Simply that the clock has started ticking for the Return ... and we only have a limited time to prepare. Today is what date?"

Specs is quick to answer, "Today is Wednesday. It's just after midsummer, June twenty-second."

Gerald turns to the elderly couple on the settee. "Gumpa, do you happen to remember the date that gran'ma was captured by the Wizard?"

As if Gumpa could forget! "It was nine days ago. The worst nine days of my life! It was the evening of last Monday, June thirteenth."

Gran'ma breaks in, surprised that someone like her should be in a vision of an ancient seer many hundreds of years ago. "The goblins put me to work in the laundry the next day. That was Tuesday, the fourteenth. I tried to see if I could get loose, but although I pulled as hard as I could, I couldn't manage it. I ended up with sores on my ankles."

The children lean forward, listening keenly to all that's being said.

Gerald continues. "Now what do lines seven and eight mean?" He reads them again.

    7.   *Two spheres of night only you stay,*
    8.   *You shall not have longer a day.*

Specs wants to answer and waves his hand over his head.
"Yes, Specs?"

Specs is called Specs because he wears eye glasses called spectacles. He's a twelve-year-old English schoolboy from one of the London suburbs. Away from his school uniform, he looks like any regular boy. He wears short jeans with ragged legs, socks around his ankles, and black sneakers. He enjoys solving problems, especially problems with numbers. 'I'm so enjoying this summer adventure with the Twith. I'll never forget the exciting rescue of gran'ma from Goblin Castle. It's the high point of my life.' He's been busy scribbling and calculating even while Gerald was talking. He speaks with assurance about the facts he gives. One of his hobbies is watching the night skies. "Well, I think it's pretty clear. A sphere of night would be a full moon. The length of time between one full moon and the next varies but averages twenty-nine and a half days. Two spheres of night would be fifty-nine days. That's eight weeks and three days. Since gran'ma was chained to the floor on June fourteenth, that would make it the twelfth of August. What do you think, Gerald?"

Gerald has already traveled this way in his thoughts except that he only counted twenty-eight days in a lunar month. Specs' figures give them another two days. "That's good, Specs. Because of line eight, we're told that we have only until that date to complete the Return. There won't be a single day more! We have to start moving fairly soon to allow for all the obstacles the Wizard will place in our way as we get closer to the castle. Since the clock is now ticking for us, it seems unlikely that we'll get another chance some other year if we fail with this one. We just have to succeed this summer!"

The children are thinking how this will affect them. Will there be enough time for them to help? The time falls within their summer holidays, but for Stormy and Bajjer whose school in America restarts in August, there will be only just enough time.

Gerald continues, "Let's look at line nine."

9. *From the water the shield will come,*

"We think Dayko would have meant the shield of King Rufus. At the time he wrote this, the shield was in the king's possession, but later, he was wounded fighting at Fowler's Bridge. A javelin was thrust into the king's shoulder through the shield. You saw the hole in his armor where he was pierced. Crusty caught him in one claw and was able to lift him and carry him out over the lake back to the castle. While swinging around to approach the wall, the shield slipped off the king's arm and fell into the lake. So where is the shield now? During the work on enlarging the lake so that it surrounded the castle, it could have been found. There was a time the lake was dry. We don't know if the Wizard found it. If it came into his possession, he might have destroyed it. More likely, though, he would have kept it in the castle as a trophy of war. At this time, we don't know about the shield. Does anyone have anything more to add about the shield?"

Stormy breaks in. "When Dayko wrote this Rime, the shield was in the place where the king usually kept it. Maybe in a cupboard or the armory. Yet he knew for sure that the shield would come from the water. We know that it fell into the lake. So, as the line says, it doesn't matter if it's been found. It will have come from the water. I believe it means that, although we don't know where it is at this time, it will be found in time for the Return."

Gerald commends Stormy. "You are right. Dayko didn't know the shield was going to be in the lake, so he certainly 'envisioned' correctly. Now let us go on to line ten."

10. *The sword will come forth from the stone,*

Jock breaks in, smiling at Gerald. "Let's wait on this line awhile. Bimbo has gone back to Gyminge to try to recover the sword from the stone. Cydlo had some information that he shared with me, and we felt it was worth taking the risk of sending Dr. Tyfuss back to Gyminge with Bimbo to see whether it can be located and recovered. Bollin is with them only as far as beyond the waterfall. If all goes well, he'll be back soon to tell us how things are in Gyminge."

Barney hears something. He signals Bajjer to come and take him down off the table. He says, "I think I hear Buffo ringing, Jock. I'll just go and see."

He's off down the little winding staircase. While they wait for the boy to get back, Ginger asks, "Does the line about the sword and the stone mean like King Arthur and the sword Excalibur? That was in a stone, and only the boy Arthur was able to remove it." Ginger is into King Arthur and is ready to explain the details of the story further, if Gerald needs them.

Before Gerald can reply that he doesn't know, Barney is back. Lifted back up onto the table, he explains. "Buffo had a visit from his nephew, Bingo. One of the returning mother toads met one of the Little People in Gyminge and brought a message from him. Here it is."

It's a note from Bollin.

The Cloth and the Crown

Bollin's note is brief and simple. Jock reads it out loud. "*King Haymun hurt.*" He explains, "That's the goblin king." He continues reading the note. "*Vyruss helping him to castle. I'll stay and help Bimbo.* It seems the boys have resolved what could have been a sticky situation with the goblin king. They probably won't get much sleep tonight though. Let's leave the matter of the sword until we hear more from them. Gerald, please continue with Dayko's Rime."

Gerald sat down while waiting for Barney and now returns to his printout of the Rime. He reads out line eleven.

11. *The dirk from the dust will return,*

"Do we have any comments about that one?"
There's an outburst of laughter.
"That's a line that you can all see displayed on the table in its pouch. We can mark a tick against that one, can't we? Stormy already told us it was very dusty. Yet without gran'ma having been kidnapped, we would never have known about the dirk. I'm beginning to get a sense that everything that's happening to us, even including the bad things, is working towards one great end — our Return to Gyminge. Next is line twelve."

12. *And the cloth will give up the crown.*

"Well, this one is a puzzle. Does anyone have any ideas about this one? We already have the crown from the goblin king here on the table. It's unlikely that Dayko was referring to any crown of King Haymun's in his poem. It's more likely to be a crown belonging to King Rufus. He had several crowns that he used on various occasions. There's the one on his helmet that you have already seen, but the cloth doesn't seem to fit along with the helmet. Then there's the great State Crown that's used for Coronation and State occasions. It's very valuable and is kept safely in the castle. We presume, unless it's now in the Wizard's possession, that it's still there. I think it's unlikely that the Wizard would turn the State Crown over to King Haymun although it's possible he might have done so. Then there was the king's working crown, a much lighter headpiece. Presumably, that was in his quarters in the castle because he was wearing his crowned helmet when he was wounded in battle. We have no idea where that might now be. Does anyone have any comments? If not, we'll leave the line unsolved and move on to the next lines."

Gerald looks around the room. Everyone is thoughtful.

Katie raises a question. "I wonder whether King Haymun might be using the king's working crown? Especially since he lost his other one. Bollin said Dr. Tyfuss was helping the goblin king. If he was wearing a crown, couldn't they take it from him?"

Gerald answers. "King Rufus was much bigger than Haymun, so it wouldn't fit without being altered. But it's certainly possible that a smithy could have resized it."

Cydlo sits on a stiff-backed chair. Elisheba sits at his feet. Her full blue skirt is draped around her folded legs. Her long auburn hair is caught in a clip at the back of her head. Cymbeline sits next to her, leaning against Stumpy's legs. The girls have been holding hands. Elisheba reaches under her spread-out skirt and removes something wrapped in cloth. The diameter is slightly larger than her head and the depth is the size of her upright hand. Her voice is sweet and musical as she lifts the object up for all to see. "Is it possible that Dayko is referring to this?" She passes it to Gerald.

Jock jerks forward, and his mouth drops open.

Taymar looks at Elisheba with utter amazement written across his face. No one had seen her carrying anything into the room. He wonders, 'Where did she get it, and what is it?'

Gerald doesn't uncover what Elisheba passed to him. He has an idea what it is, but he wants to know more before he removes the cloth.

Dayko's Rime

His voice is strangely hoarse and strained. "Elisheba, before we look at what you gave me, can you tell me about it, where it came from, and how it got here?"

"My father can tell you better."

The wounded woodsman is relaxed and smiling. Taymar looks at him very keenly as though he's searching his memory for a past recollection of the man.

A big smile is on Cydlo's face as he looks around the room before speaking. "You have already seen the dirk that Bimbo found in the toad tunnel at the border of Gyminge. In that same place, he later found the item that Elisheba just handed to Gerald. When he brought it back here, he left it with me. He had not looked to see what it might be. He felt one of the Twith should do so."

The room is completely empty of sound. Gerald looks around at all the Twith. 'If this is what I think it might be, this is a very special occasion. From the same hiding place has come the Royal Dirk. Who shall open it?'

He goes over to Stumpy, gives him an encouraging smile, and hands the object to him. "Stumpy, will you please uncover this for us and show us what it is?"

Stumpy is overwhelmed. He doesn't move. He just sits there. He studies the size and shape carefully. Whatever color the cloth covering might once have been, it is now the color of the dust that dropped on it year after year for many centuries. 'This may be the king's crown. Who am I to open it after it's been hidden away for so long? I'm just a nobody. All my life, I've put other people first. This time too.' He appeals without words to Cymbeline.

The girl looks up at him from between his knees. Her smile is broad as she shakes her head. "No, Uncle, you have to do it."

Barney adds to her remark, "Yes, Uncle, you must do it."

Stumpy's rosy face is ringed with white hair and a short beard. His clothing is the regular leather vest over a cloth shirt and the pants that all the Twith men wear. On his head is the red woolen hat with a bobble on top. He looks back at Gerald. 'Hasn't Gerald made a mistake?

I'm nobody special, and this is … well, this is…this is Dayko's Rime coming true in my hands. Well, isn't it?'

Nobody else is willing to take this honor away from him.

Cymbeline encourages him, "Go on, Uncle. Show us what it is."

Tears begin to roll down the old man's cheeks. He isn't the only one crying, but he can't see that through his own tears. His fingers fumble as he works to remove the ties holding the cloth to its content. There are laces wrapped tightly around the dusty cloth.

No one moves to help him. Everyone is content to wait until Stumpy himself reveals whatever is inside.

At last the various knots and loops yield and the cloth is loose and free. Slowly, the cloth, and the dust with it, drops away. Shining in the woodcarver's hands and unseen for centuries is a crown of gold, lavishly decorated with jewels.

Cymbeline passes her handkerchief up to her uncle and whispers, "Here, Uncle. Clean it with this." Rough, hardworking hands worn by toil and scarred with many cuts from knives and chisels softly wipe away dust from gold, rubies, emeralds, and diamonds. The full glory of the crown blazes in the reflected light from the lights above.

There's spontaneous clapping.

Jordy, the talkative northerner, can't believe his eyes. He rubs his hand across them and shakes his head. He, like Jock, isn't native to Gyminge. The pair came south together to help King Rufus fight off an invasion. That defense failed. They fled with the others. His mind is whirling. 'The Twith have only had Dayko's Rime to encourage them that one day, there will be an end to the exile. Now the beautiful young stranger who just arrived among us is offering a solution to one part of the Rime. What else might be revealed?'

The crown is clearly for a large Twith head. It has an open center. It isn't an ornate crown for state occasions but is fashioned more on the style of a coronet. The circumference is a deep band of gold decorated with three parallel rings of precious stones. The upper and lower rings are pearls, and the middle ring is rubies. The crown has a scalloped top consisting of eight waves. The peak of each wave is the same height as the depth of the gold band and is decorated with a gold oak leaf. In the center of each leaf is a precious stone, ruby alternating with emerald or diamond. One wave, indicating the front of the crown, is higher than the others, and in the center of its leaf is the largest of the rubies. Below it, on the gold band itself, is the Royal Crest of the Twith — a crouching lion, a rearing horse and a crown. There's no doubt which royal house this crown belongs to.

Stumpy looks around and smiles broadly. The weight of the centuries is dropping away. He feels almost young again. The joy of the occasion catches hold of him. He forgets his natural humility. For once in his life, he is center stage. Surprisingly, especially to himself, he's actually willing to be there. Rising carefully from his chair, he gains and holds his balance.

Raising the crown high and forward so all can see, he shouts, "Long Live the King!"

All in the room echo back, "Long Live the King!"

Stumpy, his face glowing with pride, turns to Gerald and Jock who are both standing and clapping. Lowering the crown to chest level, he looks at it carefully. His mind whirls as he drinks in what he sees. 'I may never be this close to it again.' At last, he tries to hand the crown to Jock, but the Scot steps aside and points towards Gerald.

Gerald is the keeper of the treasures, and one more has now come home. The scribe accepts the crown and puts it down on the table on its cloth. His obvious joy spreads all around the room. None of them will ever forget the drama of this moment. All of them are hanging on his every word.

"We have just witnessed the fulfillment of line twelve of Dayko's Rime, 'The cloth will give up the crown.' Things seem to be falling into place."

The Dog Shall Win

When things settle down, Gerald picks up his pointer. "Let's continue our study of the Rime. Look at verse four."

    13. *The open door's better to guard*
    14. *Than one which is bolted and barred.*
    15. *Though conspire the foe and his friend*
    16. *Yet the dog shall win in the end.*

"Perhaps Taymar can throw some light on this particular verse."

Taymar stands up for the comments he wants to make. "Jock charged us to defend the farmhouse. We took the advice of this particular verse. We decided to defend the house by allowing all the doors and windows to be completely open. Even though the huge SnuggleWump was at the front door, he wasn't able to get in. The bat and the raven that did get in both had to flee very soon after they got inside. The foe in the verse is the Wizard and his friend is Mrs. Squidge. They thought they had everything under control, yet it was the farm dog, Ollie, who was in control of everything. He started the fighting, and it was Ollie who won in the end, even though he lost his own life doing so."

Specs interjects a comment. "That was like Lord Nelson at Trafalgar. Ollie could have been called Horatio instead of Oliver."

With sadness in his voice, Gerald adds, "Ollie made it possible for us to put a checkmark by verse four. It might have just been a coincidence that he came across at that time and found the SnuggleWump. Yet Dayko saw that happening all those years ago. We will remember Ollie as one of the heroes making possible our eventual Return."

Gerald continues. "We are almost halfway through the Rime. The various lines are falling into place as though they are parts of a jigsaw puzzle. Even though some parts are still missing, a pattern is clearly developing and closing around Gyminge and the Wizard. Now for the next two lines."

> 17. *You go through the heart of the log,*
> 18. *Though the way is hid in the bog.*

"These two lines have already been solved for us. Barney recognized the first one before most of you Beyonders were born. He used it as an argument for us to move here almost thirty years ago. The log is beginning to rot away. It won't last much longer, but the entrance to Twith Mansion is still through the log and that's why Buffo stands guard there.

"Although the Twith have been on the Brook for such a long while, not one of us put two and two together about the trail across the bog. It wasn't until Buffo and Bollin started talking that we learned about the spawning trail of the toads. Now there's steady traffic across the bog to the waterfall and on into Gyminge. We and the Wizard's forces are both using it in both directions. Line eighteen is no longer a mystery. However, we have to expect that the Wizard will soon take steps to block that way in. He knows that we have discovered it, but up until this evening, it's still open. Now we come to line nineteen which is puzzling."

    19. *Black and white the flag high will rise.*

"What can this mean? Why is the word *rise* and not *raise*? Is it just because it needs to rhyme with prize? Is the flag supposed to be black-and-white? The Wizard's flag is all black. Does it instead mean a black skinned person and a white skinned person? Two people holding up the flag? You can't have one person with two skin colors. But is the Rime talking about skin color? Couldn't it be clothes? What about a harlequin wearing a jester's suit that's half black and half white? But why? There has to be a reason. Can it be something other than a person? There are creatures, even if there aren't people, that are black and white. There's Maggie the magpie, and there's Bandy the badger. There are black-and-white horses and ponies, even dogs and cats. Somehow though, that seems contrived and not the kind of thing Dayko might have been seeing."

    Specs puts his hand up. He's all smiles as though a great shaft of sunshine has just hit him, and he is warm all over. "It's all over. It's already done. You can tick that line."

    Gerald blinks. "What do you mean, Specs? So far, no one else has carried the flag except you and Bajjer."

    "There you have it! Bajjer! He carried the flag when we left here, didn't he? We call him Bajjer because he collects badges, but a badger is black-and-white, isn't it? I'm sure that's what Dayko's Rime means in a secret way. Maybe he was seeing someone who looked like a badger as he looked into the future. We have such a badger with us right now, and we all saw him carry the flag. Let's go on to the next line. I'm sure this is right."

Gerald looks at Jock. They weren't thinking along the lines of a nicknamed boy, but the other Twith are all nodding. Bajjer sounds like *badger*, and a badger is black-and-white.

Gerald says, "You see, we would never have come up with that answer by ourselves. Specs may well be right. If so, it was in front of our faces the whole time. It was a kind of riddle. The rest of the Rime seems easier to understand."

"We Need a King!"

It's time for another stretch break. The children and the Twith stand, twist their shoulders, lift their legs, and swing their arms. They chatter among themselves until they're once again seated and settled.

Most of the children, especially the newer arrivals, are learning a good deal about the struggle of the Little People. They're gaining new understanding of the long, long stretch of time between the exile and now. The Twith have been so patient, waiting for the pieces in the Rime to fall into place. They begin to see how everything is now building to a climax. There are now only a few hidden mysteries left to solve, but there's also little time. Solutions still have to be found before the Twith are free to return to their own land. They silently wonder, 'Will all the riddles be solved in time? Or will August the twelfth arrive before they're able to complete the Return?'

Gerald looks around. It's getting late, and soon, Gumpa will call time for bed. Some of the younger children are already rubbing their eyes. Lupus, the wolf-dog, is asleep beneath Gumpa's feet. Back home in Gyminge, it was Cydlo's foot on the animal's shoulder. Although the woodsman is unchanged in size, the dog moved from Twith-size to Beyonder-size on his arrival on the Brook. Gumpa has his eyes closed. Although no one can tell, he's most likely still listening intently.

"Is everyone settled and comfortable?" Heads nod. "Good. Does anyone need an extra cushion?" Heads shake. "Okay. What do we make then of the last line of this verse?"

20. *The Child shall lead on to the Prize.*

"This can mean two things, I think. The first is that there's a competition with a prize and a Beyonder child, or a team of them, will win the prize. We know that the Child in the Rime is a Beyonder child because the word is capitalized. It could be that he or she will be like our team captain to receive the prize. Although that's a possibility, I don't really think that's what this means. More likely is that the Child will lead the Return to Gyminge, and the castle itself is the prize to be gained. If this is so, then it means that at some later stage, when our Return is closer, that we can, indeed we must, appoint a Child to lead us in the Last Battle. We don't have any idea whether the Child is a boy or a girl, but"— he grins as he speaks — "we have plenty of both when the time comes. What do the rest of you think?"

Six children in particular are focusing on the fact that Gerald said there may be a competition.

Bajjer wonders, 'Will Jock ask for volunteers? I hope so. I want to be involved.'

Nick has his own concern, 'I wonder if Jenn will help me write an application?'

Jenn, on the other hand, wonders, 'Should my application be just a folded note or sealed in an envelope?'

Stormy thinks,' I wonder if I'll make the athletics team? Which events should I enter?'

Lucas is interested in something else. 'I hope there will be a band I can play with.'

Austin is curious, 'Who does Dayko think will be offering the prize — the Wizard or Jock or someone else?'

Specs is the one who answers since no one else makes any comments. "I think this is just something that we'll see happen, and we'll recognize it after it happens. Until then, we should just give the line a check mark and go on. If it hasn't happened by the time we're on our way back to Gyminge, then it would seem we should appoint a Child to lead us."

Gerald agrees. "You are probably right. Alright, let's continue."

21. *The goblet holds no draught of wine*
22. *And yields but a drop at a time.*

"There's no trouble understanding these lines. The answer to this couplet is right in front of us. Here on this table is Queen Sheba's treasure chest, and within that is the Goblet of Consecration. It yields but a drop at a time because there's so little oil left from when the monarchy in Gyminge was first instituted. Only a drop at a time is now used. Now here are the next two lines. We're getting to the end of the poem. What do we make of these? This is an answer we must get right."

> 23. *The king will arise in the wood.*
> 24. *The Rime is at last understood.*

"These are the central key lines of the poem. When the king arises in the wood, we shall understand everything else in the Rime even though there may still be things left to happen before our Return. I don't know whether you've noticed it, but somehow, this Rime and our Return to Gyminge are closely related to a king. Just now, we don't have a king because the king is missing. But look at what's on the table, the goblet and the oil of his consecration, his ring of accession, his dirk, his armor, and his crown. It's all just waiting for the man himself. Some items are still not with us — his shield and his sword. But Bimbo and Bollin have gone seeking after at least one of them. We hope they will be successful. But until then, we aren't fully prepared to welcome our king, even if he should turn up right now.

"Our king used to be King Rufus. If he is alive, he is still our king. If he died of his wounds, we are saddened. Yet somewhere, there's someone to succeed him even though we may not know who he is. King Rufus was a good king. After we return, we'll want to see our land governed in the same wise way it was before the Wizard came. Perhaps Dayko requires that we find our king before we return and not wait until afterwards. Perhaps now is when we need his leadership and example the most for the journey is soon ahead of us. It may be that we should not travel until we do have a king. We need a king!

"This line is a special line for it's a key to the others. When the king arises in the wood, we'll understand other mysteries in the Rime. I used to think that Stumpy would be the one to solve this for us. He takes a piece of oak or walnut, and as he cuts away, he allows the wood to tell him what's inside. This is the way that he uncovers birds. Although it's mostly birds, sometimes there are other creatures he sets free. No one had any idea they were inside the wood before he revealed them. His workshop is filled with carvings that have, as the Rime says, arisen in the wood. Through the years, I thought that one day he would discover the likeness of King Rufus as he carved away. Or possibly, a future king that we might recognize, or perhaps even an unknown king. Even if what he carved was a head wearing a crown, it would fulfill this line of the Rime.

"However, it hasn't happened this way, so there must be some other meaning. Let's look elsewhere for our answer. The word *wood* has another meaning besides the part of a tree that Stumpy carves or what is used to light a fire. It also means a grouping of trees smaller than a forest and larger than a grove. Cydlo, you are a woodsman, and, Elisheba, you too are acquainted with the woods. You've lived in the forest in Gyminge and must have seen many comings and goings during your years there. Can you help us in our search for a king?"

Cydlo's Response

Elisheba makes no sign of responding to Gerald's invitation. She gives a wry little smile and looks up at her father. All eyes are on the man behind her. When he arrived at the farmhouse, he was close to death. His broad twirling mustache and his wild mop of red hair were both matted with blood. Stumpy, his barber, not only trimmed his hair and beard, but shaved off the mustache altogether. It was as though a disguise had been removed. This evening, he looks like a totally different man. He's still recuperating and doesn't move from his chair. However, he sits straight up in it, alert and confident.

Gumpa studies Cydlo. He thinks, 'Occasionally, you enter a crowded room and meet a stranger about whom you know nothing. It can be in a classroom that you are entering for the first time, meeting your fellow students. One person sticks out among all the others, even without a word being said. There's a kind of personal magnetism that attracts you, some vitality inside that radiates and invites you to come closer. You are intrigued and want to get better acquainted and know more. Whatever it is, Cydlo has it. I notice that even Micah is no longer fiddling with the things in his pocket.

The quiet woodsman explains to Gerald, "What I have to say may take a long time. Is it not late?"

Gerald looks over to gran'ma. She's anxious to hear what the man has to say. "I'll be breaking one of my own rules, but the children can sleep in tomorrow. Take as long as you need. If it's too long for one sitting, we can resume tomorrow."

Broad smiles adorn the faces of all the children. There's complete silence. No one dares to move in case she should change her mind.

Cydlo speaks loudly enough for everyone to hear easily without straining. "Let me start by telling you what happened long ago when

Gyminge was struggling for its life against its stronger neighbor in the north. As you heard from Jock, King Rufus was severely wounded. He was left in hiding in a secret room behind the great fireplace in his residential quarters in the castle. He had some food and water and a few other essentials."

Something strange suddenly happens on the table where the Twith are sitting. Not a word, other than what Cydlo says, is uttered. It's as though the lights of a theatre are dimmed, and the audience is lost in darkness while the single figure on the stage is caught in focused spotlights. Jock and Jordy and then the others noiselessly slip from their chairs. All the Little People, including even Elisheba, cluster in a part circle before Cydlo to look up at him. Several of them are crying. Those without handkerchiefs pull their sleeves across their eyes to dry them.

Taymar alone doesn't look at Cydlo. He's seated at the edge of the group and looks with complete fascination, almost awe and wonder, at Elisheba.

"The king knew his kingdom was lost and turned the task of its recovery over to a Scotsman he recently met. It was Jock, of course, who came from the north to help. He left with a few others on an eagle headed for the Beyond. The king could not do anything more. He was now alone to face whatever might come. His greatest concern was for his family, perhaps separated from him forever.

"His daughter, Princess Alicia, was sent into hiding before the invasion happened. She and her nurse were in a cottage deep within the southern woods of Gyminge, the ones you know as Blindhouse Wood. Unknown to Alicia, the king secretly betrothed her to be married to the son of a friend, Earl Gareth. Queen Sheba left the castle even as the Wozzle attack developed to go inform her daughter of the plans for marriage made by her parents. The queen had only a small escort of loyal servants.

"The king, who was lying behind the fireplace ill and delirious, thought and expected that he would die. He had a raging fever. When eventually the fever broke, he recovered, but he was almost too weak to stand. He had no idea how long he had been in the room. His clothes were loose and damp to the touch. The lamp had long ago used its oil, and he was in the dark. His eyes adjusted to benefit from the little light there was so he could, with difficulty, make out the contents of the room.

"He struggled to stand up and groped for the jug to gulp down some water. It tasted so sweet. The dim light was a beam from a small spy-hole in the door from the fireplace. He moved silently and slowly, leaning against the wall, to take a look. The Wizard, the victorious enemy from Wozzle, was seated at the great round table surrounded by subordinates. Servants moved to and fro. The king couldn't hear what was being said, but there was a clear atmosphere of exuberance. He didn't recognize any of the faces, but he looked long and hard at the Wizard, imprinting his features in his memory. His right eye twitched with an uncontrollable twitch.

"The king turned away. He needed to build up his strength. As he ate the dried fruit, nuts, and other edibles, he gnawed his way through some stale bread. To escape, he would need to struggle out along the tunnel to the quarry and get clear from there. For at least two more days, the king remained in his shelter. He was very weak but exercised himself to the limit of his strength. He walked around the tiny room, raised each of his legs hundreds of times, and exercised every muscle he could to make himself fit to venture outside. The pain of his wound had to be disregarded.

"He was intent on reaching his daughter and locating his wife. As long as he had life or breath, he would do so — come-what-may. There were weapons in his hideaway. The Royal Sword and other royal weapons would attract attention once he was out in the open. He decided to take only a knife and a good-sized axe. He left all the finely made royal clothing behind. He had other clothes to choose from and selected simple clothing such as that worn by any workman.

"Eventually, he was ready. From the spy-hole, he watched the day recede into darkness. He had traveled the tunnel before and began to make his way as soon as the light faded. There was little that he took with him except the knife, axe, and enough food to last him for a day or two. He could drink from streams. Initially the tunnel, built within the thickness of the outer wall of the castle, went down several flights of steps connected by flat landings. At the foot of the last steps, he felt around with his fingers, searching for something that his father once showed him. He found it. His memory didn't fail him. As he moved on down the continuing slope, he was now below the level of the ground and underneath the lake.

"The slope of the tunnel leveled out and then began its climb. He smelled fresher air. Tiny noises reached him. There was a faint tinkling ahead that he recognized. The noise came from jangling metal discs that hung near the entrance of Mad Jack's cave at the quarry. He wasted no time looking around the cave.

"As dawn broke, he was well beyond the quarry and the edge of the forest and into the trees. The journey was a long one. He had little strength and had to rest frequently. He was about to look for somewhere to sleep for a while when he came upon a clearing. There had been fighting there. He could tell it was a sword fight because there were the sprawled bodies of two men on the ground. They had been dead for several days, perhaps a week, perhaps even longer. There were many hoofprints, scuffed and deep and in all directions as though horses were whirling and rearing in a frenzied encounter. There were no horses around now and no discarded weapons. Only two dead men. The king turned them over. With dismay he recognized them as the men who had accompanied Queen Sheba as her escort.

"There was no sign of Queen Sheba. He wondered whether the dead men were on their way to the princess or returning from leaving the queen with her. The hoofprints retraced their path back in the direction of the castle. There were no signs of such prints on the way ahead. The queen never reached her daughter. The king's heart was utterly broken.

"The king pushed on deeper into the forest. He rested when his energy gave out but pushed on with increasing concern for the princess. By evening, he was close by the cottage where she had been sent into hiding. It was back on a narrow linking path away from the tracks wandering through the forest and was selected for its isolation. Driving himself forward with only little rest, he was at the point of complete exhaustion.

"The king was too late. Where the cottage had once been, he saw only empty land. A fire had consumed most of the cottage with its thatched roof and left only dry, powdery ash. There were no glowing embers wherever the king poked. Nothing smoldered. This fire was old and cold, so it had happened days ago. He couldn't tell how many days ago though. Only a few of the oak beams, rock hard, weren't fully burned. They were twisted into awkward angles as they fell, propped against each other. There was no sign of survivors and no apparent attempt to salvage anything. The king sank to his knees and wept."

A Blackbird Sings

It's as though everyone in the long room has been frozen into position, like figures on a photograph. No one moves a muscle. Cydlo makes no gestures nor tries to catch and hold attention. He simply tells a story that somehow he's well acquainted with and remembers well.

"That was the lowest point of the king's life. He had lost everything — his kingdom, his family, his friends. He was sunk in despair all night. As the light crept back into the sky, he heard something that broke into his grief. It was a bird singing. Since before he fought his last battle at Fowler's Bridge, he hadn't heard a bird sing.

"It was a blackbird. It was probably one of the last birds flying south on its way to the Beyond. It may have just stopped in for a rest on its way. The king wouldn't hear a blackbird again until many, many years passed. It didn't matter. The bird's song was the start of the journey back for the king. The bird's singing was a song of hope. Darkness had wrapped the bird around, but now light had come, the day had begun, and it was time for the bird to move on. It did so, and the king heard it no more. It was time for the king to move on as well.

"He pulled himself together. He was still a king although he no longer had a kingdom. A king's duty is to be a king, not a broken reed or a woman weeping for the past. Around the perimeter of the fire, there were hoof imprints, at least three or four differently shod horses. The king searched through the ashes of the cottage. He wondered where Alicia and her nurse could possibly be. There were no signs that anyone died in the fire. More likely, the women were taken away captive, or perhaps Alicia had escaped after all. He could hope.

"His thoughts turned to the queen. The king doubted that she had died. He would surely feel that within himself if that had happened. The scene of the fighting along his journey suggested that she was captured. If that were so, then he could still do something. The Wizard would surely use the small dungeon for special prisoners, even if he used it only temporarily until he put her into a bottle. Only his family knew the way back into the castle that he just used to escape. He also knew something further, that there was, from that tunnel, a way into the dungeons as well as into the fireplace.

"From the dungeon for special prisoners, there was a secret link tunnel to the escape tunnel. The entrance doors on either end were hard to find. It had been built in by the castle stonemasons in anticipation of a possible coup and imprisonment of the king. As far as the king was aware, only he and no other in Gyminge knew of the secret link tunnel or the ways to enter it. He himself had only been in it once when he was shown its existence and the ways of exit and entrance by his father.

"After lying in the secret room behind the fireplace with a burning fever for so long, he was relieved to feel his mind working rapidly once again, thinking clearly. He felt like a king once more and welcomed the challenge to regain his kingdom. The king thought about the princess and where she might be. Several things could have happened to Alicia if she were still alive. She could have been taken captive by the horsemen who were at the cottage. They would have most likely taken her to the Wizard. His daughter, he had no doubt in his mind, would try to escape. Alternatively, she could have escaped the horsemen and fled with her nurse into the forest where she would hide. What would Alicia do then? She would not waste her time crying. His daughter was resourceful and had initiative, very much like her mother in so many ways.

"He knew without a doubt what his daughter would do, and he knew what he had to do without wasting any more time. If she had succeeded in staying free, she would make her way with great care back to the castle only to find it had fallen. Many would have seen the king wounded in battle and reported it to her. She would hear that he had gone to the Beyond on an eagle, but she would not believe them. She knew that he would not flee without her. She would make her way through the tunnel back to the hideaway behind the fireplace to search for her wounded father. As a clever girl, she would make the attempt at night to remain unseen. The king needed to return to Mad Jack's cave in the quarry and wait for her there.

"Several times on the way back to the quarry, the king had to avoid goblin soldiers. Some were mounted, some on foot, but all were rounding up any free Twith they could find. Long lines of peasants and farmers, herders and woodsmen, husbands and wives and children were trailing towards the castle. The king could see that in the distance, the traditional central gathering ground for the people, despite its great size, was slowly being filled.

"No one recognized the king. He was unshaven and unkempt. He pulled a peasant's cap down over his face and looked down at the ground as he shuffled by any local people he met. At last, he reached the quarry and the cave. His heart leapt! Hope was springing into joy. On the ground beneath the dangling fragments of tinkling metal hanging from the tree at the entrance to the cave was a small fragment of cloth. It wasn't there when he passed through earlier. It wasn't accidentally dropped because it had a small rock on top so it wouldn't blow away. He recognized the finely woven handkerchief embroidered around the edges. It was Alicia's! This was more than he could have expected!"

A great sigh of relief and joy passes around the long room in the farmhouse. Rarely have so many people sat unmoving for such a long time. Their sigh releases some of their tension.

Cydlo smiles with pleasure. "Before the king picked up the handkerchief, he examined the ground carefully. There were footprints, most likely Alicia's. They crisscrossed the cave. She was there for some time. There were also animal prints on the floor. He studied those carefully. It was possible they were dog prints, but more likely, they were wolf! He was fearful the cave had become a wolf's den, but he hadn't smelled wolf when he passed through earlier. The animal was a large one, not a pup. One of the animal's prints overlapped the edge of the girl's footprint. The animal was later than the girl. The clutching white hand of fear seized his heart. However, the handkerchief was clean and undisturbed, so he put his fears aside.

"He replaced the handkerchief with a coin of the realm he had in his pocket. It was of little value, but the face stamped on it was the face of King Rufus. As he examined the ground further, he saw traces of a girl's footprints disappearing into the darkness of the tunnel, but none were returning. And in the last of the light from behind, he noticed that the wolf's steps were ahead of the girl's, for her prints erased part of the wolf's prints. They must both be up ahead. He held his knife in his upraised right hand, ready to plunge it forward in a split second for self-defense. He moved very quietly, not wanting to frighten his daughter if she heard approaching footsteps. He went down, then along, and then up the tunnel. He couldn't hear anything ahead, until there was suddenly a growl and a sharp commanding bark. A wolf's bark, but not a full-blooded bark of anger and intent. More a warning to stop.

"The king continued on. His grip tightened on his knife. In his left hand, he had his axe. He would have only seconds to react. Past the place where the link tunnel connected to the dungeon, the escape tunnel climbed flights of steps to the hideaway room behind the fireplace. He couldn't avoid making noise. He could barely see, but ahead he sensed a living presence. He expected a furry missile of intense fury to come hurtling towards him at any time. Yet the animal wasn't barking again. He wondered if the something ahead was only the wolf or was there a person also. He heard the deep menacing growl growing in the wolf's throat. He didn't want to frighten Alicia if she was somehow trapped behind the wolf. He called out into the darkness in a low, urgent voice, using the nickname that only she knew. 'Ashy? Ashy! Ashy, do you hear me?'

"He would never forget the relief he felt as an answering call came back. 'Oh, Daddy, Daddy, yes, I can hear you. I'm here. I'm coming.' He felt a lump in his throat, and his eyes were moist."

Princess Alicia

Cydlo has never told this whole story previously. There was no one, except his daughter, whom he could trust completely. Even to his daughter, he has only shared parts, never fully. However, that was for her own protection and peace of mind. He's surprised. 'That was easier than I thought. But for at least three of those present, life will not be the same again once I finish my story. No matter. Events and people move on, and the future is never the same as the past.'

As he pauses in the telling, he wonders, 'What must Elisheba be thinking?' He notices she grips Cymbeline's hand tightly. 'She is intent on what I've been saying. Her eyes haven't moved off my face.' He wonders about the young man Taymar too. 'His gaze is so intently fixed on Elisheba. Is the lad falling in love with my daughter? What is he thinking now?'

Cydlo continues. "After the two embraced, Alicia led her father up to the hideaway room. The animal, half dog-half wolf, was a friend protecting her. The animal sniffed and smelled around the stranger."

Beneath Gumpa's feet, Lupus, who was half asleep, is suddenly awake and alert. His ears prick upright, and he lifts his head. He barks once and then again as though acknowledging the talk is of animals like himself and settles back with his muzzle flat on the floor. Cydlo smiles affectionately at his dog and resumes his story. "Alicia knelt and talked to the dog, explained the stranger was her father, and they were all friends together. She admonished him to not bark until they were back in the daylight lest they be heard and discovered. They retreated back to Mad Jack's cave. There the father had a chance to look at his daughter in good light. She was footsore and weary. Her green dress was torn, her hair was untidy, and there were smudges and signs of dried tears on her face."

Elisheba will tell her story later. She's glad to have the company of her father, but wishes her mother could be with them. She hasn't seen her mother since she said good-bye as she left for the south forest with her nurse, Nettie.

"The news of her mother's intended journey to see her was a surprise. The queen never reached her."

The queen would not have found her daughter even if she had arrived.

"The king and his daughter were left to hope that if the Wizard had captured her, she would still be alive. The king told his daughter nothing about her betrothal. He would wait for some later opportunity. Alicia related what happened to her. She was uncertain how many days previously it was."

The Twith take little account of the passage of time or its sequences.

"She told her father that she and Nettie were living quiet lives in their hideaway cottage. They decided against having other local people in to help them. It was good for them to have to do things themselves. They had brought enough supplies with them to see them well into the days ahead. One day ran into another. One midmorning on a gloomy day threatened by low dark clouds, the house was surrounded by five horsemen. They were not knights or soldiers, but rough, uncouth, ill-dressed men accustomed to violence. They hadn't bothered to disguise themselves in any way. Their dialect suggested they were native to Gyminge, not from Wozzle. The women thought they were likely a band of robbers living in the forest. Nettie told the girl to hide in the closet. The men hammered at the door and pushed their way in. When they searched the house, they found the princess. They tied her hands, but Nettie was too old to cause any concern, so they didn't bother to tie her. All that was of value and portable was removed and bundled onto three horses so that there was hardly room for the riders.

"Each woman was seated in front of one of the two leading horsemen. The house was deliberately set on fire using sticks of wood taken from the cooking fire. The raiders waited until the fire was well underway before they left. They went up to the main path through the forest and headed west along tracks the girl had never traveled before.

The path rose towards the top of a hill. Suddenly, they were hit by a storm. Alicia was on the leading horse, and the heavy rain was in her face. She wondered whether it would douse the fire at the cottage. The going was difficult, and as the muddy path sloped up, the horse stumbled. Struggling to stay upright, his feet went in all directions. Because Alicia's hands were tied in front of her, she was able to grab the reins. At the same moment, she knocked her head hard back into the face of the rider holding her. Kicking back against his legs, she jammed her heels hard into the flanks of the horse. In normal conditions she would not have succeeded, but the weather was advantageous — lightning, quickly followed by thunder and heavy rain. All the animals were having difficulty as the rain intensified and the hard path got more slippery.

"Her action was a surprise. The horse reared, and the horseman's foot slipped. He leaned awkwardly to the left and tried in vain to hold his balance. His other foot also slipped from the stirrup, and he fell to the ground landing on his back. Before there could be any reaction from those behind them, Nettie, who was waiting for any chance to escape, grabbed at the reins of the second horse. The stallion responded to her pull to the left, slipping and scrambling, and spun around into the fully loaded horses behind. For a few moments, there was chaos.

"Alicia snatched a quick look behind. Nettie screamed, 'Ride for your life! Ride! Ride!' The dismounted rider, hurt in his fall, slipped as he climbed to his feet. He caught hold of the wet tail of the stallion, but it slipped from his hands. The princess was a good horsewoman. She had been trained well by her father, by her mother, and by the stable master as well. Although her hands were tied, she kept her balance. The horse gained good ground ahead of the others behind. Alicia held on well with her knees and was bent low over the horse's shoulders. In moments, there would be pursuit behind her. The path twisted and turned. She was around one bend and then another. Then still another. She gave the animal its head, urging it with her knees and her coaxing voice. Where the paths divided, she couldn't guide the animal onto which path to follow. The horse chose the way.

"Alicia didn't want that. The horse would head for home. That would likely lead her into a camp of robbers. Just around a bend where there was plenty of thick vegetation for shelter, she pulled the horse up tight. He slowed and stopped. Resting her hands on the animal's shoulder, she swung her leg over its flanks, slipped under the reins, and dropped to the ground. There was no time to waste. As hard as she could, she gave the horse a whack to hurry it on its journey home. She scurried into hiding. The horse, with no burden, picked up its gallop towards familiar pastures. Its sound disappeared into the distance.

"The princess forged her way through the undergrowth to a nearby tree. She leaned against it and worked at getting her hands free. Now she heard the galloping pursuit. She threw herself to the ground. Fortunately, that day she had chosen to wear her dark green dress and not her red one. First, there was a single-pursuit horseman, not laden with any baggage or prisoner. He galloped as fast as his horse would go and looked neither to the left nor to the right. Finally, after an interval, the three remaining horses galloped by. Nettie, who was on the leading horse, was still captive with her hands now tightly tied.

"Alicia wondered whether the men would come back to search for her. If they had seized her for ransom, then they would surely come searching for her, especially if Nettie should let slip she was the king's daughter. She finally managed to free her hands from the rope binding them together. She needed to move, but she didn't know where she should go. This was all new territory to her. The storm continued unabated. She was soaked through. She had to find shelter somewhere. She also needed to find food to eat, but had no idea where she could go. She was in thick forest with wolves and wild boars in its depths. Soon, the light would fade."

Cydlo pauses for a moment. There are worried looks on many faces. The girls feel sorry for the wet, bedraggled, and hungry princess. Many shudder with fear thinking about wolves and wild boars. The boys are impressed with her skill in handling a racing horse while her hands are tied together. None are sure they could manage that. Everyone is thinking what a brave little girl she is and are anxious to hear what happens next.

Cydlo looks around. "It's long after our bedtime, and I've been talking a long time. There's much yet to tell, and I don't want to shorten the story. Will it not be wise to break now and continue later? We don't want to be too tired to think. How about it, Jock? Gumpa and gran'ma, you have the care of the children. What do you think?"

Micah is quick to say, "Oh no, we can't stop now, Gumpa. This is the really exciting part! We're not tired, really!" A chorus of agreement radiates from the children, even from some of the Twith.

Gumpa has heard that chorus at the end of a bedtime story many times before. It's almost a ritual response. "Thank you, Cydlo, for the story. You are right. It's getting late, and the children need their rest." It's actually Gumpa who needs his rest more than the children do. "We'll meet here an hour after lunch tomorrow to continue. All you children, scurry off to bed. I'll help gran'ma with the dishes. Good night now."

There's a reluctant stirring and stretching of limbs, even a yawn or two as the youngsters make their way up to bed. They may climb into bed, but there's likely to be chattering among them for a while before they drift off to sleep.

Thursday on the Brook

At Squidgy's cottage, Mrs. Squidge is preparing to leave for her daily trip to the village post office to pick up her mail and buy supplies. Thinking it's about time to spice up the menu for her guest, she plans to buy a pound of yeast and wonders about alternative recipes for her yeast buns.

The SnuggleWump has become withdrawn since the loss of two of his ears. He pretends he can't hear although he still has as many ears as any other creature so he shouldn't complain. Squidgy is worried about him. 'He's so listless. Just doesn't seem to have any energy.' She speaks a few encouraging words to him on her way to the village shop. After all, she is a kind of mother to the poor creature.

The Wizard is having an inspection of the goblins in Mole Hall and thinking that somehow he has to train a whole new lot of senior officers. 'The current ones have bungled a perfect scheme at the farmhouse.' He's perturbed. 'Where are the qualities of leadership that I have a right to expect from my subordinates? Missing! Zero! Zilch! Nil! Only a blur! They're no better than horses on a merry-go-round.'

Even as he inspects, he reviews details of a final massive blow against the Twith. It's his double-track thinking again. 'It will be a strike of staggering brilliance and simplicity. It cannot fail. My forthcoming *Games on the Brook* will have new events introduced. The deformed MoleKing has the build for a weightlifter. For the time being, I'll have him stay indoors at Squidgy's cottage away from prying eyes.

His mind goes back to the task at hand. 'The goblins are very crowded in Mole Hall. I'll have the son of MoleKing develop a second hall near the first with its own entrance. Then, by linking the two halls, air can circulate between the two entrances. The goblins will appreciate the improvement. A general's first regard is for his men!'

He thinks further ahead. 'On Sunday, I need to make a brief visit to Gyminge to inspect King Haymun's progress on the fort at the border. I'll also check on the situation at the castle. Once the *Games on the Brook* are set in motion, I don't want any distractions from Gyminge. I intend to clear the enemy off the Brook once and for all.

Thoughts of his loyal and most trusted ally cross his mind. 'Rasputin must have been a casualty of the failed strike against the farmhouse. Poor faithful bird! After so many years together, I miss him more than I thought I would.'

Over at the farmhouse, it's a leisurely morning. Breakfast and devotions are both over, and the children stay in the long room sharing what they make of Cydlo's story so far. Time passes quickly, and it's lunchtime before they know it.

Since gran'ma's return from captivity, she wants to ease the load on Cymbeline. When the second batch of children first arrived, gran'ma was missing, so they were all shrunk in order to take their meals in Twith Mansion. The arrival of Elisheba and her father has given the Twith girl two more mouths to feed. She doesn't have to worry about the five Shadow children; they don't get hungry while they're on the Brook.

Gran'ma prepares meals for eighteen — herself, Gumpa, and sixteen children. Her two long tables can each seat eight. With the extra leaf in the larger one, ten will fit around it, but it's a bit of a tight squeeze. Occasionally, Nick and Lucas are invited to eat over at Mike's house. His mother doesn't mind the extra company and is quite a good cook. Gran'ma is able to manage and guide the many willing workers in her kitchen. She has identified who among them can be trusted to wash dishes properly — most of the girls, but as can be expected, no boys.

Mealtime gives gran'ma the opportunity to measure up each of the new children. She can get a better idea of what they are capable of, how well they work in a group, and if they are independent enough to work by themselves. Stormy is gran'ma's main helper and makes the list of duties each day.

Gran'ma has fourteen American children to feed. They like different food than English children do and she knows what children from the States really like. She brought up five of her own.

Lunch in the farmhouse today is designed for the majority. They are having chili-dogs. Gumpa chooses to have something else — anything else — which means he'll eat whatever leftovers he finds in the fridge. Gran'ma warms up twenty or thirty hot dogs in a large saucepan. To Gumpa they look like long anemic-looking sausages. He thinks, 'They may as well be called dogs because they certainly aren't sausages. An English butcher worth his salt would have rejected them out of hand.' The largest pan gran'ma has is full of multiple cans of chili. The enticing flavors float from the kitchen, tickling the children's taste buds.

Spread on the dining tables are bottles of ketchup and mustard, pickles and olives, packets of potato chips that Gumpa calls crisps, a platter of large flat buns, raw sliced carrots, and sliced tomatoes. Gumpa brings his bottle of chutney sauce from the fridge, even though he has no intention of using it on something as vile as hot dogs! For dessert, gran'ma has made brownies. There's milk to drink. Austin is in charge of guarding the table against predators until after thanks are given. However, he was unable to prevent Micah from going out to the kitchen. He returns with ten black olives adorning the tips of his fingers.

Gran'ma assures Gumpa the children will love the meal. To his great surprise, they do. When lunch is over, everything is gone. Everything, that is, except Gumpa's Branston pickles and chutney sauce. Gumpa is amazed. 'It's like the plague of the locusts! If they continue to eat like this, then by the end of the summer their clothes won't fit. The girls are as hungry as the boys!'

Uncle Andy comes across to hear the end of Cydlo's story. He played it safe for lunch and ate at home, but he does nab one of gran'ma's brownies before they all disappear. He's less concerned over the successful understanding and completion of Dayko's Rime than he is intrigued by what Cydlo is telling and wants to hear the end of it. 'The grass cutting can wait until the story is over', Uncle Andy thinks.

Lunch cleanup is done at last. The dish crew has washed, dried, and stacked the dishes and tidied the kitchen. Everyone is settled and comfortable. Gerald has the Twith treasures beside him, but hasn't displayed them as he did yesterday. In case it should be needed for reference, he brought the Book of Lore. However, the Shadow Book is locked in its hiding place below, and the front door of Twith Mansion is bolted from the inside.

The children are all in their places before any of the older folks. They think they know what they're going to hear, but some of their guesses are a long way off. They wait anxiously for more of the story.

Gerald is eventually ready to start, and he smiles his welcome around the room. "It's time now to resume our study of Dayko's Rime. You'll remember from yesterday we're on line twenty-three."

23. *The king will arise in the wood.*

"Our new friend, Cydlo, is helping us understand the meaning of this line. We'll ask him to please continue where he left off yesterday."

Cydlo is brief. "Yesterday, I told you how the king saw his daughter's handkerchief in Mad Jack's cave at the quarry and went on to find her in the hideaway in the escape tunnel from the castle. I've asked Elisheba, who also knows this story well, to tell about Princess Alicia's adventures until she met her father again. The two of us have gone over the story many times during the long evenings in Gyminge. Come up here, and sit beside me, my child so that everyone can see you."

Elisheba is a favorite with everyone. The love lavished on Cymbeline is similarly lavished on the new girl. She's a little older than Cymbeline and slightly taller. Today her auburn hair flows loosely around her shoulders and down her back. There are four of the Little People who have red or ginger-colored hair. Cydlo's is slightly brighter than his daughter's while Taymar and Jock's are shades of ginger. The girl wears a simply cut, full-length, dark-green dress with gold trim at the neck and hem.

She has a clear resemblance to her father. Although her face is less rounded and more oval. She has green twinkly eyes, rosy cheeks, and naturally red lips. Her pearly-white, even teeth create a brilliant smile. Her hands and feet are small although her fingers are long and slender.

She overflows with vitality and latent humor. Cymbeline thinks, 'She's the most beautiful girl I have ever seen.' Across from Cymbeline and unknown to her, Taymar has the same thoughts.

Before she starts, Elisheba looks around and smiles happily. She's completely relaxed. 'I already know most of them by name. I'm talking to family.' She begins, "At the point where my father stopped his story yesterday, Princess Alicia had escaped from the robbers and was into the forest. She was soaked through, and the storm didn't let up. She rested beneath a large oak and pulled her wet shawl around her. Alicia feared wolves and wild boars roamed about in the forest. It was important to find shelter. She was also hungry, but shelter was more urgent than food, and she needed to find someplace safe and dry before nightfall. She was close to tears, but she knew she must not give way to feeling sorry for herself.

"A break came in the clouds. The rain stopped, and sunbeams showed which direction was east. That's the way she needed to head. She pushed through the undergrowth, nettles, and scrub brush between the trees and came to a pond. She followed a faintly worn path around the south edge of it. Tracks along it showed animal prints, but then she stopped in surprise. What she saw were small footprints, a woman's or else a child's and only one pair. There was someone like herself! She placed her foot beside the print — it was the same size. The prints didn't continue around the pond but turned away southeast along a barely visible footpath into the thick forest. Alicia followed them. Wherever they led, it would be better than being lost in the forest at night. The rain resumed, and the girl found difficulty following the tracks. Suddenly, in the distance, still far through the thicket of trees, she saw a light! She walked faster. She took the straightest path and dared to hope it wasn't a robber's hideout."

Pru

E lisheba pauses and looks around. Everyone listens with rapt attention. She builds descriptive word pictures and suspense into her story and enjoys telling it to the best of her ability.

"The princess came to a small hut with a light shining through the window. The cob walled, thatched cottage was half the size of the one she saw burned to the ground that morning. She looked in the small window. The lighted oil lamp hung from the ceiling. There were a few simple furnishings. She didn't see anyone, but gave an urgent knock at the door. That caused barking and a call from inside. It was a woman's voice telling her to come on in. Alicia lifted the timber latch and entered.

"The woman spoke to a pair of dogs, 'Down, Loopy, down. Stay down! You too, Lupus. Come in, girl, come in. Down, Lupus, what did I tell you? Down!' She was an old woman, apparently the only occupant of the cottage, and sat in a low easy chair."

Gumpa sits in his regular chair, his slippered foot resting on the shoulder of the large brown-and-tan wolf-dog. Lupus has made the foot of Gumpa's chair his regular place to relax. He jerks his head at the sound of his name and gives a short bark to indicate he's awake, alert, and available.

The children also jerk a look away from Elisheba to the dog. Questions crowd into their minds, and they express them aloud. "How can a dog in a hut in the forest of Gyminge a thousand years ago be in a farmhouse on the Brook now?" "Is it really the same dog?" "It couldn't be, could it?" "It must be a different dog." "Who's who in the story?" "What's happening?"

Elisheba doesn't acknowledge the questions the children ask or make any attempt to answer them. She smiles with amusement at the reaction she caused and carries on with her story.

"Quickly, Alicia closed the door behind her. That blocked out much of the natural light. There were two small windows opposite each other. The oil lamp was hung from the ceiling beam between them, its wick turned only high enough to dimly light the room. To the right of the door was an old cabinet with plates, bowls, cups, and saucers all neatly arranged. Beside it was the bottom step of a steep, narrow, winding staircase.

"Against the side wall to the left was a big, wide fireplace almost the full whole width of the wall. A wood fire was burning, and its warmth beckoned the girl. The fire glowed red rather than blazed. A large covered cooking pot hung above the fire. The contents were warm if not hot. The heat of an open fire couldn't be wasted. Two brown-and-tan dogs were lying on the hearth in front of the fire. Alicia thought they were probably siblings. They didn't look like any of the dogs she knew in the castle though. They looked more like wolves.

"The woman had a shawl around her thin shoulders. There was a warm patterned blanket over her knees. Another shawl or blanket draped over the back of her chair. On her head was a high, loose, white cloth headpiece with a band at the brim to keep it tight on her head. She probably used it both indoors and out and maybe even wore it to bed. She was knitting. The interruption was little cause to stop.

"Handy beside her was a scuttle filled with coal so she could occasionally add some to the fire without needing to get up. She turned to face the girl. Alicia saw the kindly, wrinkled face of a woman she would, during her short stay, grow to love. When the old woman spoke, her voice was cheery and musical. 'I've been expecting you. Make sure the door is closed tight, my child. Then come over here by the fire and warm yourself. Bring over some of those sticks, and we'll blaze the fire up a bit. You'll be wet through and chilled. Never mind, a bowl or two of hot vegetable stew will make you feel better. Hang your shawl over the back of the table chair to dry. There are no men around here, so you can take off your clothes in front of the fire to get yourself warm. Take one of the towels from the clothes basket, and dry yourself off.'

"Alicia was surprised by the trust the woman showed in her and asked, 'Don't you want to know who I am and why I'm here first?' The girl went forward to stand in front of the old woman so she could be seen and inspected.

"But the woman wasn't interested, 'Goodness, no! There are things more important than that. I know enough about you for now. You're alone. You're a stranger to these parts. You're wet through, and you're cold. And I'll guess that you're also hungry and thirsty. Most importantly, you need shelter. You are probably lost — no one comes this way unless they're lost. You'll find what you need here, girl. I won't turn you away. In fact, I'll enjoy your company for as long as you care to stay. By the time you leave, I'll know as much about you as you care to tell me. I don't move easily myself, or I'd get up and do things for you, but you look as though you can manage for now if I tell you where things are. My name is Widow Brewer, but you can call me Pru. It's short for Prudence. That's what my mother called me. You can tell me your name, dear.'

"Alicia told her what her name was, but didn't mention she was the king's daughter. The old woman had the same nurturing nature as Nettie. The girl felt totally at ease. As she walked to the fireplace to dry herself in front of the fire, the wolf-dogs made a place for her. The lovely warmth enveloped her. When the girl sat down in the high-backed chair and wrapped herself in a couple of blankets, the animals returned to the space they considered their own. All the girl's anxieties had left her for now.

"Widow Brewer told her guest, 'We'll have some fresh bread and stew as soon as the stew is hot enough. I bake once a week, and today is the day I have done so.'

"The cottage was a poor man's cottage. Its walls were built of cob — mud covered with thick plaster. Straw and manure were used as binder for the plaster. When it had been built, the walls had been lime-washed. Now the lime was a light brown — discolored over many years by the smoke of the fire. The shelf above the fireplace wasn't straight. It had been made from a huge awkwardly curved rough-hewn limb of oak. It was strong enough to hold the weight of a wall and the short crossbeam from which the cauldrons and pots were suspended.

"The mantel held kitchen pots, jugs, and canisters. It wasn't level, but that seemed to fit with the roughness of the cottage elsewhere. Inside the fireplace, on each side, were shelves at fire level where the hot cooking pots or cauldrons could be swung aside and lowered to rest. A kettle was there, and a large pot for the pond water that the old woman used as her water supply.

"Between the door and the fireplace was a roughly made table, which was both work top and dining table. Pru explained the small bench beside her chair, 'Most often, I pull this forward to use as my table to eat from.'

"The widow put her knitting down, eased one of the dogs out of her way with her foot, and told the girl, 'Don't stir yourself. I'm used to managing for myself.' She struggled to her feet. 'Don't be concerned, my dear. It's my hip that gives me the trouble. I took a fall years ago, even before my husband decided there was little use in carrying on after his long illness. He didn't want to burden me any longer with his care as if I wouldn't rather have had his company. The years since have been lonely for me. The dogs are good company though. They're half dog, half wolf. No one is likely to cause me any trouble while they're around.'

"Alicia thought Pru was a very brave woman. She asked Pru if she should tell her story, Pru said, 'Later on, Alicia — what a pretty name you have — I'll want you to give me all the news from outside the forest. It's been ages since I last had a visitor. This cottage has two bedrooms. You can make up the bed in the room at the top of the stairs. There are linens in the cupboard under the staircase.'

"At last the meal, the talking and sharing news was over. For the old woman's sake and safety, Alicia still hadn't shared that she was *Princess* Alicia. The stew pot was swung away from over the dying embers, and the last ashes were spread. The dogs' rug was pulled back in case of sparks. A small oil lamp was lit, and the wick of the large oil lamp was turned down. The two women made their sleepy way upstairs. The dogs remained on guard below.

"At the top of the stairs, Pru turned to Alicia. 'I trust you will sleep well. Good night. Sweet dreams. I'll see you in the morning.'

"Alicia smiled gratefully and wished Pru the same."

The Black Flag

Elisheba pauses in the telling of her story. "I realize my story is taking a long time. Perhaps everyone might like to get up and stretch a bit. I don't have much more of my story about the princess, but my father will take over and finish what he has to say."

The children stretch briefly and then quickly settle back to listen. The Little People on the table have scarcely moved. They have a sense that this day is a momentous day in the life of the free Twith. When it's through, things will never be the same again.

Elisheba leans forward in her chair. "Princess Alicia spent a full week with Widow Brewer. She did spring cleaning throughout the house as her way of saying thank you to someone who was kind to a stranger. She attacked dust as though a herd of wild horses had been trampling through the house. Cobwebs got swept away from a hundred hiding places. The tiny window panes sparkled. She brushed down walls, swept the floors, and swept them again. The lamps were cleaned, and the wicks trimmed. The clothes and bedding were washed and ironed. The linens folded and put away. When Alicia went out to gather in a supply of wood and twigs, Pru sent Lupus, the larger male dog, with her. The old woman didn't want anything to happen to her visitor while she was her guest. Loopy, the smaller female, liked to stay close to her mistress.

"Lupus and Loopy had the same brown-and-tan coloring and were from a litter of seven puppies. As soon as they were strong enough to be away from their mother, Pru's brother walked them over to her. It was a full day's journey. The wolf-dogs have been with her ever since."

As Elisheba goes on to describe Lupus more fully, the children silently check out the description against the dog at Gumpa's feet. 'Yes, he would of course be slightly larger than his sister. His upper parts are dark brown and his under parts, a light tan. His face is broad. He has a white muzzle and sharp alert ears rarely relaxed. His thick brown tail curls over naturally until the tip touches his back. He has strong broad legs and thick fur. He gives an impression of intelligence, alertness, and strength.' The details seem to fit even if they can't make sense of the time difference.

"Occasionally, Alicia went for a walk in the afternoon. Lupus was always ahead, sniffing, checking, growling a warning, and refusing to go in a direction he didn't approve of. Those were occasions for Alicia to think about her mother and father and how worried they would be about her if they had gone to the cottage. And she wondered what might have happened to her faithful old friend and nurse, Nettie. She thought about what she must do next.

"On her return from one of those walks, Alicia shared with Pru, 'I feel the time has come for me to try and return home. I'll be sorry to leave such a kind and good friend, but it's possible my parents could be very worried about me. I've sorted out that I'll need to head northeast. That direction will take me to the lake for sure and on to the castle where my parents are. If you will permit me, I'll leave early in the morning, as soon as breakfast is over, so that I can be at the castle before it gets dark.'

"Pru had also been thinking. She shares her thoughts. 'You have become like a daughter to me, and you are welcome to stay as long as you wish. If things prove difficult for you, you must come back and make your home here. I have a spare shawl in the drawer upstairs that will suit your hair coloring. You must take it with you. You must also take supplies of food and water to nourish you along the way. Take some tinder and flint. You may need to make a fire.'

"Pru was thinking of everything. 'Do you have any money in case you need to buy some supplies or rent lodging for a night? I have some savings, and I insist you take part of it with you. There will still be enough for my own needs. What's an old woman like me going to spend money on at my age anyway? It won't be safe for you to travel alone. I'll send Lupus with you. He will protect you. The dog has a mind of his own, so don't worry if he wants to stay with you once you are reunited with your parents. If he wants to return home, he will and no one will be able to stop him.'

"Alicia flung her arms around Pru's neck and cried with both thankfulness and sadness. She was going to leave such a good friend, and it was unlikely that she would meet her again. She burst out, 'If things do go well with me, then for certain, I'll find you again, Pru. I want to give my parents a chance to meet and thank you. I'm deeply grateful for the offer of Lupus. He will be a wonderful companion. We love each other already, and I'll have no fears along my way with him alongside. Thank you so much for everything.'

"The old woman and the princess spent the evening in quiet, farewell conversation. The next morning, Alicia and Lupus walked for several hours. The first signs of weariness reached her legs. The dog was still fresh, but didn't waste any energy chasing rabbits. They didn't exchange much conversation. Lupus wasn't much for just talking but more for action although Alicia understood him very well when he did choose to say anything. The recent storms had left everything fresh and green.

"Lupus led the way, usually a few feet ahead. It was almost as though he knew where they should go. It even seemed that he had traveled this way before. At any junction, he sniffed the area, chose the path to take, looked around, and barked for Alicia to follow him. She didn't try to direct him. She knew he was heading roughly in the direction of the castle.

"The trees were less close together. The paths became more used and well-trodden. Animal tracks were increasingly replaced by human prints — both shoes and boots — but they weren't seen by a single person throughout their journey. The path joined other paths successively and broadened into one of the main trails through the forest. At last, they were out of the forest and into a large grassy meadow that was covered in yellow buttercups.

"The view ahead refreshed the girl's heart. Familiar childhood scenes were before her. In the far distance were the hills of Wozzle. The Dark Forest, north of the lake, was a melody of greens as the summer sun lit up the foliage of a variety of trees. They reached the crest of the meadow, and before her was the castle lake — *her* lake — where she used to play and swim.

"She had promised herself a short break once they were through the forest, but instead, she dashed ahead into a run. She didn't want to stop and eat. She could do that as soon as she got home to the castle. She knew her father would be sure to send out a rescue party to recover Nettie from the robber band. Lupus could lead them back to Pru loaded with gifts. The old woman would be welcome to live in the castle if she wanted to move from her cottage.

"Alicia reached the edge of the meadow and stopped dead in her tracks. She gasped with horror and dismay as her eyes searched the scene ahead. The distant flag at the castle wasn't the flag she knew so well. It was a black flag. The flag of Wozzle! The footbridge across the west brook from the castle to Dayko's house was no longer there.

"On the ground in front of the castle gate were soldiers on parade. For certain, they weren't Twith men. Other soldiers — some mounted, some on foot — were alongside long lines of peasants and farmers. Whole families were making their steady way towards the traditional gathering ground to the south of the castle. A huge crowd was already assembled there.

"At Fowler's Bridge a squad of soldiers were crossing the west brook and marching towards the junction where the track she was following met and joined with the track around the lake. Suddenly, Alicia realized they were goblins! She shouted to Lupus, 'Come on, Lupus. Back into the forest. Quick! Run!' What was the princess going to do now?"

Panic!

No one stirs. The girls, even the Shadow girls, picture themselves in the place of the princess, facing the realization that an awful calamity has befallen her and her family.

Elisheba nears the end of her story. "Princess Alicia ran back into the forest. Panic caught hold of her. Thorns and brambles caught at her dress and left several small tears. The shawl was pulled off her shoulders. She left it where it fell and ran on. Her heart was beating furiously. Her mind refused to work except to say, 'Run, run, run!' Lupus bounded beside her. Panting and out of breath, she stumbled and fell headlong on the ground. She began to cry, but picked herself up, brushed her hair back out of her eyes with muddy hands, and ran on.

"The landscape was blurry. She could only half see through her tears. She wiped a hand across her cheek to dry it off. The situation was worse than when she escaped from the robbers. Now there was no hope at all! The black flag meant that the Wizard had conquered Gyminge. Her father and mother could be dead, and she was the only one left. She tried to think. She must hide! But where could she go? She didn't know what she should do.

"The princess turned off the main track and took every path that was smaller in size. They were more likely to lead her to a hiding place. Somewhere, she could curl up into a small bundle of herself and be away from everything — except the quiet dog close beside her. The trail led to the home of a stonemason. He had obviously left in a hurry quite some time ago. The embers of a fire were cold, and the hammers and tools of his trade were still on the shelf.

"Alicia sat on a cushion that had also been used as a pillow on the straw mattress bed. She stroked Lupus gently. The calm of the creature communicated itself to her. He, at least, was taking everything in his stride. Slowly, her panic subsided, her rapid breathing steadied, and she too felt calm once again. As she talked to the dog, she was talking to herself as well. She confessed that she had panicked. Wondering what they were going to do, she sat down to try and figure out what that might be. She tried to think what her Mum and Dad had taught her. They would have told her to keep calm and think of three good things. Things are never as bad as they seem.

"Alicia searched her mind. The first good thing could be that she was grateful to have Lupus. She didn't know what she would do without him. The second was relief that the goblins hadn't captured them and they were still free. And for the third thing, she knew that they could always go back to Pru. She would give them shelter, and Lupus could certainly find the way.

"The princess thought of something else to add to the list. She could hope that perhaps her Mum and Dad may not be dead. She didn't know what might have happened to them. If the goblins got in through the gate and the fighting went right through the castle, her Dad would try to save her Mum even if he couldn't save himself. He would make her hide in the hideaway behind the fireplace while the fighting was going on. She would do that if he told her it was for the best. Then, if there was no other way, he would join her there. If they weren't injured, they would try and find her. But if they did go to the cottage, they would only find ashes. If they had any chance to leave a message, it would be either in the hideaway or in Mad Jack's cave. That's where she needed to get to before giving up and trying to make her way back to Pru's. She decided to search for them at the fireplace hideaway.

"As she rose to her feet, Lupus barked sharply twice. He was on his feet and ready to go. It was early afternoon with still a good part of the day left. The princess didn't know that her father had just passed through the tunnel and Mad Jack's cave and was headed towards the cottage in the forest to find her.

"Alicia's panic and fear were gone. She absorbed the shock of seeing her home in the hands of the Wozzle troops and decided on her next course of action. Helped by Lupus, she retraced her journey of flight, picked up the shawl where she lost it, and also recovered Pru's basket with supplies. She remained in the shelter of the trees. The pair made their way eastwards, not daring to venture out onto the meadows where they would be within sight of watchers on the castle walls.

"They passed by Dayko's home. She had visited there many times in the past. There was no sign of activity, and she wondered what might have happened to him. The two went down the slope to where the brook from the lake flowed southwards. They stayed well back from it and kept in the woods. Alicia heard the sounds of the crowds in front of the castle gates. Occasionally, angry orders that were shouted by distant goblin soldiers pierced the air. Lupus scouted ahead, weaving to and fro, and uttered sharp little barks of warning to indicate that the princess should stop and hide. Occasionally, they saw wild animals — an otter, a fox, and some rabbits — but nothing dangerous. The girl used the stepping stones to cross the brook. The water was clean and clear, and both of them drank thirstily. Alicia refilled her water bottle.

"Now, they climbed the slow rise towards the quarry. There was a long way yet to travel. The ground was rough, rocky limestone similar to that at the stonemason's home. At last, they reached the quarry! The great opening had been cut from the hillside over centuries. Laborers developed skills in shaping stone into usable building blocks. The stone used to build the castle came from there. The narrow path up the left side of the quarry led to Mad Jack's cave. In front of the cave was a small gnarled tree clinging precariously to the rock. The roots grew in cracks and fissures filled by windblown soil over the years. Streamers and tinkling bits of metal chiming eerily in the wind hung from its branches.

"For many years, a madman — unshaven and half dressed — lived in the cave even while quarrying was going on around him. The citizens steered clear of the cave. Mad Jack was inclined to violence if anyone approached and he showered visitors with stones the size of his fist. Then he just disappeared. Local people said his bones were found back deep in the cave. They believed that his ghost waited to surprise anyone who dared enter his home.

"Alicia had been to the cave with her father and wasn't frightened by the stories about Mad Jack's ghost. She searched anxiously for signs of any message left for her by her father or mother, but there were none. Her hopes were dashed, and she dropped to her knees in despair. The princess saw footprints on the dusty stone floor that were not hers. They were the footprints of a big man, and she felt sure they were left by her father. She looked carefully, but there were no woman's footprints. Perhaps her mother was still in the hideaway.

"The girl placed her handkerchief out of sight of the entrance, but where it could be easily seen by someone inside the cave. A small stone on it made sure that no breeze would blow it away. Alicia knew there was a tunnel that led from the quarry into the castle. She wasted no time. 'Come on, Lupus, we're going through a tunnel to check the other end. Perhaps we can find out what's happening in the castle when we get there. Now don't you dare bark.' The princess fervently hoped that she would find her mother in the hideaway, but would she?"

"Who Are You?"

E lisheba has finished what she wanted to tell. She looks back to her father. Around them, the whole mixture of Beyonders and Little People sit unmoving and waiting. Elisheba might be finished, but the story isn't over, and they want to hear how it ends.

Gran'ma breaks the silence. "We've been fascinated by Elisheba's story. We're going to need to take some time to think about what it all means. But you children need exercise. All of you who are Beyonder-size, with the exception of anyone over fifty, run down to the croc' pond and back as fast as you can. Stay in pairs. Gumpa and I will make some tea, and we'll have cookies and cake when you get back. Off you go. The last one back serves the tea."

Bajjer is first out of the door, followed by Micah and then Rachael who is determined her brother isn't going to get back before she does. The stream of children — shouting, laughing, and jostling — floods out onto the grass from all three doors. Crusty takes off and hovers high overhead to see and protect the whole line of children running from the farmhouse to the pond.

Uncle Andy offers to help make sandwiches. Gran'ma tells him, "The children's favorite sandwiches are peanut butter and jam." He makes a face and decides to leave that task to her. Instead, he arranges the biscuits artistically on the plates. He's learning new words all the time. What he calls biscuits, gran'ma calls cookies. Sweets are candies, jelly is jam, custard is pudding, and afters are known as dessert. Gumpa carries in and arranges the cups and saucers ready for pouring tea.

Cymbeline, Elisheba, and the three Shadow girls are downstairs in Twith Mansion preparing the smaller snacks and taking the opportunity to ask a few questions of their own. Elisheba just smiles and says little. "My father will soon finish the story. I don't want to spoil the end of it for you." She changes the subject, "I wonder how Bimbo and Bollin are getting along in Gyminge?"

Cymbeline knows where Cydlo's story is leading. Carefully and quietly, she compares Elisheba's hands with her own as they work alongside each other.

Upstairs, the Twith men are alone with their thoughts. Gerald looks at the large copy of Dayko's Rime he used yesterday. He realizes that none of the lines beyond line twenty-four is yet marked. Two of the previous lines, those about the shield and the sword, remain unmarked, even by a question mark. He hopes that the two boys in Gyminge will bring back some answers to those two lines. Answers are needed before they can move on. Meanwhile, time ticks away towards August twelfth.

Jock wonders about the two boys he sent back to Gyminge. He has a feeling that they may be in grave danger. He would have liked to go along with them. He's having second thoughts about putting his trust in Dr. Tyfuss. 'It's possible he's leading the boys into a trap.'

Taymar is lost in his own thoughts. His fingers reach up and fondle the small pouch around his neck. Things seem unreal to him at the moment, but he has a great sense of peace as though he is being overtaken by events beyond his control. 'I'm merely a watcher through a glass, an observer at a drama, a dreamer within a dream, and a prisoner within a bubble floating in the air. It's all going to happen the way it's going to happen. Everything will be alright. Someone else is calling the tunes, and the tunes make beautiful music, like water trickling over pebbles.'

Jordy's thinking is more practical. 'I wonder how the Return will be managed now that the flight hole for Crusty and Tuwhit to enter the skies of Gyminge is closed off?' The eagle and the owl between them have made possible all that has been accomplished so far. The Twith from the very beginning have always had the birds at hand. His brow furrows. 'In order for the attack on the castle to be successful, it will surely be essential to have birds in Gyminge. Without them, can there be anything but failure? Will they, can they, find a way to get through the curtain?'

Stumpy is thinking about his memorial to Ollie. 'I'll do the two necks of the SnuggleWump last of all. That will protect them from breakage as I work on the larger part for carving the dog.'

Barney has been thinking on lines similar to his sister. 'I'm way ahead of Cydlo. I have everything worked out ... and, boy! Am I excited!'

Cydlo is thinking of his lost wife, and then of his daughter who resembles her so much. 'Have I ever seen her so happy?'

Gumpa finished his assignment to oversee the tea and is dozing. Lupus left him and is running with the children.

The children, puffing and panting, come bustling back from their race to the pond. Specs ended up with a pain in his side and walked back slowly with Ginger. He serves the tea. Slowly, the hustle and bustle settles. Dishes are cleared away and necessarily, according to gran'ma's rules, washed and dried before anything else is allowed to happen.

Cymbeline, as she settles back to listen, brushes against Taymar. Unseen by the others, and without a spoken word, something transfers between their hands. He sneaks a glance down and grins, first to himself and then at Cymbeline.

Gerald asks, "Cydlo, do you or Elisheba have any more to add to the story of the king and the princess?"

The woodsman nods, waits for silence to fall, and continues. "The king had met up with Princess Alicia in the hideaway behind the fireplace. They couldn't stay there indefinitely, but for the time being, it was good shelter. Lupus was sent out to guard the entrance from the quarry just in case any goblin soldiers came snooping around. If they did, they would certainly turn tail and race away to report that the cave was inhabited by a pack of wolves. They spent a lot of time watching and listening at the spy-hole into the king's apartments. They hoped to get news, any news, about the missing Queen Sheba. They overheard talk that the king was in the Beyond, but at the point of death, and Princess Alicia had either fled with him or was drowned in the lake. There was no mention of the queen. That suggested that she was either already in the Wizard's grasp and he was keeping quiet about it or that something even worse had happened.

"The king knew that the tunnel branching into the castle dungeons from the escape tunnel would be a secure hiding place. No one else knew the secret of finding the way into it from either end of the link tunnel. The door from the dungeon side had a spy-hole looking into the cell for special prisoners. The king was hopeful that his wife was being held there, and he could easily rescue her. But, once again, he was grievously disappointed. There wasn't anyone at all in that cell, so he returned to the escape tunnel.

"They ate meals from Pru's basket until that was empty, and then they turned to the stored supplies, but didn't dare cook anything. Over the next week or so, the two of them moved almost everything of value from the hideaway into the more secret and safe link tunnel. That included weapons, armor, clothing, tinderbox, and candles. A few small pieces of furniture were brought down also. The link tunnel would become their hiding place if goblin soldiers managed to get past Lupus guarding the entrance at the quarry.

"The days gave the king time for reflection. It was becoming clear to him what he needed to do. He talked it through with Alicia. The Twith had been soundly defeated, and the Wizard was in complete control.

Dayko had foretold not only the defeat of the Twith, but their eventual Return. He didn't know how long that would be — years or centuries — but the free Twith would one day Return. He was sure of that.

"The king had appointed Jock to be in charge of bringing them back. They would need evidence that the king yet lives. He decided that somewhere along the path of the Return, he would hide his crown and the Royal Sword or the Royal Dirk. It would have to be in some secure place where they would eventually be found. However, that task had to wait until later. For now, they needed to act without delay and hide, not things, but themselves, against discovery. The Wizard would sweep the land clean in his search for any who opposed his control or objected to his reign.

"Both the king and the princess adopted new names and changed their identities. He became a woodcutter and supplied charcoal and firewood to the castle. That kept him in touch with events there. She was still his daughter, only now a woodcutter's daughter. If they discovered that the queen was alive, they would try to locate and free her. They decided to settle to the south of the castle, on the edge of the forest, but not within it. It was near the path of the Return that Jock would one day take.

"Together, they built themselves a cottage near the stream that joined the brook that flowed from the lake to the border. They designed the cottage to have a safe hiding place big enough for both of them. The only weapon the king brought from the link tunnel was his fighting axe which he hid in their home. He would use it to defend them if defense became necessary. When any strangers approached, no matter who they were, the princess just shook her head and pointed to her mouth. They needed to believe that she couldn't speak. Voiceless mouths tell no lies and betray no secrets."

All the children who were on the team to rescue gran'ma are nearly jumping out of their seats. Micah can hold himself back no longer. "Then... Are *you* King Rufus? And... Is Elisheba *Princess Alicia?*"

The King's Ring

Cydlo doesn't answer Micah's question about whether he is the king and Elisebaa is the princess. He smiles knowingly at the impetuous boy who has given voice to the thought that is present, in some way or other, in everyone's mind. Some are sure of the answer, but others are uncertain.

It is Gerald who responds to Micah. "First, let's return to Dayko's Rime. Before we are through verse seven, we shall have that answer from a different source than either Cydlo or Elisheba — a source that will accept no falsehood and be absolutely certain. Let us bide our time just a little while longer for the answer to your very important question, Micah. Let's look at the first of this verse and the first line of the next verse to start with. They can be interpreted together."

> 25. *The armour the flame will withstand.*
> 29. *The belt is restored from the fire.*

"When Dayko wrote this, there was little connection between his belt and a fire or between pieces of armor and flames. Dayko himself could have no reason, except his gift of sight, to have both objects share the same fate. Uncle Andy, do you have any thoughts about this?"

The mixed audience of Twith and Beyonders is enjoying going through the poem. For the children, it's something like the quizzes they get from the teacher at school or quiz games they have seen on television. This one is easy. These lines were resolved by Uncle Andy. They wait for him to say so.

"These are two of the items I retrieved from Squidgy's cottage. For hundreds of years while they were in Smiler's cottage, flames and fire were only a few inches from both Dayko's belt and the king's armor lying beside it. They have come through it all completely unharmed. I think you can put checkmarks against those two lines."

Gerald asks, "Do we need another break? Maybe you would like to at least stand and stretch. We're more than two-thirds through the poem, but there are tricky lines ahead to look at." His audience wastes little time in stretching and settles back quickly into quietness. They are anxious to get to the answer to Micah's question.

"Now here's line twenty-six, the second line of verse seven."

26. *Salt wind shall blow over the land*

"At present, because of the curtain, the salt wind that blows from the sea doesn't blow over Gyminge. Even the weather is different there. The sea is only four miles away, but it's hard to see how the salt wind can get through to Gyminge. The line must mean that the curtain will disappear or be lifted in some way or develop enough holes in it that the wind can blow through it. The Wizard certainly won't want that to happen. If the wind can get in, so can our bird friends. He doesn't want that. He's afraid of the birds, and so is Rasputin.

"Does it mean that after we have returned and the Wizard is gone, that the curtain is removed so the salt wind will blow over Gyminge? I don't know, but the other lines seem to refer to what will happen before rather than after we're home. Does anyone have any ideas?"

Specs has questions, lots of them. "The curtain has been there for a very long time. Can it be it's just wearing out? What is it made of anyway? Has anyone tried cutting holes in it at ground level or even up in the air? Maybe a welding torch could be used to cut through it. Mike's dad has one, and it cuts through most anything. If that doesn't work, Max has a chainsaw. What about using a hot electric wire? Could the curtain be set on fire? Has anyone tried that? How deep into the ground does the curtain go? Do we know?"

Gerald shakes his head. "I don't know the answers to those questions."

Jock, however has been listening carefully. He stands up and shares his thoughts. "This seems like a project some of the children might like to tackle in a more focused way. Answering the questions Specs raised would give us the solution to line twenty-six. How *is* the salt wind going to blow over Gyminge? We need to find an answer in a hurry. Whichever children would like to join in can do so." He turns to Specs, "I'll let you arrange the meeting and discussions. Is that okay?"

Specs nods. "Yes, I can manage that. The Shadow girls and Barney should be in on this too. And also Tuwhit and Crusty and Blackie. It most likely won't be today. How about ten-thirty tomorrow morning? Anyone who's interested or has any ideas should come along and help. Barney, will you let the birds and Blackie know?"

Barney grins broadly and says, "Sure."

Gerald moves along to the lines in the poem that he is most interested in. "Let's now move on and consider the next lines."

27. *For light in the heart of the ring*
28. *Shall end the restraint of the king.*

"Yesterday, we saw the Ring of Accession, the ring that is fit for our king. We heard about the light that glows in the heart of the ring. It's the light that reveals who is really the king. Without the light we should have no assurance that the wearer is indeed our king. Let the king's ring answer for Cydlo, Micah. Wait and watch."

He stands up, walks across the table and carefully removes the ring from Queen Sheba's treasure chest that he showed them yesterday. "This is the Ring of Accession. Should any other but the king wear it, the ring will remain a dull ruby red. When our king wears it, and only when he wears it, the ring will take on the life of the king himself. It will shine with light borrowed from the king. We have not seen it do so since King Rufus ruled over Gyminge. This will be the test. Will you hold out your right hand, Sir?"

Cydlo remains seated. His hand is not the manicured hand of someone of royalty. It's a broad hand, fingers bruised and thickened by long hours of hard work. The man behind the hand is dressed in the simple clothes of a laboring man that Elisheba made for him. It isn't kingly garb. The gold ring is large in diameter, made to fit a large finger.

Even so, it's too small to slip on Cydlo's middle finger easily. With difficulty, Gerald works it into position. The woodsman's hand has no other adornment.

All eyes are now focused on the ring. Everything else loses significance. Only the ring matters.

Light!

As soon as the royal ring is placed on Cydlo's finger, the ring begins to glow with a warm red light. It gains strength from within itself as though needing no light from any other source. It's as though the mere fitting of it on his finger has turned on some powerful switch. To be certain the ring isn't reflecting the electric light above, Gumpa motions to Stormy who is sitting on the staircase, to reach up and turn off all the lights. The room is much darker, and the rich red glow looks even brighter. The whole room is bathed in rich, soft red light streaming from the ring. It continues to brighten. The light from the ring, though ruby red, is as bright as the lights in the room were before Stormy turned them off.

The absolute silence gives way. There's a rustling sound as the Little People move off their chairs. Nothing is being said. The Twith on the table all kneel, left knee touching the tabletop, both hands on the bent right knee, and head bowed. Even Stumpy is down among the others. The peg leg on his right foot appears to be no problem. This is his king he is honoring. Elisheba has slipped from the chair where she was sitting and kneels beside her friends, showing loyalty to the king, her father.

The three little Shadow girls, who are accustomed to covering their heads as a sign of reverence, use handkerchiefs instead of chiffon scarves and bend on both knees as though in prayer.

Gumpa strides across the room to gran'ma. Taking her hand to help her to her feet, they quietly stand at attention looking straight in front of them at Cydlo who doesn't stir. Their eyes are moist, and the tears aren't far away. There are other quiet movements. All the Beyonders are now standing at attention. The tiny sounds die to nothing.

For a long moment, there's neither movement nor sound.

Stumpy, remembering the crown from the cave that he was allowed to unwrap yesterday, blurts out, "Long Live the King!"

He's joined by the others. "Long Live the King! Long Live the King!" The sound of clapping rolls around the room.

The ruby light now dims. Cydlo is removing the ring, easing it off. Stormy turns on the lights. He passes the ring back to Gerald who quietly replaces it in the chest. The king is a leader who has acknowledged and reassumed responsibility. He speaks with assurance and confidence. "Please, all of you, sit down and relax. This isn't a formal state occasion, although my heart has been warmed by what has just happened. Yes, indeed, I am King Rufus. I bear the scar of the wound I received at Fowler's Bridge. Some of you who tended me then would recognize it. Indeed, your doctor Gerald did recognize it as he cared for my most recent injury. I swore him to secrecy until the time was right to reveal who I am.

"My daughter combined the sound of her own name Alicia with that of her mother, Queen Sheba, to make the name you know her by, Elisheba. I do ask you all, until the happy day when we are once again back in Gyminge Castle, to continue to call me Cydlo. I have grown accustomed to that name. And please continue to call Princess Alicia by the name you are already accustomed to using. When you refer to us, we are still the woodcutter and his daughter, not the king and the crown princess. We don't want to allow the Wizard to know any information about us that might help him or draw even more attention to this place.

"There are several matters to make clear. From Dayko's Rime, there's no doubt in my mind that the time for the Return is now, this summer. We must seize our opportunity. Before this summer ends, if we show courage and wisdom, the Wizard will be overthrown and banished forever from both Wozzle and Gyminge.

"Before we were conquered, I made certain decisions concerning three of you who are with us here. I need to make clear how these decisions now stand in these very different circumstances. First, I granted Jock both a title, that he appears never to have used, and a charge. The charge was simply to appoint him as Leader of the Twith in the Beyond, to serve for an indefinite period of time. He was given authority to act in my stead at all times until the free Twith return to Gyminge. Jock has led us to this point with faithfulness and with courage and wisdom. My charge to Jock continues unchanged."

He turns to Jock. "You shall continue to lead us, Jock. The only change to your instructions is that you are no longer limited by the event of our Return. You will continue to lead us until I, the king, shall determine. I will act as subordinate to you and you will refer to me as Cydlo, not the king. Unless I inform you otherwise, I fully accept your leadership. We need you. Do you understand and agree to this extension of your charge into Gyminge itself?"

Jock finds it difficult to treat King Rufus as Cydlo the woodcutter. He controls himself. With great effort, "Yes, Sire" becomes "Yes, Cydlo."

"Next, I placed a restraint upon you, Jock. Only my ring used on my behalf might overrule any order of yours. Have you ever been overruled on my behalf?"

"No, Cydlo." Jock is puzzled by this question. Surely no one has the king's ring but the king himself.

"In the last days of my reign, I gave my ring to an old and beloved friend as a token and a sign of a covenant with him. He isn't here just now. Yet I must ask whether anyone here has with him the king's signet ring which represents the authority of the king himself?"

For a moment, there is silence, and then there is stirring among the Little People. Taymar stands up. He reaches up to the pouch around his neck and pulls its leather lace over his head. Shaking his ruffled hair back into place, he unties the knot securing the pouch. Reaching inside, he selects from among the contents one item.

Taymar is solemn and thoughtful, not his usual lighthearted self. These recent events are opening doors that he thought had been closed long ago. And, if by chance, they hadn't been closed, he was sure it would be far into the future before they did open. As he walks forward, he gives a long look towards the two Twith girls. The lad hands something to Cydlo.

The king takes and examines it. He smiles with pleasure as he recognizes it. He holds the ring up for all to see. "This is indeed the Royal

Signet Ring. It has on it the Royal Crest — a rearing horse, a crouching lion, and a gold crown. I wore this ring on my finger during the years that I was king until at last the kingship was wrested from my grasp."

Surprisingly, he neither fits it on his own finger nor does he return it to Taymar. He gives it to Elisheba who sits on the table in front of him next to Cymbeline. The girl looks at it and then back to her father, puzzled by his action.

He looks at Taymar. "Is this ring yours or mine, my son? Did you perhaps steal it while the owner slept?"

The Betrothal

There's a gasp of surprise from everyone around the room at the king's remark. All eyes are on Taymar.

The young man thinks only a moment. "No, Sire, it isn't yours. It is mine. It was given in fair exchange. A ring for a ring. My father gave you his gold ring, and you gave him this as a token of your mutual agreement. My father passed it on to me the last time I saw him."

"You are right, Taymar, and I agree that it is yours. Sadly, my son, your father's ring never reached where it was intended although I did indeed receive it from him. You have heard how the queen was journeying to see her daughter, but she never arrived. Where the ring is now, we don't know. What can I do to replace the ring that has been lost?"

"Sire, I knew my father's ring would not fit. It would be far too large, but it was merely a token of another that would be made later of the correct size. I had no opportunity to have it made in Gyminge for the enemy was at our door. Here in the Beyond there aren't craftsmen who have the skills needed to make a ring small enough suitable for the hand of a Twith maiden. They can't work in such tiny detail. Instead, while I was in Cornwall, I had a bracelet to suit our size made of gold and then had engravers work decoration into it with tiny instruments. The pearls are from the sea near where I lived."

He reaches into the pouch again. "Here it is, Sire. You may look at it. I also have a small and simple ring of what I believe is the correct size to fit the one for whom it's intended." Taymar takes from his trouser pocket the tiny ring that Cymbeline secretly slipped to him earlier in the afternoon.

Cymbeline truly had been way ahead of events. Even earlier, noticing the looks between Taymar and Elisheba when they thought the other wasn't looking made her think, 'What a wonderful couple they would make.' She gives Elisheba's hand a squeeze of encouragement.

Elisheba tries to hide the joy flooding through her and keeps her eyes demurely cast down before her. 'This day is on its way to becoming the happiest day of my life!' Since she has been at the farm, her heart has been anxious for the health of her father, but in every other way, it has been singing. 'Cymbeline told me that there was nothing between her and Taymar and never has been. She said he was like a brother to her and could never be anything else. When I heard that, I allowed my secret emotions free rein to dream and imagine and build pictures in the sky of what life might be like if he felt the same way.'

The king doesn't take either the bracelet or the ring offered by Taymar. Instead, he calls both Taymar and Elisheba to stand before him. The others on the table shuffle back to make plenty of space in the front.

He asks Taymar, "See if the bracelet will fit Elisheba's wrist." It's a tiny bracelet, but her wrist is also tiny. It's a narrow gold band with a clip which tightens against the natural springiness of the band. The front of the band broadens and divides to create a frame for seven perfect pearls, all of the same size.

Elisheba lifts her eyes slowly and turns to look directly into Taymar's eyes. 'Oh, I love him so much! How can this have come to pass in such a few days?' As a girl she dreamed of love; now she has met it face to face. 'It's been such a short time since I arrived, yet I feel as though I've always known this man standing beside me. At last I have come home to the place where my heart will forever rest. Can there ever be disagreement between us? I can't imagine it.'

Taymar is clumsy, unaccustomed to fitting bracelets. He's more accustomed to a sword or a dagger or a staff. The catch snaps closed. He holds and turns her hand to show the pearls on the outside of her wrist. 'I wish I were wearing my best clothes instead of my everyday clothes. She's so beautiful, and I'm so... so plain!'

The king is not yet done. "See if the ring will fit also, Taymar."

Taymar knows that the ring finger is on the left hand. He takes her hand, raises it, and slips on the ring. It has a single pearl.

Stumpy recognizes it. 'That's the one my brother used when marrying Cymbeline's mother. I carried it at that wedding. Now it's betrothing a princess.'

It fits perfectly. Cymbeline got it right. She has few pieces of jewelry, but several precious pieces she managed to bring with her when she fled her home in Gyminge. In *her* dreams, she had thought that she, like her mother, would receive that same ring from the man she loved. But it was not to be.

Cydlo continues. "Elisheba, you have a ring in your hand. I doubt that it will fit young Taymar's hand. However, do you wish to try it and see whether it fits?"

The happiness of the two young people is contagious. The children recognize that they're witnessing the betrothal ceremony of the Crown Princess of Gyminge to one of their very own Twith.

Gumpa whispers to gran'ma, "This is probably the longest engagement in history. I hope they won't take as long to get married!"

Elisheba makes no further pretense at modesty. She is totally happy. 'In the two days since I arrived on the Brook, my world has been turned wonderfully upside down. I wish that this day will never end.' She takes Taymar's hand and looks at it carefully. She has never held his hand before. They have never even been out for a walk together. Well, they had once, centuries ago, when she was nine years old, but they didn't hold hands. She slips her father's signet ring, the ring of royal authority, onto a finger and hand that is so like her father's they could almost be from the same stock.

Cydlo rises slowly and cautiously from his chair and stands before them. He takes Taymar's hand into his own, places Elisheba's hand on top of Taymar's, and then his other hand on top of his daughter's. "I, King Rufus of Gyminge, call upon all of you present to bear witness to the betrothal of my daughter, Crown Princess Alicia of Gyminge to Taymar, also of Gyminge, the oldest son of Earl Gareth and the Countess of Up-Horton. Let none try to divide them or frustrate the union between them. I, the king, so declare."

The Twith on the table congratulate the couple. Taymar and Elisheba are just enjoying holding hands. For the first time, Taymar slips his free arm around Elisheba's shoulder. The girl snuggles up against him to acknowledge her pleasure. She has come home. There will be a lot of getting to know each other.

Uncle Andy suggests, "If you don't want to wait until you return to Gyminge, a wedding could be arranged in the cow barn. It has a sunroom large enough for everyone to fit in. I'm sure Julie and Max would be happy to make it available."

Specs and Bajjer decide to make some music. Their instruments seem to emerge from nowhere, and they are ready. A little physical exercise is clearly needed to celebrate the occasion. Jock has the children clear space on the hearth as a dance floor for the Twith and anyone else small enough to join in. Jordy holds out his hands to anyone who might want to shrink. Gran'ma pulls Gumpa to his feet. Stumpy too holds out his hand to help the children shrink to dance floor size. He looks as though he's lining up to dance himself and wants a partner. Even Uncle Andy is there, paired up with Ginger.

There's going to be a celebration!

Party Night

More than an hour has passed. Gran'ma needs to bring some order to the occasion. She calls, "Attention everybody!"

The activity doesn't stop immediately, but slowly, the pause becomes effective as Specs and Bajjer lower their instruments and the accompanying percussionists banging on borrowed pots and pans cease their drumming.

When it's quiet enough for everyone to hear, gran'ma says, "It's time to break for supper. After the dishes are washed and dried, I want you children to go get dressed for a party. This is an important occasion, so everyone please choose your very best clothes. That means you boys wear neckties, and you girls wear dresses, not jeans. No tennis shoes unless that's all that you have."

The necktie bit doesn't bother the English boys; they're used to wearing ties. Most of the American boys wrinkle their noses in disgust. Gumpa grins and says, "Don't worry, boys. I have plenty of ties for you to choose from."

Rachael is the only girl who didn't bring a dress. She *never* wears dresses. 'Well, I'll make an exception this time. But who's the right size for me to borrow from?' She looks around. 'I'm taller than most of the girls.'

Vickie senses her concern. "Perhaps I have something that would work for you Rachael."

Gran'ma continues. "There's a long evening ahead, so Jock, Gerald, Cydlo, and Taymar, you will have forty-five minutes between you for speeches and announcements. Gumpa will fill out any time which isn't used with a story about something strange that happened long ago in Cornwall. Uncle Andy, would you be willing to sing your song from the Italian opera?"

Uncle Andy had rather enjoyed his performance as an Italian opera singer for Squidgy's benefit. "Yes, I suppose I could do that."

Gran'ma has still more ideas. "We need some other entertainment. I want everyone, Real children, Shadow children, and Twith, to gather into groups and come up with a skit. That part of the program can last as long as we like. There will undoubtedly be dancing and wild celebration after that. Before bedtime we'll have cocoa, cookies, cake, and candy."

The children all cheer at this announcement.

She looks at her husband. "If Gumpa will start a fire, the coals will be right for toasted marshmallows later."

He grimaces, but nods his head. He doesn't like toasted marshmallows.

"The party will start at seven-thirty to give you time to prepare your skits. Now my kitchen crew can get busy setting the table and helping with supper."

She decides on curry and rice with mixed vegetables as the quickest option. Gumpa makes a fresh pot of tea, although most of the children will choose milk to drink.

As gran'ma bustles about the kitchen, she thinks, 'People need parties. Not only children but even people as old as Gumpa need parties. We've been spending so much time thinking about what Dayko was saying in the Rime that we're in danger of getting burned out. A party will be a much needed diversion.'

Even the boys join in willingly in cleaning up the dishes after supper. They don't want any delays in starting the party.

Not all the new children brought party clothes, but Specs and Bajjer and Stormy and Ginger are ready to share from their stock. Clothing worn by one child regularly can look bright and exciting and fresh when worn by someone else. All kinds of exchanges are taking place. Jenn is quite popular as she brought her curling iron. It is difficult to find any space at any of the mirrors. As soon as the boys leave, the girls use the nice long one over the dresser in the guest bedroom.

Gran'ma finds ribbons among her Christmas wrappings that the girls can use in their hair. Some of the girls also decorate their dresses with ribbons. She also has some sweaters with silver or gold threads and pretty buttons that will add sparkle to everyday clothes.

The boys hang some of the Christmas decorations from the ceiling beams for a festive atmosphere.

Clusters of children gather to discuss ideas for skits. The three big bedrooms upstairs reverberate with sound as actors and actresses practice their lines. Two groups are in the attic with the dividing door closed against distractions. Several of the skits will emphasize differences observed or experienced between the Twith and their friends. The Wizard and Mrs. Squidge feature in two of the skits. Uncle Andy is going to demonstrate how Mrs. Squidge cooks yeast buns. That should be hilarious. Gumpa plans to sing the song of 'Ivan and Abdul, the Bulbul Amir,' and gran'ma will recite a poem from her childhood, "Pea Little Thrigs." Vickie is preparing a skit involving an Italian stonemason.

The Twith aren't as organized as many of the children. Performing skits is something new to them. Barney leads the group that's working on the reactions of a Twith suddenly enlarged to Beyonder-size. It's going to be difficult being ready in time.

Gran'ma searches her special store of treasures for something to give the engaged couple to start them off right. She chooses a pretty teapot and two bone china cups with saucers. She ties a blue bow around two special teaspoons with a royal crest she bought in an antique shop. To complete the gift, she includes some packets of the special blend of tea that Gumpa uses. Everything will be shrunk before it's time to give it to the young couple.

Ginger rings the bell at 7:30 p.m.

Jock calls those gathered in the long room to some sort of order.

"May we come to order, please? Everyone find a place to sit down."

He wears his most formal Scottish attire — black shoes highly polished and a sprig of heather from the garden in his lapel. His blue eyes sparkle with fun and happiness. He looks around at his Twith friends and the bright group of children dressed in their best for the party. Over half the children are already Twith-size. The others are waiting until it's time for the dancing to begin. Jock smiles. 'Interesting how easily they adapted, and enjoy being Twith-size. What a wonderful bunch they are.

These children are so stimulating to work with! I'm enjoying myself in spite of many uncertainties.'

Jock begins with a short summation. "Because of the examination we made of Dayko's Rime, we have suddenly received a great forward impulse by the reunion with our king. We had no idea this reunion would take place in the Beyond. We rejoice that we have our king back to join in the fight for truth and justice. We look forward to the Return. For the Twith, it means going back to our homeland.

"I do have some concerns though. I know that across in Squidgy's cottage, the Wizard and Mrs. Squidge must be plotting mischief for us on the Brook. Otherwise, the Wizard would have left for Gyminge. Tuwhit confirmed he's still around. He must be planning another attempt to get hold of the Book of Lore.

"However, the confirmation that Cydlo is our king and Elisheba is the princess has boosted my faith that, within a month or so, the whole struggle will be over. The time between then and now, though, promises to be the most difficult fighting of the whole campaign.

"We're at the edge of a great and risky adventure. Dayko's Rime lists twenty-one events that must take place before our Return. Several are yet to be fulfilled. We still need to see the shield and the sword. We expect to see at least one of them when Bimbo and Bollin return. Events of these last few weeks fit together as though they are pieces gathered for a pathway — stepping stones to the way back home.

"We spent yesterday and today looking at Dayko's Rime. It's time to move on and enjoy being together. Gerald, I call upon you to postpone until tomorrow afternoon, if you will, the final consideration of Dayko's Rime."

Gerald has had his world transformed by the afternoon's events. Lines in Dayko's Rime are clearly coming to pass here and now. He thinks back to when he was an apprentice seer. 'I frequently watched from the porch of Dayko's house as my master crossed the footbridge to the castle to greet and talk with the king and his daughter. Those days had seemed gone forever. They were mere dreams lost when the sun of freedom went down. Now today those dreams are strangely renewed. Centuries later, that same king, and that same princess, are right here in the long room at Gibbins Brook Farm. The foresight of our ancient seer confirms that there will be a Return, if not to the good old days, at least to Gyminge. Things are well!' He voices agreement. "Yes, we'll wait to continue with the Rime. How about two-thirty tomorrow?"

"Alright, two-thirty will be fine. Let's continue with our celebration."

The Celebration

Cydlo has no royal attire and wouldn't wear it if he did. He didn't want any brought from the hideaway to the hut in the woods once it was built. Instead, his daughter made the kind of clothing he needed for the life of a woodcutter and charcoal burner. Softened calf leather and goat and lamb skins were the base materials she used with increasing skill. The best of those clothes the girl brought from her last visit to their home. The clothes the king wears may be simple and ordinary, but he commands a presence, a royal presence, that needs no fine clothes to confirm who he is. Fine clothes are everything to the puppet king, Haymun. The purple cloaks and ornate crowns make him what he claims to be; without them, he's pitiful. Cydlo struggled to hide within the woodsman the nature of the king, but now that he's revealed, his royalty shines forth.

Elisheba brought many of her clothes from the castle hideaway. She has chosen a deep-blue dress, with a flowing skirt and half sleeves, which complements her auburn hair. The sleeves, skirt, and neck are trimmed with plain silver ribbon. Ellie and Margaret braided her hair and tied it with a matching blue velvet bow. She wears a simple necklace and her new bracelet and ring. 'Pearls are special somehow', she thinks, 'probably my favorite gemstone.'

She and Taymar are sitting next to each other. Taymar too wears his best clothes. His white ruffed shirt is patterned on one of Jock's, but of a larger size. His pants are green, full-length and tight to the leg. His jacket is made of soft, brown tweed. His shoes are also brown. 'I'm more relaxed now that I'm suitably dressed for the occasion. I can hardly fathom that this beautiful young woman beside me will one day be my wife. How happy my mother and father would be if they could see the pair of us together.' Taymar looks at the king's ring on his finger.

He has carried it for hundreds of years in the pouch around his neck. 'It's strange to be wearing it openly.'

Cymbeline is the seamstress for the Twith and keeps the men folk equipped with clothing. Their preference for everyday is soft leather, salvaged from Beyonder handbags and shoes. Gerald gets some of his shoe materials that way too. Cymbeline runs short of very little since she's been at the farmhouse. Gran'ma sets aside all leftover quality material that can be used for a jacket or pants for a Twith. She also has a great jar of buttons that she spreads out for Cymbeline to make up sets. Once gran'ma shrinks with them in her pocket, they are suitable for what the girl needs.

Jock has a formal speech he wants to make. "This is indeed a very special occasion we are celebrating today — the betrothal of two of our Twith friends. It has never happened in the Beyond before. I'm not expecting it to happen again. I expect all future Twith betrothals will take place back in our own land of Gyminge.

"We had no idea when our rescue team sent Bimbo and Bollin to scout out the woods for the ambush site, that it would lead to the eventual discovery of our king and his beautiful daughter. She has won our affection, but especially the heart of one of us. We didn't know, few did, that Taymar's heart had long ago been given to the princess. She didn't know herself."

Excited chattering breaks out all around the room.

Jock holds up his hand and the chattering falls silent. "We join in their happiness as they begin to enjoy their love for each other. We hope that we'll be able to journey safely together back to their future home. It's so near to the Brook, but for so long it's been so far away. All of us want to see them settled in a home from which they will never again have to move.

"There are still a couple of speeches and gran'ma was clear about the time for talking. I want to give the king an opportunity to speak. Then, his future son-in-law should have a chance to respond to his betrothal. Cydlo I invite you to share any thoughts you might have at this time."

Cydlo remains seated. "I urge everyone to make yourselves comfortable although I don't intend to make a long speech. Over many years in the forest, I often found myself remembering and regretting much of the past. One of my regrets was that I had put off the enjoyment of happiness until it was too late. Before events overtook me and we went into hiding, there were many days of happiness I could have had and should have taken. Because I never claimed them, they were — and are — lost forever. They would have helped me bear the pain of dark days if I had remembered to seize every day of happiness with my lovely queen. I chose to defer those joys and thus they never came.

"A gift that children have, and which I see in all of you before me, is that you leave tomorrow for tomorrow and wring your utmost pleasure out of the day you are in. It's as though there will be no tomorrow, and you are made to enjoy the present. Your smiles and laughter show that you do. I hope that when we do return to Gyminge, I'll be a wiser and a better king than I once was. I'll try to be like you in the days we spend together. I'll look to you to teach me how to laugh again. If you can do that for me, then you will enable me to pass it on and teach my people once more to also laugh and be happy.

"We have with us this evening two young people dear to our hearts that are learning, after many delayed years, to seize happiness. Long ago, I was with my good friend, Earl Gareth of Up-Horton at Count Fyrdwald's Castle in the Dark Forest. The three of us were planning how to face the difficult days ahead when we would be battling the invading forces of Wozzle. I took time to be alone to talk with Gareth. He pledged to me that his oldest son, Taymar, would care for my daughter. If necessary, he would even take her with him into the unknown Beyond. He assured me that his son would care for her and give his life for her.

"Then I wondered if he would love her? My daughter had grown up being loved and not only by her mother and her father. All of our people loved her. If she found herself in some far country and wasn't loved by the people there, she would wither like a flower starved of water. I could not commit my daughter to flee away without assurance she would be loved.

"My friend gave me those assurances. We agreed to the betrothal of our children. In our land, parents, with their greater wisdom and experience, arrange for the marriage of their children. We exchanged the rings that would bind us into the agreement. Neither of us would break it against the other's will. It has taken until this day to tell my lovely daughter that the love that has already sprung between her and Taymar was set in motion long, long years ago in the middle of the Dark Forest. Now we must seize the day, or rather, allow them to seize their day and permit us to join with them in it.

"I ask all of you who know the customs of the Beyond, to advise me how soon their marriage should take place. It can be here at Gibbins Brook Farm. We will gratefully accept Uncle Andy's offer of the use of the cow barn. As Dayko foretold, the brides shall process to the barn, and it shall be the Princess Alicia who is the bride. We now have the opportunity to see his prophecy come to pass. There are plans and arrangements to be made. Gerald, today is Thursday evening. Can the wedding be on Saturday?"

"I don't see why not. The sooner the better."

Great cheers ring out from, not only the Twith, but the children as well.

Gran'ma Has Her Say

"Cydlo." It is gran'ma speaking. "That doesn't give us enough time to arrange everything! There's more to a wedding than most people realize, and you've caught us completely by surprise. If Elisheba is going to be a bride, she's going to look like a bride. You do want her to look like a bride, don't you? She needs a wedding dress, and you can't make a wedding dress in five minutes, you know. And she'll need new shoes. Gerald will need time to make those. Does anyone have a sixpence? She'll need that in her shoe. She'll need her hair done and a manicure. We can't have her looking like a woman shopping in the market or hanging out the washing or going to a cemetery! Cydlo, you'll need new clothes also. You're the one who gives the bride away."

This catches Cydlo by surprise. He was thinking that he would be the one performing the ceremony.

Gran'ma has the bit between her teeth and is charging full-speed ahead. "Is the wedding going to be in the cow barn for sure? There'll need to be preparations over there. It will probably need to be redecorated. The Rime says that there will be a procession. That means at least four bridesmaids. They need dresses. We need groomsmen as well. What about the wedding rehearsal? Then there are bouquets for the bride and the bridesmaids. And boutonnieres for the groom and groomsmen. We need corsages for special guests and flowers for up front. There's the special wedding cake to make, and we'll need to get food and prepare it for the reception. Not just the food for a meal, but also fancy nuts and mints. Then we have to decide what kind of punch we want. We have to organize the dishes too. We'll need plates, cups, and saucers, glasses, and silverware.

"And who's going to do the service? We have to decide the order of service." Gran'ma doesn't wait for answers from the bemused king, but allows her thoughts free rein out loud. "Then there's the music. Do the Twith have hymns? Once the hymns are chosen, hymn sheets need to be made up so a choir has time to practice. There's an organ we can use, and maybe our dear friend Gwen will play for us. Where is the couple going for their honeymoon? That's something more that needs organizing. We'll need to arrange things ahead of time. How are they going to get there? I guess Crusty or Tuwhit could take them. We could have silver ribbons trailing from their wings. Maybe the magpies could carry a banner ahead of them. A massed bird escort could be very impressive and quite unusual, especially if we matched the colors of the birds and arranged some special flight patterns. We could have a bird acrobatics team." Gran'ma is letting herself get carried away.

She notices the amazed expressions on everybody's faces. "Well, the birds themselves could organize that. But we have to work on the photographs. Twith photos don't come out, and we just must have pictures. Gerald, maybe you can come up with something. The wedding rings need to be made. I have a class ring we can use for the gold bands themselves. Jordy, could you get started on that right away? What about the invitations? We need to work on the guest list. How many are we planning for? Are we going to invite the rabbits and the badgers and the birds? How about the toads? That will affect where the wedding and the reception are held."

She pauses for breath and looks over at Cydlo. "You see? It will all take time."

Cydlo blinks and swallows hard. If he had been standing rather than sitting, he would have stepped back at least two feet in sheer surprise. 'I may be a king, but this is on an entirely different level. Fighting the Wizard is one thing, but I've never encountered an American woman determined to get things right for a wedding.'

Gran'ma has been involved in many weddings apart from the weddings of her three daughters. She knows what is essential if it's going to be a proper wedding and not a fiasco. She expresses more of her thoughts. "Every wedding is a special wedding, but after all, this is the Crown Princess of Gyminge getting married. They are the future king and queen! It's essential that everything is perfectly timed, or there will be chaos. A wedding is a wedding after all, not a stroll through the garden to look at the roses! There needs to be someone at the center of things making sure that everything is done right."

She allows herself the thought in passing, like an express train past a signal box. 'Men just don't seem to realize that the various parts of a wedding require precise timing and coordination. I'm definitely on my own for this one.'

Cydlo, with his question about how soon the wedding can be, has put himself on the sidelines as one of the objects to be coordinated. He's one of the pieces on the chessboard rather than the hand moving the pieces. Without knowing it, he's launched a ship that, as soon as it hits the water with a splash, is out of his control. It proceeds with increasing speed due south with a different person at the helm.

Even Gerald is taken aback at how complex a wedding is. 'It's an iceberg where suddenly the great bulk below water has moved to the surface and is exposed. Cydlo has unleashed a whirlwind. Who would have thought a simple wedding of two people in love could become so complicated so quickly?'

The two men exchange startled glances. Cydlo shrugs his shoulders helplessly and surrenders the meeting back to Jock.

Jock takes a deep breath, coughs gently and breaks into gran'ma's thought process. "The wedding of Taymar and Elisheba is an exciting challenge. We came this evening prepared for a party. Perhaps, in view of the urgency to move forward on preparations, we should defer the party until after the wedding when it can be part of those even bigger celebrations. The really important matter as far as we Twith are concerned, is the conduct of the wedding ceremony in accordance with our practice and customs. We'll be guided by the Book of Lore and our traditions. It isn't necessary to us that the father present the bride. However, it isn't forbidden.

"The other matters we'll be happy to leave for gran'ma to arrange. Perhaps, in order to keep everything in harmony, Cydlo, Gerald, and I, Taymar and Elisheba, and Gumpa and gran'ma should meet frequently to agree on the details. Gran'ma, you seem to have a good idea of what's involved in arranging a wedding. Would you please tell us how we go forward? Can you give us an idea when the earliest date and time could be?"

Gran'ma is only half listening. She has Stormy beside her rapidly writing a list of the tasks to be done. They're grouped into roughly similar activities, and already have names of children and Twith against them. Cymbeline's name appears in several different places, but gran'ma will edit that later. She realizes that from now on, someone else will have to see to the Twith cooking. 'Cymbeline will be busy full time making dresses for the bride and the bridesmaids and supervising a team of all the girls who know how to use a sewing needle. Ruthie did a good job of preparing meals for us in Gyminge. She won't mind taking over.'

To answer Jock, she stops dictating and looks up. Stormy hands her a calendar. She turns over the page from June to July, thinking hard. "Today is June twenty-third. We don't want to have some awful, rushed affair that we'd be ashamed of. I think that if it's going to be any kind of a wedding at all, the earliest time is probably two weeks from tomorrow. That's Friday, July eighth. That may sound like a long time, but it isn't. We'll have to cut out some things just to meet that deadline. I'm allowing very little time for something that normally takes a minimum of three months."

Jock raises his eyebrows and looks at Cydlo. Cydlo nods slowly. While listening to gran'ma, he was afraid the wedding wouldn't be possible until long after the date Gerald set for the Return. He's relieved it's only going to take two weeks. He looks questioningly at Taymar and Elisheba.

Taymar also nods and answers for them both. "Okay, gran'ma, it's up to you!"

The Rush Is On

Gran'ma is five foot one when she stretches. She's a long way from the environment where she grew up, high in the Colorado Rockies. She thought when she married Gumpa, she would enjoy a quiet life in a picturesque English village. She imagined herself without a care in the world, totally at peace and completely relaxed, enjoying the soft, tinkling sounds of distant wind chimes. She expected the most dramatic event of each day would be the gurgle of water down the kitchen sink drain after washing the dishes. Or, perhaps, measuring how much the amaryllis plant grew from one day to the next. She has never seen a plant grow so fast that its stem could be measured in inches.

She didn't realize that by marrying a quiet, reserved Englishman she would be introduced to two sons and seven Twith — now nine — who are only half-a-thumb high. Further, the peace and quiet she envisioned is now a thing of the past with sixteen exuberant children having free run of the house. She watches with amazement as they shrink and grow between one inch and sixty-seven inches, depending on whether or not they want a ride on a bird! Such things never happened in the Rockies.

Neither did she expect to be kidnapped by a slimy young man claiming to be from Heathrow wearing a purple jacket with brass buttons and red pants. After she shrunk going through a waterfall, he had his goblins take her to a castle in a lake where she was chained to a ring in the floor of the laundry, and set to work ironing their uniforms. Standing at the ironing board, she began to revise her understanding of a quiet life in England. Suddenly, chaos broke out all around her. Men in carts cracking their whips and driving like Ben Hur raced around the castle courtyard chasing each other. Suddenly, some of the visiting children burst in and right behind them was her laidback husband behaving like one of the Furies in Greek mythology.

Now once again back at the farmhouse, she gains new understanding. "It's quite clear to me what the real underlying reason was for me to fly across the ocean and marry a retired missionary from Pakistan. No one else has any idea how to organize a wedding! They needed to have someone here to do that, and I have experience as a wedding hostess."

The eight girls in the farmhouse gather around the large dining table. Cymbeline and the three Shadow girls sit cross-legged on top of the table. Elisheba thinks that Taymar's hands might be cold, so she went to snuggle close and warm them up for him. Paper and pencils are everywhere. The girls have been looking for pictures of weddings in the illustrated magazines scattered around. There are also one or two books with pictures of royal weddings.

Austin represents the boys, but they aren't expected to be involved in these early stages of planning. They are the laborers to be called in when things need to be moved. Weddings are for girls, and boys have just no idea. Austin thinks he's present because he can contribute wisdom from the other half of the human race.

Gran'ma begins assigning duties. "It's obvious that what will take the longest time is making the clothes for the wedding party. So, we'll look at that first. To start with, who will be in the wedding party? Cymbeline, will you go ask Elisheba if she will be happy with four bridesmaids and who they should be? Also check to make sure she wants a traditional white wedding dress and veil. It's possible the Twith have some other color for brides. I know in China they wear red. Does she also want a flower girl? Lynette would be perfect for that. I'm thinking of a variety of pastel shades for the bridesmaids' dresses. See if that will be okay with her too. Those are all things we need to get settled right away."

Cymbeline scurries off to find Elisheba.

"Now, who else in the wedding party besides the girls will need new clothes?"

Austin ventures a guess. "Just the bridegroom, the best man, the father of the bride, and whoever does the service will be enough."

Gran'ma rolls her eyes. "Who is going to escort each of the bridesmaids? The flower girl will need a ring bearer as an escort. I wonder if Barney would be willing to do that?"

Austin makes a suggestion. "Perhaps, owing to the shortage of time, the number of bridesmaids should be reduced to two. That way, the best man could escort one of the bridesmaids, and Cydlo the other."

Gran'ma shakes her head. "No, Cydlo escorts *Elisheba* to the ceremony. Afterwards, Taymar will escort his bride away. The best man will indeed escort the maid of honor down the aisle, but the other bridesmaids need their own escorts."

Austin is warming to the idea of organizing a wedding. 'A man somehow brings a more mature perspective to planning something so serious and important.' He adds another suggestion. "Perhaps, apart from the bride and the groom and Cydlo, the people taking part should only be those who already have suitable clothes. Jock could wear his kilt. Specs brought his suit. So did Bajjer. Stormy brought some fancy dresses. Cymbeline just has to be a bridesmaid, and she already has some pretty yellow dresses."

Gran'ma shakes her head again. "You don't understand, Austin. Nothing in the present wardrobe is ever good enough for a wedding. Even Gumpa and I will go shopping in Ashford for a dress for me. We'll need to go in on Saturday anyway to buy the first load of groceries. 'Although,' she thinks, 'I could wear the one I bought when I married Gumpa. That one still looks new.'

Cymbeline is back. "Elisheba says whatever we decide will be alright with her. A white dress is fine. She'd like Stormy and me to be two of the bridesmaids. She doesn't know what a flower girl does." Cymbeline's eyes twinkle as she says, "Taymar's hands must be *so* cold. Elisheba didn't let go of them once."

Gran'ma moves on. "Which of you girls can sew?"

All of the girls have done some embroidery, but few of them have done any serious dressmaking. However, the three Shadow girls have been taught how to sew by their mothers. Cymbeline says, "Barney can do simple sewing things if we need extra help."

Gran'ma is surprised at that. "Well, let's see whether we can prepare for four bridesmaids. If we run out of time, we can cut it back to three or even two. Cymbeline, you concentrate on the bride's dress. Gretchen, you can be in charge of the seamstresses. They can either make dresses for the bridesmaids full-size and then shrink them or they themselves can shrink and make them Twith-size which will save on material. Why don't we all go upstairs and look at the material that's available?"

The Beyonder girls carry the Shadow girls and Cymbeline, and troop off upstairs.

Cymbeline's mind races ahead of events. "Gran'ma, I assume that Gerald will conduct the marriage ceremony, but I have never seen a seer's formal clothes for state occasions."

Gran'ma beckons to Rachael and Jenn. "I'm giving you two a free hand to come up with a suitable robe for Gerald."

The girls waste no time in getting started. They search through the books showing royal weddings and find one where the Archbishop of Canterbury officiated at the wedding of the crown princess in Westminster Abbey. They will pattern Gerald's robe on that. Gran'ma has wonderful white satin material that somehow didn't get selected for the bride's dress. In order to get things right they choose to be Twith-size while they work. The stitch work is smaller and neater and mistakes won't be as noticeable. Gerald won't be allowed to try it on to see if it fits, or even see it at all before he wears it for the ceremony. They use Barney as their mannequin, and the boy enjoys being part of a secret. It makes him feel like he's someone special.

The girls are disappointed when gran'ma calls a halt and says, "It's time for bed." She shepherds them and the other children off to their rooms.

Everyone is still thinking about all that Cydlo revealed. They're trying to work through and understand what his story means for the Twith. From the moment he began speaking, the whole course of the future for the Twith changed. Each of them draws their own conclusions. In bed, the children are slow getting to sleep. They share their views, and are reluctant to lose out on hearing what the others think.

Salt Wind Blowing

The next morning, a group gathers promptly at 10:30 to discuss the assignment from Jock to find the answer to line twenty-six of Dayko's Rime.

Specs makes a suggestion. "Let's go out and sit on top of the well. Why don't we Beyonders adjust to Twith-size? That way we can understand the birds and Blackie without translation."

The others agree, and they stream outside. Barney shrinks them when they get there. The day is a perfect summer day. The sky is blue. A few lazy cumulus clouds drift high overhead. It's warm almost to the point of being hot. There's hardly any breeze; the leaves are almost motionless.

Gumpa has his chair in the sun and Lupus is in his usual position propping up Gumpa's feet. Gumpa learned long ago how to communicate with birds and animals and doesn't need to be shrunk. Gran'ma has sent regrets for herself, Stormy and Cymbeline. She will try to attend for part of the time, though.

The meeting is soon under way. Gerald is glad so many of the others are present, there are fewer missing than he expected. "The line of Dayko's Rime that we're here to discuss is line twenty-six."

26. *Salt wind shall blow over the land*

Gerald invites Specs. "You may carry on. Do you have anything to share about the salt wind over the land?"

Specs stands on the edge of the well cover. "Will everyone please sit down somewhere? And could you please be especially quiet? I'm not used to leading a meeting like this, so I hope everyone will help. We've been given a task by Jock to figure out how the salt wind is going to blow over Gyminge. We need to find an answer in a hurry because unless the salt wind blows over Gyminge, there may not be a Return.

"First, let's think about what we know about the curtain. Even before the Wizard conquered Gyminge more than a thousand years ago, he used a curtain around his own land of Wozzle. Taymar told me during the invasion of Gyminge, the Wizard made at least one special curtain and placed it over Fyrdwald's Castle. That curtain was roofed over, so it made a bubble. People couldn't get out from under it to join in the fighting. We may face the same problem later this summer ourselves. Taymar said the rabbits were able to dig beneath the curtain to get into Wozzle. But the Wizard improved the curtain around the combined countries. It hasn't proved possible to dig beneath it or to get above it. I don't know if anyone has tried to cut through it.

"The Wizard can alter the curtain whenever he wants, but he does it by magic. He made a hole in it at bird height, but presently, that seems to be closed off. The curtain has some strange properties. It's invisible for one thing. Beyonder birds and animals shrink when they go through into Gyminge and return to size when they come back. Beyonders themselves also shrink and enlarge unless they've been made Twith-size before they go through. The Twith stay the same size, and so do the toads. They were going into Gyminge long before the curtain was erected, so that must be why the curtain doesn't affect them.

"The curtain falls into the bog in front of the waterfall. There's a slit in it there that Buffo knew about. It was once full Beyonder height because gran'ma went through it. The team that rescued gran'ma used that way to get into Gyminge. After she was rescued, the Wizard shrunk that entrance so it prevents anyone larger than a toad from going through.

"Now let's think about the salt wind. We're close to the sea here, so wind from the sea could well be salty. We think that the land Dayko refers to is Gyminge although we don't know that for sure. If it does, then the sea breezes from the south will blow over Gyminge. If it doesn't happen naturally, then we have to find a way to make it happen."

Specs repeats, for the benefit of the birds and Blackie, questions he raised yesterday. "Yesterday, I asked several questions, and that's why we're here today, to try and answer them. Is the curtain soon going to wear out and be filled with holes to allow the wind to blow through? We know that it's centuries old. Is that what Dayko was seeing? Is there any sign it's wearing out?

"Has anyone tried cutting holes in it? Perhaps, if it's weaker higher up, it would be easier to cut it there rather than at ground level. A welding torch goes through most things. What about a chain saw? Can the curtain be set on fire? Has anyone tried? How deep into the ground does the curtain go? What's it made of anyway?"

Crusty lifts up a claw and the noisy chatter of responses to these latest questions slopes to nothing.

"Yes, Crusty?"

"Stormy came early this morning with her little book of notes and shared the discussions of yesterday with Tuwhit and myself. Why are you worrying about this line in Dayko's Rime? I think you're worrying about nothing. I don't see what the problem is. Allow me to share my thoughts. The curtain has been in place for more than a thousand years. If it was going to wear out, it would have done so before now.

"However, Dayko's Rime says that *salt wind shall blow over the land.* He says just that, and he says no more than that. You are thinking he says more than he does. The salt wind couldn't blow over the land of Gyminge after it was conquered. The curtain surrounded the country. And it still surrounds it, so no salt wind blows over the land today.

"Dayko, however, looking down the years, knew that one day salt wind from the sea would blow over the land. He didn't say how long it would blow or how much would blow. Simply that some salt wind would blow for some period of time, nothing more than that. Thirty years ago, the Wizard betrayed himself, and it will cause his eventual downfall. He's the one who has fulfilled this line of the Rime for us. He alone, not any of us, allowed salt wind to blow over Gyminge. He made a hole in the curtain so that he and Rasputin, and later Mrs. Squidge, could fly through it. I flew back with Cydlo three days ago before the Wizard closed the curtain completely. As I approached the hole I could smell the salty sea air. The southerly wind from the sea tossed me about in the Gyminge sky as I made my way to the hole that would let me back onto the Brook.

"The Twith don't need to do anything. The Wizard can't turn back what has already happened. The salt wind has already blown over the land!

"The Wizard learned to fear us birds. We are so many we can overcome him here on the Brook. He saw where his weakness was, so he closed the curtain. He did it for good, his good! It would be very unwise for him to open it again. He's not that foolish. Your battle in Gyminge will most likely have to be without our help, but this line from Dayko's Rime doesn't need to hold you up. It has already been fulfilled."

Great cheers go up from all the children as they agree wholeheartedly with Crusty. There's clapping from behind, near the sycamore tree. The four Twith men were quietly listening. Gerald also nods his agreement and approval.

Specs is beaming. "Thank you, Crusty! You have solved the puzzle for us. The Twith won't have to bother with this line any further. There's no need to try and find out whether the curtain is inflammable enough to burn down or whether we could cut through it. I agree with Crusty that the Wizard made a serious mistake. By opening the hole for Rasputin to go through, he himself fulfilled this line in the Rime. The salt wind has indeed already blown over the land. And once was enough to count as fulfilling this line of the Rime."

Brides to the Byre

For lunch, there's lots of Gumpa's famous seven-day stew loaded with leftover vegetables and chicken from the frig. The children eat sparingly of that but go for seconds on the cookies and ice-cream. Gran'ma is too busy today to be distracted by precautions for healthy eating. Children are survivors. They could probably eat anything that was peanut-butter flavored spattered with chocolate chips and included ice-cream.

After lunch, the children stream into the long room, chattering excitedly as they go. Even gran'ma has decided it's important to be present.

Gerald doesn't intend to be caught up by the general rejoicing of recent events. He calls the afternoon session to order. "We need to move on quickly. If we can, I want to close the discussion on Dayko's Rime today. Time is beginning to squeeze up on us. We're waiting for Bimbo and Bollin to return and tell us about the sword and possibly the shield. It's possible, even probable, that they won't succeed in their quest. If that happens, the difficulties we face ahead may prove insurmountable. However, at this point, we must wait and see and take heart from what has happened already.

"The fighting in Gyminge when we get there is likely to be long and hard. We need to have some idea of when that will be. We'll be short of days rather than have too many. Soon, we should try and set a date for launching our return attempt. Most of us were present with Specs this morning when Crusty made it clear to us that the salt wind has already blown over the land of Gyminge from the moment the Wizard opened a hole in the curtain to first let Rasputin through. We won't take further time on that particular line. I believe we have mutually agreed that it has already happened. I'll put a checkmark by line twenty-six. Now, let's take up where we left off and look at line thirty in the next verse."

He points to his large printout of the poem.

30. *Brides shall process to the byre.*

"What does this mean and how can it happen? It's a puzzle. The Rime says brides will go in procession to the byre. Brides is plural, so it means more than one. We certainly now have a bride in the offing, but brides? That's a different matter. Does it mean that a whole lot of brides are in procession together? Is this some kind of mass wedding that Dayko was seeing? Cydlo told us that a byre is a cow barn. Why go to a cow barn? What do cows have to do with brides? The only thing they give in the byre is milk. Are the brides going to ride to their weddings on cows? It sounds ridiculous.

Gerald turns to Cydlo. "Cydlo, I understand that in Gyminge you had cows. At any time while you lived there, did a bride or brides ever go in procession to your byre to maybe have a look at the cows?"

Cydlo shakes his head.

"Does anyone have anything to add to this line? It's difficult to make sense of it. If not, then we'll have to leave it for now and go on to the next line."

Gerald is teasing and enjoying the tease. He knows something most of the others don't.

"Oh no, not so fast, Gerald." It's Vickie speaking. There are several others ready to speak up, but Vickie is first. "Ask gran'ma."

"Can you throw any light on this question, gran'ma?"

Gran'ma looks over at Gumpa. They aren't the only ones smiling. Uncle Andy, Mike, and Vickie are all grinning as though they have one big secret from the others. Gumpa flicks his eyes from face to face, wondering what the children are thinking. The seven original Twith who were there when it happened are keeping straight faces.

Gran'ma is one big smile. "Gumpa and I were married only four years ago. I came from America, and we were married soon after in a ceremony in Ashford. However, we wanted to celebrate our wedding in an old-fashioned way, so we turned the barn into a chapel for the occasion. My daughters flew here from the States. Uncle Andy came to me at the farmhouse to escort me across to the barn. The barn is right next door to the old cowshed, so the wedding procession, which included my three daughters, proceeded towards the cowshed and then past it on to the barn beyond it. There Gumpa was waiting for me. I think I can say that I was a bride who processed to the byre. Dayko saw me chained to the laundry room floor in Gyminge. Perhaps he saw me process to the byre as well.

"But brides isn't limited to just two. Perhaps others have also processed to the byre in the past that we don't know about. Or," she looks over to Elisheba, "will do so in the future. I wish Dayko had managed to give us a little more advance warning. But the plans for Elisheba's wedding are underway, and there's no doubt at all that a feature of the whole ceremony will be the procession. We expect it to be a very special procession that no one will ever forget.

"There's little doubt the old seer must have seen the wedding of his princess. He must certainly have known about the betrothal from the king even though it was secret. He saw what we have yet to see, the crown princess married to a handsome bridegroom who was probably also known to him. I think as far as this line of the Rime goes, we can just let what we are planning come to pass, and the line will be fulfilled. We can just enjoy it happening."

The Loss of the Lore

Gerald inclines his head in agreement, adds no more to what gran'ma says, and turns to the next section of the poem. He shares his thoughts. "Probably nothing in the whole Rime has given me more concern over the years than the next two lines." He reads them out slowly, following the words with his pointer.

> 31. *The loss of the Lore gives grief,*
> 32. *Though what is that to a life?*

"I'm the present Keeper of the Lore even though I was only an apprentice seer when Dayko was alive. To my knowledge, there are no other seers left since Zaydek and Haymun betrayed us. Cydlo may know."

He looks questioningly at the king. Cydlo just shakes his head sadly.

"From the day I first read these lines, the fear of the loss of the Lore has been with me. I have dreamed about it often. In my mind, I've gone a thousand times to the hiding place of the Book of Lore and found it missing. Many times to reassure myself, I've gone to be sure that the Book of Lore is still where I left it last. Sometimes, I get up in the night to check that it's still there. I fear to have it out of my sight lest an intruder stole it in my absence. Just weeks ago, Jacko might have stolen it. Fortunately, the ferret took the Shadow Book instead. Jock was able to recover that with only a little damage to it. The Wizard would give almost all he has to get hold of the Book of Lore.

"I wonder if there is more that we can do to protect it. Are our present precautions good enough? When we return to Gyminge, will the Book of Lore travel with us? This has been our thinking, but as soon as we begin moving into Gyminge, it will become even more vulnerable to enemy attack than it has been previously. A sudden ambush, a hundred goblins around us, and the Book of Lore could be gone forever. The precautions we've taken over the years have kept it safe, but they may well prove inadequate for what lies ahead of us when we return to Gyminge. For safety's sake, perhaps it should remain here. Will we leave it unguarded or lightly guarded?

"For some time I've been thinking we should have a fake Book of Lore that looks like the real one but isn't. This might serve as a decoy and provide added protection. We had one before, but it could quickly be seen to be a poor copy. We need something that could fool an expert."

He holds up his ink-stained fingers. "That's what I'm now working on downstairs and why you see so little of me. I'm very close to finishing it. Gumpa gave me some old leather suitable for the binding and scraps of old paper from a friend of his who works in a museum. I have already made and bound the book, and now I'm copying the original text into it. I'm only copying those parts that can be of no use to the Wizard if he should ever get his hands on it. Much of the Lore is like that.

"We don't know what the word *loss* in the Rime really means. It can mean it just gets mislaid. It can mean it gets lost, just simply lost, not only for a period of time but forever. It could even mean it gets burned up in a fire or destroyed in some other way. It can also mean the Wizard himself gets hold of it by outwitting us or that someone like Jacko steals it and sells it to him.

"A possible guide to us is that Dayko wants us to read the line about the Lore in connection with the line that follows. The pair of lines together suggests that loss of the Lore is to be compared to a life, likely one of our own lives. It's as though the Book of Lore is on one side of a scale and a life is on the other. We can't have both. When the choice has to be made, it's better by far to save the life and lose the Book of Lore.

"I can't help but feel that what Dayko is saying, at least to me, is that it's better that the Keeper of the Lore be saved and the Book of Lore itself be lost. I would not want that. I would gladly sacrifice myself to protect our precious Book of Lore so that our past can be carried forward into our future.

"However, the life that Dayko sees might be the king's life or the princess or any other of us. Dayko is telling us that whenever and for whomever the choice is to be made, there should be no hesitation in making the choice. His counsel to us is that we must be prepared to let the Book of Lore go. Perhaps now that we have a king, we need to look afresh at the appointment of a High Seer so that someone else takes care of the Book of Lore. Dayko told me that when the time came, I would know who to give his belt to, but up until now, I have had no clear direction who that might be."

Gran'ma breaks in. "As you've been talking, Gerald, I've sensed and can feel the great responsibility you've been carrying, carrying for centuries. All the recorded wisdom of your people has been yours to care for. If the accumulated wisdom and experience should be lost, how would it ever be regained? Before writing was discovered, wisdom was passed orally from one generation to the next. The appointed living bearers of the ancient records had a heavy burden to carry. That must be the kind of burden you now carry.

"Yet in these modern days, even if the intrinsic beauty of the Book of Lore itself might by some disaster be lost, surely it should be possible to save the information in it. There's no need for the Twith to lose the wisdom itself. My computer is upstairs and working. To be certain, the Book of Lore is a miniature and a computer scanner might not pick up its contents. Nevertheless, if the scanner doesn't work, I can type it in myself. You will just need to dictate the wisdom to me slow enough for me to enter it. As soon as we're free, come up to my office with the Book of Lore. Together, we'll put all that it says into my computer and save it before it's too late for anything but regrets. I doubt that I'll be able to save the pictures and the beautiful script, but at least we can save the words themselves. This is something that must not be put off until a more convenient time. We should have done this long ago, and we shouldn't let any more time slip by before it gets done."

Gran'ma has one last thought. "Gerald, I can't pretend to understand what Dayko is saying in these lines. They are perhaps the most ominous and worrying in the whole Rime. I'm sure the concern is not yours alone. You all need to share what you think about the meaning of what Dayko is saying. We should consider whether there's any way the loss can be avoided, although the Rime doesn't appear to suggest that."

As she speaks, Jock and Cydlo are agreeing together. Gran'ma is busy with a houseful of guests and a wedding to plan, yet she's putting the protection of the Lore before everything else. Her priorities are right, and theirs must be also.

It's Jock who speaks and he speaks to all who are present. "There are some matters that we must tend to right away. This is one of them. Let's make the remaining time until supper free time to complete any tasks you have. Or use it for exercise time. Gumpa," he grins at the old man, "will probably enjoy organizing tea. Gerald, will you please bring the Book of Lore from below? Jordy, perhaps you should go along with Gerald. The time for taking extra precautions to protect it is already with us.

"Gran'ma, we gladly accept your offer to put the Lore into your computer. Some of us Twith will, I'm sure, want to see how you do that if you'll take us upstairs when you go. Stormy, will you please take gran'ma's place and make yourself responsible for supper? Let the others know who you need to help you. We'll all meet together after supper at the usual time, but only if gran'ma has finished her work with Gerald."

The End of the Rime

Gerald and gran'ma have their tea at the computer. Jock, Jordy, and Cydlo are upstairs watching and commenting. They were surprised to find what the cure for the Magician's Twitch is. Why should that be in the Twith Lore? That must be what the Wizard is after though. There's a great sense of relief that the wisdom of the Lore no longer rests in one unique copy. Gran'ma saves the information to disc and also puts an additional copy of the Lore on Gumpa's computer as insurance against any calamity on her own computer. The accumulated wisdom of the Twith is now secure. They finish up just before supper. Jordy goes with Gerald when he replaces the Book of Lore in its hiding place in Twith Mansion.

Gerald is much more relaxed when he resumes for what will most likely be the last session. "We're nearing the end of the journey through Dayko's Rime. Some things are no clearer than they were before, but many things are. I'm grateful for all the interest shown and insights given by so many of you. Let's move on to the last verse."

> 33. *The fall will lead straight to the wall.*
> 34. *Hope is restored last of all.*

"We'll take these two lines together, although they may not belong together. We had wondered in the past about the word *fall*. We thought it might refer to someone falling. Barney once fell from Tuwhit's back onto a bubble, for instance. Or a wall might be falling or it might mean the season of the year. Summer is followed by the fall, but we can't wait for that to happen, and it doesn't seem to fit anyway.

"However, once Buffo showed us the waterfall not much more than a week ago, this line makes all kinds of sense to us. The line is suddenly understood. The fall is a fall of water, the waterfall. We already know the way past the waterfall leads us through Blindhouse Wood to the castle. Half of us have actually traveled that journey.

"It kind of tells us, doesn't it, that we do have to get through the waterfall and on our way before the Wizard blocks that way. I think the Rime suggests that this will be our way in and not any other way, even if there should be one available. The Wizard is sure to think that blocking the way of the waterfall is one of the best ways to prevent us entering Gyminge, even though it might mean annoying the toads who use it. Their season is over for this summer anyway."

"But, Gerald." Specs has been thinking hard as Gerald talks. "We've already been through the fall to the wall. Couldn't the two lines be quite separate? If so, we could check off the first one because that has already happened."

"Well, I hadn't considered separating the lines, but let's do that. You may be right, Specs. I'll tick that first line. I think the line about hope is encouraging, but who is it that is being encouraged? It kind of reads like the last line of a drama, just before we see the curtain fall for the last time — a kind of finale. Like the words in a book just before it says, *The end*."

Jordy breaks in thoughtfully. He's had little to say during the discussions on the Rime, but now is his time to speak. "Let's look a little more closely. This is an important line. There are three parts to it as far as I can see. First, it says, 'hope is.' What is hope? Hope has two parts. The first is desire of some good thing. The second is an expectation of perhaps obtaining it. We might well ask, in the context of Dayko's Rime, what is this 'good thing' being referred to? Since it involves expectation, the 'good thing' doesn't include good things that we have no expectation of obtaining. Say we go for a Sunday afternoon walk in the woods. Unless we have good reason to believe there is buried treasure under our feet or buried nearby, we don't hope to find the handles of a treasure chest sticking out of the ground. Although it might be a 'very good thing' if we did, we don't 'hope' to find treasure because it's so very unlikely. We hope for something that can be *expected*.

"Second, the word *restored* means that what has been taken away and removed is given back again. You don't restore something to people who never possessed it in the first place. You have to lose something first in order to have it returned to you. Third, it says, 'last of all,' which means what it says. It's the end. It's the end of the Return. When the Wizard is disposed of and the king is back on his throne, then, 'last of all,' hope is restored.

"It's clear to me that what this means is exciting to us and suggests the way we go about the Return. The line doesn't mean us — the Twith who are returning. We Twith never lost hope in the first place, so it isn't restored to us, and it can't be.

"The people to whom this line refers are our people still in captivity in Gyminge. They are people under the Wizard's present control. Let's look at who they are. They fall into three main groups. First, the people who are not in captivity but who work in servitude. Second, the Twith changed into goblins. Their hope to be free and to be masters and mistresses of their own lives was taken away from them. Third, the Twith who are captives in the jails and dungeons of Gyminge, captives both in bottles and out of bottles.

"What they all lost is freedom, and when they lost that, they lost hope. When we restore freedom to them, we will restore hope and the 'good things' they hope for will at last be within their grasp to attain and achieve. So 'last of all' tells me we can expect little or no help by way of a supporting uprising of the Twith who remain in Gyminge. Rather, they will remain captives of the Wizard until the very end. We ourselves, by our own strength and courage, will need to pursue the defeat of the Wizard to the bitter end. After it's all over, 'last of all,' even the goblins will become normal, restored, and like us once more. The lesson from this is that we should avoid, wherever we can, causing goblin casualties. Because when it's all over, they are 'us' once more, and we'll need them in the rebuilding of the land free from the Wizard."

There's a murmur of agreement with Jordy's analysis.

Stormy shares her troublesome thoughts. "There could be an awful number of things to do before the Return is completed. Maybe if even one isn't completed on August twelfth, everything will have been in vain. Gerald, how will we know when the Return is complete? When will 'last of all,' 'hope be restored'? Will it happen only after the very last castle in the country is recaptured? There must be many castles in Gyminge, aren't there?"

"Yes, there are as you say, Stormy, other castles in Gyminge. Count Fyrdwald's Castle is in the Dark Forest, and there were several smaller castles there as well. And there were several near our other borders. Earl Gareth lived in a fortified mansion though I don't think he would have called it a castle. I don't know what Dayko was seeing when he wrote this line. Because we don't know exactly what he does mean, I would think that we must just try to complete the recapture of Gyminge and everything in it by our deadline date unless some other meaning becomes clear to us before then. I would think that to be safe in the future, we should also need to recapture Wozzle as well as Gyminge."

Gerald turns attention back to the board. "These last two lines won't take long to dispose of."

    35. *Two reds in the night shall be green.*
    36. *All's done. I've told what I've seen.*

"That would have been a puzzle to us before the SnuggleWump came to the Brook. What Dayko is saying is that sometime, before we return to Gyminge, the angry red eyes of the SnuggleWump will change to happy peaceful green eyes.

"Well, he certainly wasn't happy on Monday. We saw his red eyes then, and Tuwhit reports they are still red. Sometimes in the past, they have been red and then changed to green. It has already happened. Let's hope it will happen again and they will stay green.

"That's the end of the Rime for now, Jock. Most of the lines are settled, or we have a good idea about them. We still have the sword and the shield to account for. Until Bimbo and Bollin return, I think we understand as much as we're able to of what Dayko's Rime is saying to us."

Bad News for the Wizard

Rasputin has, since the Wizard's first arrival in Gyminge, been his loyal lieutenant and the only one the magician trusts. During the initial fighting for Gyminge, he had his lower beak shattered by a stone fired from Barney's slingshot. It affects both his cawing and his conversation. He's a bruiser of a bird, ready to take on most of his master's enemies whatever the risk.

Ever since the battle at the farmhouse, Rasputin has been locked in Gyminge. The Wizard was unaware that his faithful black-feathered servant had fled from the scene when the attack began going wrong. By reciting a spell of his own composition, he closed the hole in the curtain, and now Rasputin can't get back out to rejoin him on the Brook.

Early Friday morning, at the crack of dawn, the raven is resting in his nest on the castle parapets. Footsteps going past waken him.

He mumbles in surprise, "What are those three strangers doing with the goblin king? It looks like he's been captured."

The two Shadow boys, Bimbo and Bollin, and Scayper, a prisoner they rescued from the dungeon, have indeed taken the goblin king captive. They plan to use the king as a hostage for securing their exit from the castle.

Rasputin quickly decides. "I better try to save him." He flies off over the lake and turns back to attack. Before he even gets close something wet hits his eyes. "Ouch! What's that?" He glances down and sees red and green splotches all over him. "Oh! Whoever they are, they're firing missiles filled with blood and green goo!" In actual fact, Bollin is using squirt bottles. One is filled with ketchup and the other with dishwashing soap.

Rasputin dives in the lake to clean himself off. "I need to let the Wizard know that Chinese goblins have attacked the castle. It means I have to go through the toad tunnel and be drenched by the waterfall. I'm certainly not looking forward to that, but my master needs to know."

The boys watch the raven take off. When he heads south, they realize he is going to report to the Wizard. They need to get back to the Brook before the Wizard decides to bring his troops back to Gyminge.

Rasputin flies to the southern border of Gyminge. Below he spots King Haymun's former doctor.

Dr. Vyruss Tyfuss was recently relieved of his medical duties as personal physician to the goblin king. He is now Colonel Tyfuss, Commander of the Southern Zone, and in charge of building the new fort ordered by the Wizard.

The raven decides, "I better find out how Colonel Tyfuss is doing. The Wizard will be sure to want to know." As he talks to the ex-doctor he expresses concern about his own welfare. "I'm uncertain about making my way through the toad tunnel. I've never been that way before." The raven is actually fearful of the dark.

Colonel Tyfuss calls one of the goblin cooks. "I want you to guide Rasputin through the toad tunnel. Take a torch to show him the way."

The goblin gulps, and his eyes widen in terror. He's afraid of the dark and should never be allowed within a hundred yards of a naked flame. Nevertheless, he steps smartly into the nearby entrance of the toad tunnel, motioning the raven to follow him.

Once through the tunnel the goblin is anxious to return. As he turns to go back, Rasputin gets singed back and front. His wing and tail feathers are on fire.

The raven dashes for the waterfall pond, getting even more drenched than he feared. "I'm not going to be able to fly in this condition! It's impossible. I'll have to ask the Wizard to trim and even up both my wing and tail feathers." Totally miserable, he walks slowly to the cottage.

Rasputin gives the Wizard an amazing report. "Boss, Gyminge has been invaded by hundreds and thousands of invisible Chinese." This report is incorrect, but the Wizard doesn't know that.

Griswold reacts immediately. "I'll order every goblin on the Brook to return to Gyminge without delay." He personally explains the "Back to Gyminge" orders to the 750 goblins in Mole Hall. "You are to return to Gyminge to fight the Chinese invaders. You will leave as soon as it's dark and proceed as rapidly as possible to the castle. I'll go ahead and place lights across the bog to guide you along the safe path and be waiting for your arrival at the castle."

Plans that the Wizard makes are usually extraordinary, exceptional, brilliant, and farsighted. However, unknown to him, those plans are doomed to failure once again. It isn't all his fault, of course. It never is. A poet — the man had to be Scottish because pictures show him wearing a kilt — once said, "The best laid schemes of mice and men gang aft agley." He didn't single out magicians, but he well might have done so if he had thought about it. The words get interpreted by the Wizard differently than the poet intended. The true meaning is that, "The best laid schemes of mice and men often go awry." The Wizard chooses to believe that it means, "There is always a fool somewhere who will prove that no plan is ever foolproof."

Griswold takes time to carefully trim Rasputin's wing and tail feathers. "Go take a trial flight, my lad. If you have problems, let me know, and I'll touch up the trim a bit." The raven now flies at an odd angle due to his shortened tail feathers but otherwise has no problems.

Almost from the start, things begin to go wrong with their journey. The Wizard reserves one of the turnip lamps he designed to light the way across the bog and through the toad tunnel. Halfway through, he receives a tremendous whack on his head when he forgets to duck at the roof's lowest point. Even worse, the lamp then catches his long hair on fire. Attempting to smother the flames with his hat, he makes a tactical error. By pulling it down over his eyes he is now blinded. He can't remove it because of the swelling bump on his head. He makes a mad dash towards the pool where the goblin king had soothed his sore and tender feet earlier. With his face just above the surface, a cloud of mixed steam and smoke floats above his head.

Colonel Tyfuss finds the Wizard and quickly cuts the rapidly shrinking hat band. Once the hat is removed, the bump increases further in size.

The stretcher squad rolls the dazed magician onto their stretcher and runs at the double. Unfortunately, the four men are of uneven height. The Wizard hangs on desperately to the slanted stretcher. It's hopeless, and the Wizard falls sideways. After the third fall, he chooses to walk.

Refusing the doctor's offer to perform surgery, he chooses to ignore his pain. "Dr. Tyfuss, did the Chinese invaders enter Gyminge by way of the toad tunnel?"

The doctor is surprised. "No, they didn't. I haven't seen any Chinese at all."

The Wizard is furious. "Your orders are changed. Send all your forces except the cooks back to the castle at once. You, my good doctor, will remain responsible for defending the border to the last man. There will be 750 goblins from the Brook arriving shortly after dark. Sergeant Major Agamemnon will be the last to arrive so you'll know there are no more coming. You will provide them food. As soon as they've eaten, they must move out for the castle. When the last of them leave, the cooks will go with them."

Dr. Tyfuss gulps. 'That means that I'll be the only man left to defend the border!'

"There is one further order. When the last of the men is ready to leave, have them first block the end of the toad tunnel with rocks. They should completely fill the last four feet of the tunnel. I want Gyminge sealed off from the Beyond."

"Now, we must be on our way without delay." In the blink of a twitchy eye, the Wizard changes into a cormorant. The bird lumbers into the air. Rasputin quickly joins him, and the two birds head north.

To the west, four horsemen are approaching, but they are too far away to see the birds leaving, and the birds aren't looking in their direction. One of the horsemen is King Haymun. The Wizard is expecting to rescue him from captivity in Goblin Castle, but once again, "The best laid schemes of mice and men gang aft agley."

The Goblin King

King Haymun isn't in the castle waiting to be rescued because the Chinese invaders have taken him with them. Bimbo and Bollin were surprised to be mistaken for Chinese, but they put the king's mistake to good use.

The boys took all the horses in the castle stable to prevent pursuit. They are novices when it comes to horses, but Scayper is an expert. They turned northeast to confuse the Wizard into thinking they weren't going back to the Brook. Approaching them was a group of cavalrymen returning to Goblin Castle. Scayper made them turn around and locked them in Fyrdwald's Castle. There he also took all their horses, and further north, he released a total of seventeen horses into the Black Forest. They had gone far enough away from the castle that they turned west. The path soon veered south into Blindhouse Wood.

Suddenly, they were set upon by a gang of robbers. Scayper and Bimbo avoided capture, but Bollin and the king, seated in front on the same horse, were taken to the robber camp. With the help of two elderly ladies and their wolf-dog, the boys rescued, not only Bollin and the king, but a stable boy as well. Each had his own horse to ride, but the stable boy had to be slung in front of King Haymun. He was sleeping off the effects of eating too much of Nettie's doctored pie. Just before leaving Blindhouse Wood, he was left on the ground; his horse tethered to a nearby tree. As the four horsemen left the woods, they emerged onto the path to the border.

As they ride, Bimbo thinks of what lies ahead. He's anxious to get back to the farmhouse with their trophies and with Scayper. So far, they've been more successful than they might have hoped, recovering both the Royal Sword and the Royal Shield. That will fulfill two lines in Dayko's Rime. He drops back to talk to Bollin, who's following the king. "I'm undecided what to do about King Haymun once we arrive at the border. I doubt whether he'll be anything more than a nuisance as a prisoner. Jock probably won't want him around. I would just as soon leave him with Dr. Tyfuss if we can get through to the waterfall without using him as a hostage. What do you think, Bollin?"

"I think you're right. Jock won't have any use for him, and he'd just be more trouble than he's worth. Let's just turn him loose. He can find his way back to the castle, and we'll be long gone before he can organize the goblins to chase us."

When they arrive at the border, Bollin, the ginger-headed brother, goes off ahead to investigate what's going on. He returns after a few minutes and talks urgently to his brother in the language they learned in Pakistan. The king can overhear the conversation, but thinks they're speaking Chinese. It must be important news and not news they're expecting for both seem surprised and excited. Bollin remains alongside Haymun. The other two take the large sword and the shield with them, gallop off in the darkness in the direction of the mouth of the toad tunnel that leads to the waterfall.

Bollin speaks two languages, and this time, he uses the language the king can understand. "Get down off your horse." He has a small broadsword in his hand, which encourages the king to do so.

The king has enjoyed having his own horse rather than riding uncomfortably in front of Bollin. It has been a distinct improvement. He hands the reins over with reluctance. He likes this horse. The animal is good for his feet, which have not yet fully recovered from the injuries sustained in returning to Gyminge from the Brook two days ago.

"Go towards that light. There are men of yours there, and they'll help you. I give you two minutes to be out of sight. Go!" The last word is a shouted command that permits no more talking.

King Haymun is plump and out of condition. The various physical activities of recent days have been a considerable strain. Nevertheless, he manages to swing on his heel and runs towards the light without pausing. He expects to hear galloping hoofs behind him, but instead, the noise of trotting horses recedes into the darkness. The king forgets his recent captors. As he approaches the light, he smells food — porridge.

The cooks are preparing porridge for the 750 goblin soldiers expected soon from the Brook. The smell reminds the king that he's hungry.

King Haymun sighs with relief when he sees, at the far end of the kitchen tent, Colonel Tyfuss and the two cooks. He knows he's among friends. There's a good deal that he doesn't know, almost everything in fact. He doesn't know the Wizard is back in Gyminge. He doesn't know that the Wizard blames him for allowing gran'ma to escape. That's just for starters. He's far happier than he should be.

The king wonders why the colonel is preparing so much porridge. 'This is more than double rations for everybody. Surely, he can't have that many men on his construction crew. Where did he get all of them? Well, time to sort that out later, after a meal, even though the meal seems likely to be porridge made without milk. I hope it at least has raisins in it.'

Haymun plans to relax and have a good night's sleep. He originally intended to inspect the development of the immigration center tomorrow anyway. He expected the Wizard to make his appearance on Sunday for his inspection. He's so puffed up with his own importance that he makes erroneous assumptions. He thinks that it must be a great help to the ruler of Gyminge to have safe hands like his to take care of the really difficult tasks.

The king is interested in protecting the image he thinks the Wizard has of him. Somehow, without being found out, he must concoct a tale that will appear like the truth and satisfy the Wizard. His story will have to cover from when he left the Brook on Wednesday up to the present. He will, of course, show himself as the wisest and bravest of the magician's underlings.

King Haymun is worried though. 'I must allow for the false evidence that will surely be presented against me by informers who haven't enough sense to keep their mouths shut. They just don't realize they all need to stick together when facing a common danger. It's a sad thing about people. So many good lies are simply ruined by people speaking out of turn because they can't stand for their tongues to be still. Rasputin, the sergeant major, the quartermaster sergeant, Corporal Pimples, Dr. Tyfuss, and even Cajjer will all get to the Wizard with their stories before I do. It's certain that they won't think to put me in a favorable light. My fabricated story will have to allow for that.'

King Haymun has been rehearsing in his mind what he'll tell the Wizard about being taken captive with a teething ring stuck on his big toe. 'That might have to be explained if Rasputin happened to see it during the encounter on the castle wall.'

The king's opportunity to explain is going to come quicker than he expects.

The Stranger

The Wizard expects his veteran soldiers, battle hardened by combat, will soon be scaling the castle walls to fight the Chinese. Once again, "The best laid schemes of mice and men gang aft agley."

At present, they are making their way across the bog on the Brook. The lamps the Wizard placed provide safe travel. Suddenly, out of nowhere, a pair of will-o'-the-wisp Shadow boys float across the bog among them, creating havoc and panic. As they kick over the lamps, the path is no longer visible. Helping them is an escaped prisoner from the castle dungeon swinging a sword around his head. He puts the fear of death into them, screaming a Twith war cry made up on the spur of the moment. A berserk owl swoops and dives at them. Tuwhit thinks that dunking goblins in the bog is better than a game of skittles on a Saturday evening. The air is filled with the sounds of screams and splashing. Pushing and shoving each other, the goblins clamber out of the bog. They head back to Mole Hall to scrub themselves clean and cook up some excuse to explain why they couldn't follow orders. Sergeant Aga doesn't want to report that the victors are a small contingent of three Twith and a bird.

The Wizard's careful planning for the attack on the Chinese has ended in disaster. Unknown to him, his goblin army is not heading to Gyminge. The complete defeat of his massive forces means that he'll wait for them in vain.

Tuwhit carries Bimbo, Bollin, and Scayper on his back from the waterfall to the farmhouse. He's still chuckling as he sweeps in to land. Behind him he has left complete chaos on the bog. He has turned a host of goblins upside down, but it is not only their plight that causes his laughter. He also recognizes, from a distant past, the stranger that the brothers have with them. He noticed the nod of both welcome and warning the young man gave him. He just winked back.

Tuwhit is aware that for everyone at the farm, and for two of the Twith in particular, a bigger surprise than anyone could have imagined is about to happen. The two returning Shadow boys don't appear to know. They can have no idea of the effect their return will have on their friends at Twith Mansion. It's hard to remain silent, but owls are accustomed to keeping quiet until the right opportunity to speak. Owls know how to keep secrets.

His usual landing place is the top of the well, a wooden cover to the well protected against the weather with a thick, stiff blue-black roofing felt. As he glides in, he remembers that the cleanup party is preparing the well top for the toad choirs to stand on during the wedding. He swings to land on the grass beside it.

Scayper has been telling the boys during the ride on Tuwhit's back. "I know Taymar from years ago. If it can be arranged quietly, before anyone else hears of my arrival, I'd like to have some private time with him to discuss what's happened to his family."

"Do you want me to wake 'em up?" the owl inquires.

Bimbo whispers his reply, "No, we'll surprise them. We'll just slip up to the entrance, and see if Buffo is alert. Thank you for bringing us home, Tuwhit."

The owl has much to share, but he remains quiet and keeps his thoughts to himself. 'I don't want to spoil the surprises that are ahead for my three passengers. They aren't going to find Buffo there for starters. I would like to see their faces when they find out about the things that have happened since they left a little over two days ago. They have no idea that a king and a princess have emerged and a Twith wedding is being planned.'

However, for the owl, the night is yet young. He tells his passengers, "I'll take a little detour to see how things are developing on the bog. I'll make sure all the goblins keep heading for Squidgy's and not back into Gyminge. I doubt they could with all the lights out, but I'll check it out anyway. I'd really like to stir things up a little more among the floundering goblins. I mustn't delay though. My duty lies in keeping watch from the ash tree at Squidgy's cottage."

He is soon lost in the night sky and the boys are on their own.

As the three travelers climb the slope to the entrance to Twith Mansion, the two brothers expect to find Buffo spread across the log entrance to block all entry while he snoozes away. He isn't there, and neither is his nephew, Bingo, who substitutes for him. Both of the toads were released from duty and are off down on the Brook rehearsing their choirs.

Instead, as they approach the log, there's a warning command that cuts the night air crisply. "Halt! Who goes there?" It's Jordy. His northern brogue is unmistakable.

Bollin, who's nearest to him, answers, "Shhh! It's okay. It's us, Jordy. We're back from Gyminge. There are three of us. Tuwhit picked us up at the waterfall and just dropped us off. We want to surprise Jock. We managed what he wanted, and we have another Twith from

Gyminge to be company for Cydlo and Elisheba. Why are you here on duty? Where's Buffo? Is he sick? Is anything wrong?"

Jordy's answer is whispered surprise and delight. "No, all's well! It's wonderful you're back! Well done! Did you have any trouble with King Haymun? We knew he left about the time you did. So this isn't Vyruss you have with you? Welcome to Gibbins Brook, whoever you are stranger. We're glad to have your company. We need everyone we can get."

Bollin introduces their new friend. "Meet Scayper. We met him in the castle dungeons where he was a prisoner. He wanted some fresh air. He's been a great help, and we know he'll be an even greater help later."

Jordy and Scayper have never previously met although they will discover they have some mutual acquaintances. They hug each other three times in the regular Twith embrace.

"Vyruss is doing okay. He told me that the Wizard and Rasputin are in Gyminge right now. And he told me that all the goblins on the Brook, 750 of them, were on their way to join the Wizard at the castle. Not now they're not. On our way back, we met the goblins as they came across the bog. I don't think they're going very much further tonight. When we left them a few minutes ago, they were lost on the bog without lights and in total chaos. I would have thought you could have heard the noise from here. Most of them headed back to Squidgy's. Tuwhit is keeping an eye on them to make sure they all go in that direction. So there shouldn't be much happening here."

Bimbo holds out the scabbard to the small determined figure standing in half shadow by the log entrance. "Here, Jordy. Feel this. It's the king's sword. And here, feel this. It's the shield! Doesn't that give you goose bumps? These are two more steps along the Rime road. There can't be too many things left to happen now. It just has to be this summer you go back."

"I'd like to come in and listen to what you have to say, but I'm relieving Buffo so he can rehearse his choir. He's determined that his is going to be the best, but Bingo has the best tenors and sopranos. Still, you'll hear all about that soon enough. I hope you are good singers; there's going to be a Shadow choir too. The girls have been waiting for

Dayko's Rime

your return before they practice really seriously. They're adapting your old school song, and it sounds pretty good. Can you sing, Scayper?"

Jordy doesn't wait for an answer. "Boys, you have a lot of catching up to do. Things have been buzzing here on the Brook since you left! Be on your way."

Bollin slips quietly down the passageway and beckons the others to follow. Silently, he eases open the door to Taymar's room. Bimbo stays in the dining room.

Gerald is disturbed from his sleep by the urgent whispered conversation between his roommate and Bollin. Poking his head out from the bedcovers, he makes a suggestion. "Taymar, why don't you go into my office and close the door? That way you can talk in privacy as long as you want."

Taymar guides the stranger to and through the office door. He pulls the door closed. What the Shadow boy overhears in those few brief moments, he keeps to himself.

The Sword and the Shield

Now that Scayper is settled with Taymar in Gerald's office, Bollin tiptoes back to Bimbo. Bimbo motions him to go hide in the passage while he goes to knock softly on the door of the bedroom used by Jock and Jordy. He darts back out of the way to join Bollin hiding where the outdoor coats are hanging.

Jock, barefoot and in pajamas, is soon at the door. His sleepy face is puzzled as he looks around searching for who knocked. He sees no one, so he goes to investigate. In the big room, on the large dining table, he sees the tablecloth is covering something that wasn't there when he went to bed. He's still rubbing the sleep out of his eyes and looks up the passage to see whether Jordy is playing a trick. He sees, not Jordy, but two boys who can hold back no longer. His face breaks into surprised joy as he sees that his two Shadow friends are already back from their secret quest in Gyminge.

Both boys come dancing and singing into and around the room the way Jock has shown them many times in the past. Their backs are straight, fingertips touching above their heads, toes tapping neat little repeated patterns as they mimic Jock's Highland Fling. They make up words as they go to the rhythm of the toads' marching song. They aren't being very quiet.

Jock, seeing their happiness, joins in the dance and in the chorus. All sleepiness is suddenly gone. He tries to keep the sound low. He doesn't want to disturb the Shadow girls and the king sleeping nearby in the guest rooms. No hope! He gathers from the gist of their words that the boys are rejoicing at more than just being back safely. This merely speeds him up in his dancing. As he whirls, his words change to some unintelligible language from the distant Highlands and become even louder.

The girls open their door. The three Shadow girls pulled bathrobes over their nighties. They reckon the lively whoop-de-do in the big room means some more excitement and are enjoying the thought. The girls believe that sleep is only for times when there's nothing more interesting to do.

Bollin and Bimbo, cavorting around the dining table, each seize an end of the tablecloth and fling it off to one side. Other doors open, and Gerald and Cydlo emerge to catch Jock's scream of delight as he goes into a double somersault in a space free from furniture.

Weathered by recent use, streaked and muddy, the Royal Sword, alongside its scabbard, and the king's shield are displayed for all to see!

Cydlo tries to dance with the others but can't manage it. Instead, he leans against the side of the table. Tears fill his eyes and stream down his face. This great strong man they all look up to is crying. He looks as though he can't believe his eyes. He touches the shield and the sword almost reverently.

He last touched the shield the day he lost his kingdom. It slipped from his grasp and fell into the lake when he was wounded. He never expected to see it again. A few moments later on that dramatic day, he threw his sword onto the castle ramparts while still on Crusty's back. Then he dropped into the waiting arms of Jordy and Jock. He reaches out and feels the marks in the shield caused by the goblin's javelin driven at him on Fowler's Bridge. That had almost cost him his life. Slowly, he wraps his huge hand around the hilt of the sword. It's only for a moment, and then he slowly releases it. He bends over for a closer look at the long blade. It's stained and marked.

The girls stop dancing and go to get Cydlo's robe. Ellie wraps it around his shoulders, and Margaret persuades him into a chair brought up to the table. Ruthie has the shoes that Elisheba brought from their cottage, and slips them on his feet.

The others also stop dancing. They all hold hands and gaze at the table top. Rejoicing at the safe return of the boys has turned into awe at what they brought back. Jock and Gerald go get slippers and robes and rejoin the others. What a story of courage and adventure the boys must have to tell. Ruthie puts the kettle on for hot cocoa. Taymar, wearing pajamas and dressing gown, emerges quietly from Gerald's office and begs a bowl of warm water from her before it begins to boil. Without explanation other than a sly grin to the others, he carries it back into Gerald's office and carefully closes the door behind him. Ruthie refills the kettle. The number of cups for cocoa will be increasing, but she doesn't know that.

Barney is the first to be stirred awake upstairs; he sleeps lightly. He renews his energy in small bursts of napping whenever he feels himself getting tired. He can keep going almost twenty-four hours a day by renewing himself in lots of little spurts rather than one long continuous sleep. He wakes Stumpy in the other bed.

"Something's happening downstairs." He bangs on Cymbeline's bedroom door to wake her and Elisheba. Then it's off to find out what's going on and join in.

He stands next to Jock, looking at the table. He has seen the shield and sword before, and he recognizes what they are. He wonders, 'How did they get here? Foolish question! It's clear Bimbo and Bollin have been successful in their secret quest. Pity they didn't need a boy along as well.'

Cydlo looks across at the two Shadow boys. His mouth trembles with emotion. He motions them to come stand before him. He can't speak. He's too full of thoughts, and his eyes still blink away the tears. He puts his hands on each of their shoulders and nods his head a couple of times. 'Yes, these are the right ones', he's saying without words. The sword is what he asked Bimbo to get on the secret quest. The shield is completely unexpected. He clears his throat. "Well done, boys. You did better than I could have dreamed. Thank you, thank you, thank you."

Gerald realizes that Jordy needs to be part of what's happening. He's on guard outside and missing everything. He has a word with Jock, slips inside his room to get dressed, and goes outside to relieve his friend.

Cymbeline and Elisheba are the next to arrive. They too have quickly slipped on their dressing gowns and slippers. They are delighted to see Bimbo and Bollin. Cymbeline naturally goes over to help serve the cocoa. She's just in time to put saucers beneath all the mugs to avoid stains on the table. Ellie takes around a plate of cookies as Cymbeline delivers the cocoa. Jock looks at Bimbo who takes it as an invitation to begin telling what happened since they left on Wednesday evening.

Cymbeline looks around, "Where's Taymar?"

Gerald points to his office.

She carries a mug across and calls out, "Cocoa, Taymar."

"Thank you, Cymbeline," comes the reply from inside the office. "Can you make an extra cup please? I have a friend of yours I'd like you to meet. We'll be out in a little while."

Cymbeline Awaits a Friend

The Twith girls look at each other, puzzled. Cymbeline raises her shoulders and opens her hands in a gesture of surprise. She wonders who Taymar means. Stumpy is just now clumping down the stairs. She knows that Gerald and Jordy are outside talking. No one else is missing. She has no idea who it could be.

Elisheba shares her friend's confusion. 'Clearly my father is as surprised as I am and has no idea who might be with Taymar.' No one offers explanations. No one knows anything that might help explain what's happening on the other side of the office door. Both girls look over at the two Shadow boys. They might know the answer since they are fresh back from an adventure into Gyminge and have obviously been completely successful. However, they too are surprised and their faces show it.

They know who is inside Gerald's office with Taymar, but they didn't know that Scayper is acquainted with Cymbeline. He didn't tell them while they traveled and talked, but come to think of it, more than once Scayper led the conversation around to Stumpy and his family. Indeed, they now remember on one occasion he referred to the old woodcarver by the name of Cleemo. This made the brothers think for a moment or so that, although it was very unlikely, perhaps he had heard of the family in the old days when Gyminge was free. Neither of them could remember mentioning Stumpy's old name to him, but in the end, each supposed the other must have done so.

Stumpy pauses at the foot of the stairs. Wearing his dressing gown, he has plunked on his red woolen hat with the bobble on top. He never goes anyplace without that on his head. Slowly, he looks around the room, taking everything in.

The king sits at the table looking at the weapons from his past. Most of the others are also sitting while Ruthie and Cymbeline are on cocoa duty. Stumpy knows Dayko's Rime, and the significance of what he sees isn't lost on him. He recognizes the worn royal insignia on the shield. He bows his head towards Cydlo. It's hard to think of his king as an equal although Cydlo wishes it so.

Stumpy walks over to the table and looks more closely. He turns towards Bimbo and Bollin. "Thank you for getting these at such risk to yourselves. It was our problem, not yours." There's a lump in his throat and tears in his eyes. He can speak no further. He swallows hard and nods instead. Barney sees his uncle's distress. He brings a chair over next to his, and Stumpy sits down. He can't yet find words. A tear trickles down his cheek, and he just nods his thanks as Cymbeline hands him a cup of cocoa and her handkerchief.

Although Stumpy is the Twith barber, he isn't the one doing the haircutting going on in Gerald's office. It's Taymar wielding the scissors. Scayper sits patiently, talking rapidly. The two talk quietly. There is so much to talk about, so much catching up to do. Scayper's last haircut was at the hands of Bimbo in the dungeon room at Goblin Castle. Although Bimbo did a fairly good job of cutting away the matted hair and beard, the light wasn't good, and the time was short. Scayper is determined that this time, he'll look near his best, no matter how long it takes. He first washed his hair thoroughly with soapsuds. After he rinsed it, he washed and rinsed it again. Then he dried it so hard with the towel that his scalp still tingles.

Scayper has waited a long time for this particular moment. He dreamed of it with less and less hope as months rolled into years, and years into decades, and decades into centuries. Now he's caught up in the thrill of anticipation. He hears voices in the large room, but his ears are tuned for only one of them.

Taymar bolted the door from the office to the passageway. After Gerald left for the outside, he bolted the door into the bedroom too. They don't want the surprise they're preparing to be spoiled by someone coming in before they're ready. Taymar finishes with the haircut, brushes the loose hair aside, and combs Scayper's hair. A few more snips of hair, a review, and then a few more snips complete the job. Taymar leaves Scayper's hair down to his shoulders. They go back into the bedroom where there's a mirror.

Scayper needs to shave because there's a beard and mustache to get rid of. The small amount of water is lukewarm, but Scayper is accustomed to much less. The water grows darker as it fills with his dark brown hair. It's already far darker than the cocoa it was intended for. Eventually, he'll find a bathtub full of hot water, soapsuds, and unlimited time to soak his body back to cleanliness. That will make him a new person entirely. For now, though, he must be content with a birdbath. Scayper strips to the waist, scrubs away, and vigorously towel dries himself.

Taymar works on getting dressed himself and then chooses the wardrobe Scayper will wear. From among the best of his clothes, he chooses a light brown shirt, a red vest, and dark-brown leather pants. Taymar is slightly taller, but they are much the same size. The pants are a little long, but fortunately, the shoes fit. When Scayper is fully dressed, he stands at attention in front of the mirror.

Taymar does a final inspection and isn't quite satisfied. He picks up the scissors. They'll cut through leather too. He kneels down and shortens the pants to Scayper's size. Standing up, he steps back and eyes Scayper carefully. He nods his head in approval.

The transformation is complete. Scayper is hardly recognizable as the shaggy young man who greeted Jordy outside. He looks only a little younger than Taymar and just a couple of inches shorter. He's well-built and muscular. His brown eyes twinkle with anticipation.

The two go back in Gerald's office. Taymar quietly slips back the bolt. He looks across at Scayper who returns his brief smile and nods. He's ready. Scayper stands to one side out of direct line from observers in the large room. Taymar flings open the door, looks around to see who's present, and steps forward into the living room. "Your Majesty, Princess Alicia, ladies and gentlemen, I have the honor to present... My brother, Ambro!"

Unfinished Business

All in the room are totally taken by surprise. Bimbo and Bollin are puzzled by Taymar's addressing someone as the king and Princess Alicia although there's little doubt who he means. The two Shadow boys have grown to love and appreciate Scayper, but he had no other separate identity. The prisoner they met in the dungeon barely resembles this smart and alert young man now smiling at them. They gasp at the transformation in such a short time. The likeness is easy to see although Ambro has broader shoulders and has a stockier build. They have the same high forehead, the same smile, and the same posture. Taymar's blue eyes and Scayper's brown ones twinkle in unison.

Jock and Jordy were aware that Taymar had a younger brother, but never had the chance to meet him.

Gerald thinks, 'I might have seen him once or twice when his family visited the castle, but I have no recollection that we ever met.'

The three Shadow girls know nothing about him at all.

Elisheba tries to remember. 'The two boys from Up-Horton came with their parents to the castle when I was a young girl. It was a very long time ago. Because Taymar was taller, I remember him more than I do Ambro. They certainly look like each other now.

The king remembers the lad well. 'Taymar's brother hid undiscovered at the top of the apple tree while I was reprimanding his older brother and the princess for scrumping green apples from the lower branches.'

Apart from Taymar, there is one entire family present that knows Ambro and knows him well. Centuries ago, they lived on the northern fringe of the Dark Forest. The Earl of Up-Horton's younger son came to their home frequently for woodcarving lessons. Stumpy puts his hand on Barney's leg to restrain the delighted boy from springing up to greet his long lost friend. He whispers, "Time for that later, lad. Not just now. You just wait."

Ambro steps forward to stand, but only for a moment, beside his brother. Almost immediately, there's a flurry of movement.

A cry of "Ambro! Oh, Ambro!" meets and merges with "Cymbeline, my love, my darling." Two figures propel themselves forward into each other's arms. Cymbeline is embraced in the stranger's arms and sobs as though her heart will break. She never cried like this before in all the years of the Twith Exile. But these are tears of pure happiness.

Only Elisheba rises from beside her father and moves across to the couple. These last few days she has come to understand love and recognizes it in others. Ambro looks down so tenderly at the head of the sobbing girl in his arms and lovingly strokes her soft, brown hair. He holds her tight as though he'll never let her escape from him again.

"Go back into Gerald's office." Elisheba whispers to him. "Take all the time you need. There's time to meet the rest of us later."

Taymar and Elisheba shepherd the pair back into Gerald's office and close the door behind them. They hold hands outside the closed office door, the redheaded princess and her ginger topped husband-to-be. Returning to the group Taymar's face shines with joy. He wants the whole world to know that his brother is alive and has to restrain himself from shouting, "Ambro is alive!"

His heart is dancing. He slips his arm around Elisheba's waist and explains to a silent room. "I didn't know whether my brother was alive or dead. Cymbeline always felt that one day they would meet again. When the Wizard of Wozzle attacked us, Ambro was guarding the border. That was where the main attack took place. The Wizard's troops poured in by the hundreds. Tuwhit brought us the news of the attack, but had no news of Ambro. I feared he was dead, and that was devastating because we were always inseparable. My father sent me with an urgent message to King Rufus while he stayed to fight. My mother stayed with him. Tuwhit took me, along with Stumpy, Barney, and Cymbeline, as far as Gyminge Castle. They stayed there when King Rufus ordered me off to Cornwall without delay. I knew nothing of what was happening behind me and had no way to find out.

"As you know, Stumpy and his family escaped with Jock, Jordy, and Gerald on Crusty's back. Later we were reunited, but they had no news of what had happened to Ambro or my parents. Today is a happy day, not only for me but for all of us. Ambro already shared some of his news with me, but he'll share with all of us later. Before he does, he needs to sort out some unfinished business." He grins down at Elisheba's upturned face as he squeezes her hand. "I wonder whether we should just all go back to bed for a while. It seems likely it's going to take him some time."

The Shadow girls groan with disappointment. Ruthie speaks up. "Oh, no! We can't do that! Even if we do go back to bed, we won't be able to sleep. We're all fully awake now. We're in the middle of the story. It's all too exciting. We still have to hear from Bimbo and Bollin. Now that you have the shield and the sword, maybe there needs to be a change of plans. Maybe the wedding will have to be brought forward, or maybe it needs to be put back. I suggest we get everybody up, even Gumpa and gran'ma. This is good news, and we shouldn't keep good news to ourselves. It won't be fair if we hear what happened, and the others don't. We *all* have to celebrate. I know, let's have an early breakfast. If we all help, it won't take long. Please?"

Jock stands up and looks around, a smile flickering on his face. He has a soft spot for Ruthie, ever since her exploits during the rescue of gran'ma. Things are buzzing, and some activity is called for. He nods assent. "Alright, breakfast will be in half an hour sharp. No, make it a bit later than that. There's a lot to do. Make breakfast at four o'clock on the dot. It can be buffet style. We don't have that many chairs. We better have raisins in the porridge today. That's the way Gumpa likes it, and after all, we're celebrating! You better cook plenty."

He looks around with a big grin on his face. "We seem to have mislaid the cook. Ruthie, will you take Cymbeline's place? Barney, you go wake everyone up. Only everyone in the farmhouse. Don't bother Uncle Andy or his family. We'll try to have a rest time this afternoon so that we can catch up with our sleep. Everyone who can find time should go get dressed. I can't see us going back to bed, so tidy your bedrooms too. Jordy, who's on guard besides Gerald? Is there somone who can take his place? Let's all try to keep what just happened as a surprise for the others later when we're all together. We'll meet in the long room upstairs at five to hear from Bimbo, Bollin, and Ambro. After we listen to them, I'll ask Cydlo and Gerald to let us know what the recovery of the sword and the shield means for our plans for the Return."

The room erupts into activity and shouts of "Yippee!" from the Shadow girls. Barney grabs the wakeup bell and dashes upstairs, ringing the bell furiously and yelling at the top of his lungs all the way up the twisting staircase to the upper level. Whoever is asleep in the farmhouse soon won't be.

Bimbo and Bollin head off to get washed and tidy up their own room. It will feel good to get a change of clothes.

Elisheba helps her father back to his room and then goes upstairs to dress.

Jordy helps to set the table.

Stumpy cuts the fresh loaves of bread into thick slices with sides that are perfectly parallel and each of equal thickness. He's pleased with his work. 'If you want bread cut properly, ask a woodcarver.'

In Gerald's office, the business is still unfinished.

Cymbeline Sparkles

Dawn brings a clear, fine day with only a few clouds. Outside The two brothers, Austin and Lucas, each full-size once again, have relieved Gerald on guard duty. They patrol together around the farmhouse, carrying large sticks. They listen to the dawn chorus of the songbirds on the Brook they now enjoy each morning. Lucas expresses the thought they both have. "I wonder why the birds in Washington don't sing like this? Maybe English worms are fatter or these birds have better choir directors."

Crusty perches on the chimney slab. Maggie is there keeping him company and sharing the Brook gossip. They don't expect trouble since Bollin reported that the Wizard and Rasputin are still in Gyminge. Tuwhit reported the steady return through the night of the muddy and discouraged goblins back down the lane to Mole Hall near Squidgy's cottage. Mrs. Squidge is still asleep, and so are the teros on her roof. All is quiet.

The long room inside the farmhouse fills fast. As they arrive after breakfast from the cleanup below, Barney changes gran'ma and Gumpa back to full-size. Stormy, Specs, Jenn and Nick also choose to resume full-size.

It promises to be another hot day, so there's no need for a fire. Gumpa places the larger carved Indian coffee table with several flat cushions on it in front of the fireplace. In front of that table is the smaller similar table with some oddly shaped items covered by a green napkin.

On the larger table are chairs brought up from downstairs. These are for the Twith seniors, Stumpy, Cydlo, Jock, and an extra one for Gerald who is more comfortable in a chair than on a cushion. There are several other tiny chairs set aside on the hearth, but Bimbo and Bollin, now all clean and spruced up, choose to sit on the cushions with the others. So do most of the Real children who have chosen to stay the same size as the Twith, thinking they'll miss less that way. Stormy lifts them onto the table.

Gumpa and gran'ma are well settled in their armchairs and Gumpa's feet are comfortably propped on the back of Lupus. Gran'ma is unusually alert for someone who doesn't really become alive until nine o'clock. Stormy and Specs sit on the sofa with Jenn and Nick for company.

The Real children all try to guess what the hidden items on the smaller table might be. None of them were present earlier when Taymar presented his brother. They don't know about his transformation. However, it isn't only the smart, young Twith stranger who attracts attention. They can see that something akin to a transformation has happened to their own Cymbeline since they last saw her. She sits next to the stranger whose fingers seek and hold her hand. Her eyes sparkle like diamonds caught in searchlights, and she can hardly keep her eyes off of his face. She's absolutely radiant with a new found happiness.

She wears her best yellow dress and shoes to match that Gerald made for her last birthday. Around her neck is a fine gold pendant necklace with a large glowing ruby mounted in its own flowered setting. Taymar recognizes it and smiles in appreciation. It was his mother's desire that it be given to Cymbeline. At last, her gift is seeing the light of day. Barney sits on the other side of Ambro as though wanting to claim part ownership of the new guest.

Sitting together on the cushion near Bimbo and Bollin are Taymar and Elisheba, holding hands and talking quietly to each other. They're delighted to be on the sidelines instead of being the center of attraction. While they wait for proceedings to begin, Gumpa and gran'ma are each wondering what might have caused breakfast to be brought forward to four in the morning. It hasn't bothered Gumpa one bit, but gran'ma isn't hungry at that time of night. They puzzle over why another conference meeting is called less than three days after the last one.

Gumpa is pleased that the two Shadow boys are back and unharmed. He was unsure whether they had enough experience to manage such a dangerous task as they were given. He gladly admits to himself that he was wrong. 'They have managed to return safely without any mishap. I'm fairly sure, from the resemblance, that the stranger is a relative of Taymar's. Somehow Bimbo and Bollin must have met up with him in Gyminge and brought him back. Obviously, Cymbeline seems most pleased about that.'

Gran'ma's mind may run on the same track as her husband's, but she's miles ahead of Gumpa. She's an express train to his freight locomotive. 'Only a superlative candidate will meet my requirements as suitable for Cymbeline. I trust the open face of this young man. I'm sure I'll be able to approve of the match. Like I have any choice in the matter! Even though there has been no mention of an engagement yet, I'm sure I'll be making more wedding arrangements! I disapprove of long engagements. A week is plenty long enough, even too long when the match is right. There's no sense in wasting time dillydallying around.

Her mind whirls with the details. 'Should the weddings be deferred to give more time for preparation of a double wedding? Especially since the chief dressmaker will be one of the brides.' She remembers the line in Dayko's Rime about more than one bride processing to the byre. 'Will it be a double wedding or two weddings in quick succession? How can the procession best be organized? The toads will need to be advised without delay. Their performance will need to encompass two couples, not just one. The composers and songwriters will want time to revise their compositions. There shouldn't be that much more catering involved.'

It's five o'clock and time to start. Stormy pulls back and releases the clapper on gran'ma's dinner bell once. Its stroke dies away. The gathering settles to silence.

Jock stands, bows towards Cydlo, and turns towards his audience. "I trust that those whose sleep was disturbed will forgive me. Hopefully, there will be an afternoon rest time." Gran'ma scowls, 'I can never sleep in the afternoon. If I do, I can't get to sleep at night.' Jock continues, "I've called this meeting at such an early hour because some quite unforeseen events may make changes in our plans necessary. Those present on Wednesday evening can consider this as a continuation of that meeting. However, several among us were not present then. So first

I need to bring Bimbo, Bollin and our new guest up-to-date on what happened on the farm since they left.

"I apologize for not introducing our new, but very welcome guest. It will be more appropriate to do so a little later. Bimbo and Bollin, after you left for Gyminge, the rest of us gathered to study how much of Dayko's Rime remains to be fulfilled." He turns to Gerald. "Perhaps you would like to share what we discovered."

Gerald gets to his feet and looks towards the two boys. "To help us analyze Dayko's Rime, we looked at the treasures Uncle Andy retrieved from Squidgy's cottage. Inside the wooden chest was the belt of the High Seer which belonged to Dayko. There was also a pewter goblet, a small vial of anointing oil, and two empty clay pots that had contained the powder used to extend the lives of Crusty and Tuwhit. Probably most importantly, there was the king's Ring of Accession. It glows with an inner light only when worn by the rightful king of Gyminge. Uncle Andy also retrieved a crowned helmet, a broadsword, and two pieces of body armor once used by King Rufus.

"We were quite surprised and pleased when Bajjer presented the pouch that you found by accident, Bimbo, in the toad tunnel. It's the Royal Dirk. The week was full of surprises, and there were further surprises yet to come. Elisheba produced, from out of nowhere it seemed, a crown. And not just any crown, but the crown belonging to King Rufus. That was what you brought back, Bimbo, when you returned from rescuing gran'ma. You were, I think, following instructions from Cydlo and passed it on to him."

The boy nods agreement.

"Our conversations about Dayko's Rime led on to Cydlo and Elisheba sharing with us the adventures of King Rufus and Princess Alicia in Gyminge after the castle fell under the Wizard's attack. We ran out of time and had to wait to hear the rest of their story because gran'ma sent us all to bed."

The boys turn and grin at gran'ma. They know well she is a stickler for getting children to bed at the same time every night, no-matter-what.

"On Thursday afternoon, there was an even greater surprise. We wondered how Cydlo and Elisheba knew so much about the royal family. Micah asked Cydlo straight out if he was King Rufus. The Ring of Accession proved to us that Cydlo is indeed our king and Elisheba is really Princess Alicia. Not only that! Before the kingdom fell, Princess Alicia was betrothed by the king to the oldest son of the Earl of Up-Horton. And guess what? That's none other than our own Taymar!"

Gerald pauses to allow the boys to absorb such startling news. He's amused to see the looks of shocked surprise on their faces.

Bollin is the one who finds words to express what they feel. "This is exciting news! It's all a bit overwhelming, but really great news all around. I can see that all the pieces are falling into place to fulfill Dayko's Rime and allow the Return to happen."

Gerald is pleased that the boys have grasped the significance of what has happened. He has a bit more to add. "King Rufus asked us to continue to refer to him as Cydlo and the princess as Elisheba. The betrothal declaration called for a celebration. After supper, everyone came dressed in their best party clothes. When it was Cydlo's turn to speak, he asked how soon the wedding could take place.

"Gran'ma wants to be sure it's a proper wedding, and that takes much planning. She said that the earliest date we can consider for the wedding is Friday, July eighth. That's well before August twelfth, the date that's predicted for the Return to Gyminge. Time is tight, but not so tight that we can't find time for a wedding. The wedding will be in Max and Julie's home, which used to be a cow barn. The significance of that is that the Rime says that brides will process to the byre. In Gyminge, a byre is a cow barn! The party was cancelled to give gran'ma as much time as possible to prepare. Since then, she and the girls have been working flat-out.

"Now to our delight, you boys returned with the Royal Sword and the Royal Shield. You also brought a guest with you. Would you like to tell us about your adventures, Bimbo?"

Bimbo's Story

Bimbo clambers to his feet and goes to the front where he can be seen and heard more easily. He isn't accustomed to speaking before a group.

Jock whispers to him, "You will have to speak loudly," and gives him a smile of encouragement. 'These two boys have never let me down!'

"Before Vyruss, Bollin, and I left here on Wednesday evening on our secret quest," the lad begins, "Cydlo told me that the king's great sword was hidden near the castle dungeons in Gyminge. There used to be an escape tunnel from the king's apartments to a quarry on the other side of the lake. That was destroyed when the Wizard enlarged the lake to completely surround the castle. But he thought that it might be possible to swim over to the part of the tunnel that was still inside the castle. If we could do that, then we could find and retrieve the sword. If any toads were still in the lake, they would probably help us find the entrance. But there weren't any toads left in Gyminge. The annual trek of the toads to spawn in Gyminge Lake is over for the year. If we couldn't find the tunnel or get to the sword, we should try to find out whether the shield that the king dropped in the lake had ever been recovered. If it hadn't been found, we could be in trouble for the Return.

"Bollin was going to go only as far as the border, while Dr. Tyfuss would go with me. We had no trouble getting through the waterfall and through the toad tunnel. But before we were able to collect Cydlo's two ponies in the nearby pasture, we heard a loud yell coming from the tunnel and hid."

The boys were unaware that right after they passed through the waterfall, the goblin king was close behind them. King Haymun gave a great cry of pain when he cracked his head on the roof of the cave where it dips down sharply.

"When we saw that it was the goblin king and he was alone, we changed our plans. Instead of having Vyruss go on with me, he went to help Haymun, and Bollin accompanied me on my secret quest. They took one of the ponies and we used the other one. We sent a message to Jock with a returning mother toad to let him know our change of plans."

Many heads nod. It had come just before Elisheba produced the king's crown.

"To avoid being seen by Rasputin, we traveled by night up to and through Blindhouse Wood, arriving at Cydlo's cottage just before dawn. The cottage was just as Elisheba had left it two days previously. We milked Daisy and Belle who were standing patiently in the barn waiting for their regular milking. We planned to rest during the day and go to the castle quarry on foot as soon as it was dark enough to travel safely. This is where things went wrong, seriously wrong."

Eyes widen in surprise. The boys have returned safely. Their former schoolmates, the Shadow girls, lean forward. They don't want to miss a word.

"While we were giving the cows a last milking, both Bollin and I felt the point of a sword sticking into our backs. Five goblins had come from the castle searching for Elisheba. Bollin and I spoke to each other in Urdu and pretended not to understand what they were saying. For some reason, they thought we were Chinese. They tied our hands behind our backs, tied our feet, slung us facedown over their horses, and took us to the castle. It was a really long, uncomfortable journey.

"When the team went to rescue gran'ma and Elisheba, we sunk the pontoon bridge, so they had to take us across to the castle by boat. Our legs were untied and we were blindfolded. Then we were led to the great hall where they removed our blindfolds."

The great hall is where the Wizard displays many of his trophies. The walls are decorated with spears, war axes, swords, shields, and armor.

"We noticed a shield bearing the king's crest above the fireplace. When the goblin king interviewed us, we continued to speak Urdu and everyone there also thought we were Chinese. I don't know why because Urdu doesn't sound anything like Chinese, I'm quite sure. The king was frustrated because we didn't seem to understand anything he said to us. He ordered us to be put in the dungeons overnight.

"In the cell with us was another prisoner. He was the only one in all the dungeons who wasn't in a bottle. He told us his name was Scayper. We had no idea who he might really be. We were determined to escape, and we told Scayper he could come too. First we had to find the secret tunnel off of the dungeon.

"Between the wall of the cell and the old escape tunnel is a link tunnel. The entrance to it is a stone door set flush with the wall. The door swings on bronze hinges set in charcoal powder so there's never the slightest hint of a squeak. Two pressure points — one at hand level and one at foot level — must be pressed simultaneously to open the door.

"Once we got into the link tunnel, Bollin took tools to break the chains securing Scayper to the floor. After we got Scayper into the link tunnel, Bimbo took the queen's crown and used that to lure the guard into the cell. It wasn't hard. There was only one guard, and he wasn't very bright. Bimbo tied his hands together behind him, stuffed a handkerchief into his mouth, and blindfolded him.

"Then it was time to retrieve the sword. King Rufus had hidden it in the stone door that opened into the escape tunnel. Inside the link tunnel, the doors are opened with a handle. We were really excited and pleased that we had actually recovered the Royal Sword."

Big smiles adorn faces all around the room. Especially bright are the Twith smiles.

"Now that we had the Royal Sword, we wanted to retrieve the Royal Shield. Just before dawn yesterday, the three of us climbed up the same staircase where we brought Gumpa down after he was wounded by the spear thrown at him. We had to creep past Rasputin's nest to get beyond the Wizard's apartments. Only the window into King Haymun's bedroom was open. He was fast asleep. We decided to take him with us as a hostage. Bollin went and recovered the Royal Shield from the great hall."

Again, broad smiles break out around the room. King Rufus is impressed with the bravery and ingenuity of these two boys.

"Rasputin attacked us on the castle wall as we made our way back to the courtyard. Bollin squirted him in both eyes with tomato ketchup and dishwashing soap. The raven dived into the lake and swam in circles, leaving behind him a line of green bubbles tinged with red.

"Six o'clock in the morning is the time for the two guards on the gate and the one at the dungeon to be relieved of their duties. Three goblins were rowed across, but only two returned.

"When the new guards came on duty, we captured them and put them in the dungeon where Scayper had been. There were several boats moored at the castle dock. We pushed all but two out into the lake. When we got ashore, we pushed the other two away so there was no way in or out of the castle. We had King Haymun order the sergeant major to bring all the horses from the stable. Then Scayper waved the king's sword over his head, let out a blood-curdling war cry, and ordered the garrison goblins to run for their lives."

Bimbo and Bollin chuckle as they remember the panicked flight of the goblins into Blindhouse Wood. Two of them chose to dive in the lake and swim for the far shore.

"Scayper took the reins of all the horses and released them later in the Dark Forest. On the way, we met a squadron of goblin lancers returning to the castle. We made them turn around and escort us to the castle they just came from. We took their horses too, made them go inside, and drop the portcullis that jammed and locked them inside. We rode on north.

"After Scayper turned all the horses except our own loose, we turned to the west and then south where Blindhouse Wood begins. So far, everything was going very smoothly although not according to any plan we made in advance. This is where things went wrong again."

The children had been just about to relax and breathe easier. Now they're on the edge of their seats again.

"It was about three o'clock yesterday afternoon when we were ambushed by a robber gang. Scayper and I got away, but Bollin and Haymun were captured. Fortunately, they weren't carrying either the sword or the shield. Scayper jumped his horse over the fallen tree that caused us to stop in the first place. I escaped by turning and going the opposite direction. Later, I met up with Scayper and we tried to track the robbers back to their camp. Instead, we came to a tiny little cottage in the woods. Inside were two friendly, elderly women who were very helpful. They gave us some fresh-baked bread and scrumptious soup to eat. We were really hungry!"

There has been absolute silence as Bimbo talked. There is obviously much more that he's left out to keep the story short, but the minds of his listeners, especially those who were recently in Gyminge themselves, are active, filling in details for themselves until they have a chance to ask questions. The story, although Bimbo doesn't realize it, has reached a point where everyone has the same question. All but the three new arrivals recently heard from Elisheba the story of Princess Alicia's adventures in Blindhouse Wood when she escaped from her captors. It's Elisheba who can wait no longer and she blurts out, "Bimbo, what were the names of the two women?"

"One was Pru. She told us it's short for Prudence. The other one was Nettie. They had a dog who was very much like Lupus here. The two dogs could be brother and sister. Loopy was a great help to us."

The long room erupts with clapping and shouting. Lupus barks once or twice to hear his name mentioned and to remind people he's awake and alert. The Little People on the table, with the exception of Cydlo and Stumpy, are on their feet. Cydlo and Stumpy are clapping, and their broad smiles show their excitement.

Bimbo doesn't understand what's caused the excitement, and he looks questioningly at his brother who is similarly puzzled. Gran'ma reaches forward to remove the cushions on the table to provide dancing space for the ring of dancers suddenly on their feet.

Jock does the Highland Fling, and Gumpa joins in by banging on the copper vase with the flat of his hand. Meanwhile, gran'ma grabs the cast iron ladle hanging from the mantel beside her head and bangs the empty coal scuttle with it. Specs pulls out his harmonica and the other full-size children rapidly organize themselves into a percussion band. The tune is "Jack and Jill" but not the words.

Stormy tries to fit words to the tune, but she has a struggle with an awkward rhythm.

> *Brothers two went up the field*
> *To fetch a sword and shield*
> *Haymun fell and lost his crown*
> *And it went a tumbling down.*
> *Pru and Nettie live in the wood*
> *With us they'd be… if they could*
> *Perhaps tomorrow, not today*
> *Bimbo's got much more to say.*

Bimbo is completely caught by surprise by what's happening. Cymbeline and Scayper join Elisheba and Taymar to dance as a foursome in the middle of the table. Three of them are accomplished dancers trained by formal dancing masters in their childhood. Cymbeline, the one not formally trained, is naturally light on her feet and quickly picks up the rhythm. She won't be left behind on this happiest day of her life. They dance an old Twith minuet from the days of castle celebrations and banquets. Cydlo and all the others who are Twith-size circle around them, facing in and clapping to the rhythm. The four in the center are moving back and forth, bowing and curtseying, turning and twirling, dancing lightly on their toes. They move aside to make room for another foursome. These are less experienced, but equally robust if not as graceful. It's Jock and Jordy facing across to Ruthie and Ellie.

Secretly, gran'ma wishes Gumpa liked to dance; she would love to join in. Bimbo and Bollin slip in beside the others. Their lack of the reason for the rejoicing doesn't stop them. Both boys clap and shout and briefly enjoy the spontaneity of complete happiness and joy.

Bollin Completes the Story

The burst of exuberance is over. Things settle down once again. Before Bimbo resumes his story, he wants to know. "What is all the excitement about?"

Elisheba explains, "We're all delighted to hear that both Nettie and Pru have met and become friends and stayed together through all the long years until now. Nettie was my nurse who enabled me to escape, and Pru helped me in my time of greatest need. It surely can't be long before I'm back in Gyminge, and the two women can be my guests in the castle for as long as they like. Perhaps Nettie can have her old rooms back if they haven't been altered by the Wizard."

Bimbo continues. "I want to hand over the storytelling to Bollin, but first, I have to explain about the escape from the robbers. Pru and Nettie knew a good deal about the robbers. They gave us a meat pie garnished with a load of herbs. It would make anyone who ate it fall into a deep sleep. They loaned us Loopy to show us the way. We wouldn't have made it without her. She warned us of a trap set by the robbers around our horses. So instead of riding, we walked to their camp. The stable boy was also a captive and agreed to help us. He fed the dog guarding the prisoner's hut for us, but he must have eaten some of the pie himself because they both went fast asleep. The robber chief who lived in a tree house ate part of the pie we left on his porch and was knocked out. We took horses for ourselves and released the others to prevent pursuit. We gave King Haymun a choice to come with us or return to the castle, and he chose to come with us as far as the border. Now it's up to Bollin to tell you the rest."

Bollin followed Bimbo's story carefully, reliving each moment. He takes his brother's place and shares with the others. "I realized, as I listened to Bimbo, that in a strange way, despite mistakes and misfortunes, there was a clear tendency for things to work out right in the end. It will probably remain a mystery how, even in most haphazard circumstances, our journey to retrieve the sword and the shield moved through to a successful completion. Somehow, I think that it must be because the Twith always tell the truth.

"We arrived at the toad tunnel just after dark a few hours ago. When Bimbo asked me to go ahead and check things out, I had little idea what to expect. King Haymun told us that he sent Vyruss to build a fort near the entrance to the toad tunnel to help control the annual toad migration. The king said the Wizard would come from the Brook on Sunday to inspect it. To my surprise, there were no guards and no signs of men working flat-out to get the buildings completed. I suspected a trap and moved forward on foot cautiously. I saw a light ahead and approached carefully with my dirk drawn. Before I attacked the man lying on the ground, I recognized it was Dr. Tyfuss! Using only a candle, he was studying how woodlice build a colony. We had little time to talk, but enough.

"He told me the Wizard and Rasputin arrived from the Brook an hour or so earlier, two days ahead of schedule. The Wizard banged his head hard in the toad tunnel. Both the Wizard and the raven were already on their way north. They told Vyruss an amazing story about Gyminge being invaded by invisible Chinese who had control of the castle. Vyruss expected 750 goblins from the Brook at any time. He was to feed them, form them into squadrons, and send them on to the castle without delay. That was a warning that we had to move quickly. Once they started coming through the toad tunnel, there would be no way we could get through to the bog until they finished moving through. The Wizard ordered Vyruss to have the last of the goblins block the toad tunnel.

"I hurried back to the others to report. Bimbo and Scayper galloped off towards the toad tunnel to get through before the goblins started in from the other side. I stayed to deal with King Haymun and the horses. I made King Haymun dismount and sent him off to Vyruss. I turned the horses loose. By the time I arrived at the waterfall, the party on the bog was well under way. There were hundreds of goblins floundering in the bog. Bimbo was weightless, flitting around kicking over all the lights and pushing goblins over as he went.

"At the waterfall, Scayper was yelling his head off, waving the sword, and waiting for any goblin to dare get close enough to engage in combat with him. He was quite hungry for a fight, but none of the goblins were. Tuwhit started at the other end of the bog knocking down lights. When he flew down the line of goblins even Bimbo and I had to duck out of his way. The whole goblin army was in chaos and completely disorganized. I hadn't realized weightlessness could be such fun.

"When we left for the farmhouse, the goblins were all in retreat, crawling as fast as they could back to the croc' pond. Tuwhit returned to the bog after he dropped us off to make sure they kept going that way. They aren't going to venture out again in a hurry if they have any choice in the matter. They'll spend today washing their clothes. The Wizard had shrunk the hole in the curtain at the waterfall. It's too small for a Beyonder to get through now, but the toads can still wriggle through and we had no problem. I can't see that the Wizard will close off entry into Gyminge now until he gets all his goblins back there."

There's an outburst of clapping and applause as Bollin sits down. Jock tells the two boys, "Your long journey isn't quite over. There are just a few more steps."

The two boys look puzzled. They see Jock nod his head towards the table, and then they understand what Jock wants them to do. Now is the time to disclose what's under the green napkin. Together they stand, walk past their friends, and jump down onto the smaller table. Each takes one corner of the cloth and folds it back. The Real children are seeing these for the first time, and there is clapping, cheering, and even screaming from the excited girls. Bollin picks up the shield he recovered, and Bimbo lifts the sword and scabbard beside it. They grin at each other, turn to face the larger table, and hop back up onto it. Side by side, they walk towards Cydlo. Each boy lowers his head as a sign of respect. They straighten their arms out before the king.

First, Cydlo takes the shield from Bollin and passes it to Jock. Then he takes only the scabbard from Bimbo and sets it down. Finally, he reaches for the sword. The clapping erupts again. The boys start to turn to go sit by their friends on the cushions, but Cydlo raises his free hand to stop them. He smiles softy to ease their fears as he asks, "Will you both kneel?"

Silence that can be cut with a knife replaces the sound of rejoicing. This is a continuing night of surprises.

Confused, the two boys look at each other and slowly sink to their knees.

Cydlo stands up, quietly reassumes his role as King Rufus. The sword he holds is a battle worn, muddy weapon still bearing the marks of the last battle. He holds it straight out in front him and lightly touches first Bollin's left shoulder and then his right with the flat of the blade. Then he does the same to Bimbo. "I establish today a new order of chivalry and bravery of the Royal Court of Gyminge, the Order of the Rime and the Return. I appoint you, Sir Bollin, and you, Sir Bimbo, to be the first knights of the new order. I, the monarch of Gyminge, representing not only myself but all our people, both captive and free, do honor and salute you for your services to our land and to our people."

Bimbo looks awkwardly at Bollin. They didn't do what they did for any kind of recognition. They did it because the Twith are their friends. No matter. The room is filled with noises of joy and approval.

Stumpy calls out, "Long Live the King! Long Live Sir Bollin! Long Live Sir Bimbo!" Others just shout, "Hooray! Hooray!"

It's been quite a day or, rather, quite a day and a night for the boys. Just a little over twenty-four hours ago, they were captives in the dungeon at Goblin Castle. Still ahead of them at that time were undreamed of adventures. Those seemed to fall into place as though future and past and present have no distinct difference. It was all orchestrated into complete harmony.

The two brothers stand and walk back to their places. Before they sit down, they look at each other, grin broadly, and give each other a big hug. It's good to have a brother. Taymar and Ambro feel the same way.

Ambro's Turn

Jock is on his feet again. He waves a greeting to Austin and Lucas who pause in their patrol to look in through the window. Maggie has fluttered down onto a low branch of the sycamore behind them. He thinks, 'Danger from the Wizard is low since he's busy in Gyminge chasing invisible Chinese. I'll take a chance and let the boys join us.'

To Barney, he says, "Will you go check that Crusty is around? If he is, have Maggie ask him to guard the farmhouse so Austin and Lucas can join us inside. Stormy, you go with him to call the boys in."

This pleases Stormy. 'What's happening is too important for them to miss. She picks up Barney and is off out through the front door in a flash. Looking up, she verifies that Crusty is perched on the chimney slab. She gives him a wave.

Carrying Barney over to the sycamore, he asks the magpie, "Will you give Crusty a message for us? Jock wants him to guard the farmhouse so Austin and Lucas can come inside. Thanks, Maggie."

The magpie takes off for the chimney slab.

Stormy calls out, "Come on, you guys. You need to hear what's going on inside." They hurry in and are back before Jock has made more than just a few short remarks. She directs the two boys onto the settee and settles back for the next episode of the morning. 'I'm loving every moment of this summer vacation!' During pauses, she fills the two boys in on what's happened in their absence.

Jock decides that it will be a shame to disturb Elisheba and Taymar who seem so comfortable warming each others hands. He'll allow Ambro to introduce himself. He merely remarks, "We have an important guest with us today. Although you may have already guessed from the boys' story that he's Scayper, he's a stranger to most of us." He turns to Scayper. "We would all like to know more about you." Jock's eyes twinkle. "Will you please start from the beginning? It seems that you have met one or two of us previously. We would like to know about that too…if you can remember." He chuckles delightedly.

Ambro goes to the front, bows to the king, then to Jock, and to Gerald. He then turns to his audience and bows to them also. It isn't only Cymbeline who thinks the young man is handsome and gracious. His voice is well modulated, and he is clearly less nervous than the two boys who preceded him. He knows he's speaking to friends, even though most of them are new ones. The warmth reaching out and enfolding him is something he hasn't experienced since he left home to go guard the border those many centuries ago. That's where he starts his story.

"Perhaps I may start by telling you that I am Taymar's younger brother, Ambro."

There are great gasps of surprise from the Real children, but they remain quiet.

"Scayper was a nickname that I received later for my attempts to escape. There were just us two boys in our family. We've always been best friends. Our father was, perhaps still is, Earl Gareth of Up-Horton which is north of the Dark Forest. Sadly, I have no more news of our parents than Taymar has.

"Before the Wizard had his forces attack us, something wonderful had just occurred that I had not even shared with my brother. It had never happened to me before, and I was trying to make sense of what was going on inside of me. I had fallen in love with the niece of my woodcarving teacher, Cleemo. I understand you know him as Stumpy. Cleemo was an excellent instructor and taught me the skills required to carve wood. His specialty was, and I understand still is, birds. However, even while he taught me, my eyes were less on what he was showing me than on the beautiful young woman who lived in his home."

He glances over at Cymbeline, and every eye in the room switches away from his face to look at the smiling Cymbeline. It's only a brief look; they're determined to not miss anything.

"She took care of her uncle and her brother, Barney. Many days, I returned to my home after a lesson and didn't remember a single word of what Cleemo had taught me. Echoing around my head instead were the few precious words Cymbeline and I had exchanged. All my thoughts, waking and sleeping, were of her.

"Occasionally, we had a brief opportunity to walk in the woods together. It was on our very last walk together that I finally told her that I loved her; that I could not live without her. I said I would ask my father at the first opportunity for permission to marry her. Cymbeline also said that she loved me, but she was sure that my family had already chosen someone of high estate to be my wife. That was indeed possible, even likely, but my father had not made any such choice known to me. He loved both of his sons deeply, and I felt sure that when he saw my happiness, he would consent to our union.

"Sadly, I never had an opportunity to ask him. However, before I parted from my family for the last time, I told my mother of my intention to speak to my father. I believe that she understood and approved of my choice. Shortly after that, unknown to me, she gave Taymar the necklace for Cymbeline that she is wearing now.

"When the Wizard of Wozzle threatened the country, our father was appointed to defend Gyminge between the border and the Dark Forest. There Count Fyrdwald would take over the defense. My father was called to meet with the king and Count Fyrdwald. When he returned, he told us boys that he wished to meet with each of us separately after the evening meal, first Taymar and then me. That was the last time I ever saw him. I went to check on my patrols west of our estate on Tuwhit rather than by horse since there was little time.

"Even that little time wasn't enough. Shortly after I arrived, we heard a cuckoo's call. That was apparently the signal for the attack to begin. Right as we heard it, the Wizard's main attack was in my section with no warning. Our patrols fell back and continued to fall back. We were completely overwhelmed by the strength of the force against us. We had no hope of more than a brief holding action. I sent Tuwhit with a warning to my father. That was the last I saw of Tuwhit until a few hours ago when he met us at the waterfall. What a wonderful surprise that was! I had thought he was lost forever among my memories. I could never have dreamed he might still be alive.

"The main goblin force was pushing down the west bank of the river. However, the Wizard had surrounded us with a new weapon that he developed. It prevented us from engaging with his men. It was invisible, very much like the curtain that separated Wozzle from Gyminge before the invasion. This was much smaller, and was closed over at the top like a bubble. Tuwhit had escaped just in time. We couldn't fire any arrows through it. They rebounded back at us. The whole of our defense north of the Dark Forest and adjacent to the border was trapped and helpless. We searched for ways to escape, but the bubble went deep into the ground, and we couldn't dig beneath it. We also tried to cut the curtain. It was impossible then, and it's impossible now. We tried fire, but it had no effect.

"Finally, dawn came. The goblin troops were moving freely all around us while we stayed trapped. They laughed at us. We were their captives to be dealt with when it was convenient. We recognized we might starve, and we rationed both our food and water. Night and day, night and day came and went. We were now eating leaves and roots. It rained, but no moisture came into the bubble. We had no news of what was going on in the rest of the country. One thing alone was certain. We had lost the fight against the Wizard of Wozzle.

"The soaring birds escaped before they became caged. But the once free men became captive with no end to the sentence they should serve."

The Rope of Hope

Ambro is now at a point of total change in his story.

"As days passed and we remained trapped, we could only believe that the Wizard had taken control of Gyminge. The best that was likely for us was that we would be captives for the rest of our lives. We had seen what happened to our neighbors in Wozzle. Now, it had happened to us. Our world that had seemed so strong and secure had collapsed and was gone, never to return. We were in despair. I had no idea what might have happened to my father and mother, or to my brother, or to Cymbeline and her family. I, who had been so full of dreams for the future, suddenly had no future. There was nothing to live for. For the first time in my life, I understood what it might mean to have no hope."

Ambro pauses. 'I need somehow to find words to share what kept me going through my years of captivity. If my listeners don't understand that, then they won't understand what is happening now, or why it happened.' Cymbeline smiles encouragement to him while fingering her necklace. Taymar is nodding him on. The rest all lean forward, keen to not miss a single word. The boy has stirred up memories of almost-forgotten times of struggle and eventual victories among his Twith listeners.

The lad continues. "It was while I was still under the bubble and before I was taken to the dungeons that a deep truth surfaced. I realized that if I should ever lose hope of freedom, I might as well be dead, even though I remained alive. I determined then and there that I would never allow myself to lose hope. Come-what-may, I would somehow hold on to happy thoughts. Whatever might happen to me under the Wizard's malicious hand, I would fill my mind with pictures of sunrises and sunsets, sunbeams in woods through summer haze, full moons rising, snow on trees, sunlight on water, and dragonflies over calm pools.

"I would make myself hear birds singing, children playing, laughter and music even when I might only hear goblin guards and chains clanking. I would not stop believing that somehow — I didn't know how, but somehow — things would get better and better. I would laugh at myself and the trouble I was in, but I would never despair.

"I would believe, even though there were no grounds for such belief, that I would one day be free. That one day, I would meet once again my mother and father. That Taymar and I would once again wrestle and spar and slide on ice. That I would once more go to Cleemo's for lessons and see Cymbeline. That my father would give his agreement to our marriage, and that one day, we would be husband and wife. I would hold on to my memories and even fashion new ones that never happened, but which I wanted to happen if they would enable me to hold on through the darkness. I would not give up hoping.

"Hope would be my rope to survival though all else failed. At least in my mind, if not with my body, I would continue to swim in cool water, climb trees, swing on ropes, gallop along the ridge, run in the valleys, walk through the rainstorms, and sing through the silences. Even in isolation, I would talk with my friends, sing in a choir, soar on Tuwhit, and feel the wind blowing off the sea in my hair. I would enjoy fragrances — even the familiar off-smell of stables and byres.

"Even if I were bound and shackled, I would not allow myself to be imprisoned. My mind would release me to the skies outside. My legs and arms would be free to run, lift, balance, climb hills, and straddle trees even if I couldn't move a muscle. I would make speeches, write books, think large thoughts, talk with poets and prophets, and challenge tyrannies though far from them. I wouldn't be silenced by misery. My mind would remain my own, and I'd keep it that way.

"We were taken in groups from the bubble. The goblins took their time. They were in no hurry. Others from among us were given a choice. Join the Wizard's goblin army or... one could only imagine the consequences of refusal. No choice was offered to me. I had been bottled once before when the Wizard captured me. He disguised himself as a pony and took me into Wozzle. The bottling was done in front of an army parade so the Wizard's men remembered me well. I was quickly sorted out as a special captive and taken straight to the castle.

"The Wizard himself questioned me. He felt I was responsible for burns he received when Taymar helped me escape from Wozzle. He wanted to know where the other members of my family were. Since I didn't know and had no idea, I told him so. He said I lied. I told him I didn't lie nor could he make me. He said he could use people like me and invited me to join his side. I refused.

"Once again, I was bottled. Many others, who refused to be goblins, were also bottled. Fortunately, these bottles were round, not flat like the ones in Wozzle. They were also a little bigger, so there was more room to wriggle around. I was put into the main dungeon with all the other bottles. All the bottles were laid out on shelves.

"While I was inside the bottle, I didn't get hungry. I don't know how long I was there. It was as though I woke up one day out of a deep sleep. I could have been asleep for years, even hundreds of years, but suddenly, my mind was absolutely clear and alert. I knew that there was a way opening up ahead for me to escape. I was completely sure about it. Time seemed to stop, but I never despaired. I had to be careful that my mind didn't go back to sleep, so I did my best to remain alert. I looked for opportunities and waited for them to happen.

"One day, the goblin who had been given the job of cleaning up the dungeons as punishment, moved me. I became the end bottle on a lowest shelf lined with bottles. That was my opportunity. I found that by shifting my body weight slightly, the bottle moved, but just a tiny bit. Slowly, I rocked the bottle sideways and then worked my way back in tiny movements so that the bottle didn't return. And then I rocked it again. It took many months, but eventually, I got it to the edge of the shelf. A few more rocks and it fell. There was a tremendous crash. Glass went flying everywhere. Unfortunately, I was knocked unconscious by the fall, and the guards recovered me. They couldn't understand what happened and thought it was an accident or maybe an earthquake tremor. I pretended to be unconscious even after I came to. They put me in another bottle and replaced me on the shelf — in the same place.

"I was determined to escape. I might have made it the first time. I would go on trying. I filled my mind with thoughts of outside. Once more, I rocked the bottle. Again, it took many months before the bottle fell. This time I hid after the bottle smashed, but the dungeon door to the courtyard was closed until the search by many goblins found me. The Wizard ordered that I be shackled to the floor in the most secure dungeon room. I wasn't allowed out except for one hour of exercise a day until he decided what to do with me. He never bothered to decide.

"This was my situation when, just a day or so ago and for the very first time, two more dangerous prisoners were put in my cell overnight. My time for escape had come. They told me their names were Bimbo and Bollin, and they had their own plan for escape. They said I could go with them if I wanted. I did, and… here I am!

"To my amazement while we were still in the dungeon, I heard the boys mention the name *Cymbeline*. The thoughts that flooded through me were overwhelming. I fainted. The boys didn't understand what happened, but from that moment on, I knew that one day I would be reunited with the girl of my dreams. Those dreams had been part of the rope I held on to through the years of captivity. This time though, the dreams would become reality. This morning, at long last, they have done so."

Gran'ma's Plans Enlarge

There's complete silence from all those listening. None of those present except Ambro himself knew the whole of the young man's story. They have each been caught by surprise and awe at the young man's long courage.

As Ambro talked of his continuing hope through the long dungeon years, they too were caught up by a strange sense of certainties. It's as though the future isn't a collection of random events waiting to be knitted into a haphazard sequence by the passage of time. Instead, the future is already a linked chain of events and consequences that merely await revealing. Dayko's Rime, penned centuries ago, is the key to that revealing for the Twith.

Ambro walks across to Cymbeline and holds out his hand to her. She takes hold of it, and he lifts her to her feet. Her cheeks are moist with the silent tears that rolled down her face as Ambro was talking. Many of the girls wipe tears from their cheeks. Hand in hand, the young lovers walk back to where Ambro was standing alone.

Ambro releases her hand and directs Cymbeline where to stand. He faces her, takes a step or two back, and kneels before her. Looking up at her lovely face, he speaks as firmly as his emotions will allow. "Cymbeline, I have loved you long, and I have loved no other but you. I have loved you since we first met. I have no greater desire than to become and to be your faithful husband. I want to protect you and provide for you in the days to come. Please, please, tell me that you will accept my proposal of marriage and will marry me."

All eyes are on Cymbeline. She, whose life has been spent unobtrusively serving her uncle, her brother, and the four men in Twith Mansion, is the center of attention. Now, she must answer the most important question of her life in front of everyone. Silently, all present are willing her on, but the answer is her own.

"Oh yes, Ambro, I do, I do indeed! I will marry you."

Without any words being spoken, Taymar helps Elisheba to her feet. They go stand by the newly engaged couple. Taymar is behind his brother, and Elisheba moves to stand behind the girl she loves as a dear sister and closest friend.

Ambro rises to his feet, his face wreathed in smiles. He raises Cymbeline's hand to his lips and kisses it. He thinks, 'I better wait to kiss her properly after we are alone.' However, the applause ringing throughout the room reminds him that the time for this is now. Barney and Stumpy dance a kind of three-legged jig in their own space. Since the two principals aren't available for hugging, all kinds of strange pairings celebrate by hugging each other. Once more, Gumpa and gran'ma are banging on the vase and the coal scuttle to make noise.

Cydlo goes forward, leaning his hand on Jock's shoulder for support. The clatter quiets and then is still as all but the two couples return to their places. Cymbeline and Ambro hold hands. Taymar and Elisheba stand to each side of them.

The king smiles with pleasure. "I have a feeling that what we have just witnessed is a betrothal although one without an exchange of rings. However, we need to affirm it. It's the custom in our country that a betrothal is arranged, witnessed, and confirmed by the parents of the two who are to marry. Is there anyone who speaks on behalf of Cymbeline?"

Barney prods Stumpy who pulls off his red hat as he struggles awkwardly to stand. There's a lump in the old man's throat that makes it hard for him to speak. "Sire, I do. I'm not Cymbeline's father, but I am her uncle. Her parents died in the plague, and since that time, I have considered myself as guardian for the maiden and for her brother. She is more than a niece. She has been a true daughter to me, and I love her dearly."

"Do you affirm this betrothal as in the girl's best interests for her future happiness?"

"Yes, Sire, I do."

"Please be seated." The king turns to Ambro. "You have told us that, due to no fault of your own, you have been unable to obtain your father's consent although you assume the consent of your mother. If your parents were assuredly dead, then your next of kin is Taymar, and we could obtain his view of your betrothal. However, we certainly hope that your parents will yet be found alive. What do we do then about a consent to your betrothal?"

Gerald raises his hand for permission to speak. The king nods for him to speak.

"Sire, we have a provision for that in the Lore. Our seers and elders foresaw an occasion where the parents or even one parent of a couple wishing to become betrothed might withhold consent. Since all parties are required to seek the happiness of the betrothed couple, the Lore states that the matter may be referred to the king for a decision. His decision will seek the long-term happiness of both man and woman and will be final."

The king is well aware of this provision although few of those present are. "I recall what you say, Gerald. You are correct, and I have exercised this power in times past. I will first of all ask those assembled here whether there is anyone present who knows of any reason why the betrothal of Ambro, son of Earl Gareth of Up-Horton and Cymbeline, ward of Cleemo the woodcarver, shall not proceed?"

Silence.

"I will now seek counsel of those present. Should the betrothal of Ambro, son of Earl Gareth of Up-Horton and Cymbeline, ward of Cleemo the woodcarver, indeed proceed?"

Gumpa's deep voice drowns out the quieter chorus of "Yes!", "Yes!" He looks Cydlo straight in the eye. "Of course it should proceed. And without delay." Wild cheering and loud clapping erupts around the room. Everyone is in agreement.

The king raises his free hand. He is enjoying himself. "This is the ruling of the Royal Court of Gyminge sitting at Gibbins Brook. The betrothal of Ambro, son of Earl Gareth of Up-Horton and Cymbeline, ward of Cleemo the woodcarver, shall indeed be confirmed. Further, we affirm that the marriage of the couple shall take place concurrently with the wedding already planned between Ambro's brother Taymar and Princess Alicia. That is, provided that gran'ma confirms the new arrangements will cause no delay in the date already set." Cydlo bows politely towards gran'ma.

Gran'ma is busy working things out. She can efficiently modify plans and adjust schedules to fit. "Yes, Cydlo, we can do it. Girls, everyone except Elisheba and Cymbeline, meet with me in my bedroom upstairs as soon as the meeting is over."

Gerald Sums Up

Jock can see that gran'ma is anxious to be moving. She set the coal scuttle down and hung the ladle back on its hook on the mantel. Her hands rest on the arms of her chair ready to rise. However, there's one last matter for them to look at.

He makes a request. "Everyone please be seated for a few minutes more. In the light of what just happened, is there any change in our understanding of Dayko's Rime?" He looks towards Gerald.

The Keeper of the Lore looks questioningly towards Cydlo, but the king nods for him to proceed. "Two things have become clear this morning, and they move us rapidly along on our list of requirements for our Return. By no means are all our mysteries yet clear, but the surprise arrival of three valiant travelers from Gyminge and what they brought with them have given us added hope. The return of the shield and the sword gloriously answers two of the events in Dayko's Rime."

9. *From the water the shield will come,*
10. *The sword will come forth from the stone,*

"There's also another line of the Rime that is now clarified."

30. *Brides shall process to the byre.*

"We now know that indeed, two brides will process to the byre. They will process together, and they will both be Twith girls. Our first assumption that gran'ma was one of the brides was not the picture that Dayko saw. Most of the verses of the Rime will be fully completed by the time of the weddings on July eighth. One of the lines that still puzzles us is the last line of verse five."

20. *The Child shall lead on to the Prize.*

"We haven't determined who the child is that will lead on to the prize. The only other lines we haven't resolved are the last two lines of verse eight.

31. *The loss of the Lore gives grief,*
32. *Though what is that to a life?*

"Otherwise, it seems Dayko's Rime is very close to being fulfilled. We just have to wait until those events happen.

"It seems likely that the Wizard will want to close all entrances into Gyminge. By the week after the weddings, we need to be clear how we're going to get back and prepare to move without delay. There may not be quite enough time remaining to gain entry to the country and regain all of Gyminge before the two moons allowed in the Rime are past.

"While we make our preparations for the weddings, we also need to arrange our farewell from the Brook. For many years, our friends here have provided us shelter and friendship. Without their help, we couldn't have survived. We'll want to show them how grateful we are for their constant help. That celebration and farewell probably needs to be just after the weddings. It would be even better if we could have the celebration either before or as a part of the wedding celebrations themselves."

Jock adds a comment. "It needs to be a worthy celebration — a kind of Farewell Festival. That could take some time to put together, Gerald. We just had a group study on the line in Dayko's Rime about the salt wind. Maybe four or five of that group could do the same for a way to say farewell to our friends on the Brook. If it seems that an athletic competition of some kind should be held, you need to consider when, where, and how it should be done, and who and what should be included. Perhaps it should include other things besides running. Maybe a tug of war between the toads and the rabbits or the rabbits and the badgers. How about a football match? What about including the birds? Is anyone interested in this idea? Maybe the skits you've all been working on could be part of a farewell revue."

A lot of hands shoot up. "I'd like to work on that! Organizing a competition to include birds and rabbits and badgers and toads as well as people sounds fun!"

Jock continues. "Stormy, I'll let you lead a small group to brainstorm ideas." He looks around at all the excited faces. "Barney... Ruthie... Nick, will you join Stormy to start with? And we should include Tuwhit. Maybe you would like to choose one or two others, Stormy. Any of you who have any ideas about what can or should be done, can share them with one of us. Suppose you report to us in a couple of days — say Tuesday afternoon. Would that give you enough time, Stormy?"

"Yes, I'm sure that would be enough to start with, Jock. Perhaps we could use the barn if part of our program is indoors."

Jock nods. "Let's leave it like that for now. Maybe you would like to continue, Gerald."

"Does anyone have any final comments to share before we close our discussions and allow gran'ma to get to work planning a second wedding?"

Specs is the first to respond to Gerald's question with many of his own. He likes to think things through carefully and analyze things thoroughly. "We learned one very important thing from Bollin this morning. Dr. Tyfuss told him that the Wizard plans to block the toad tunnel into Gyminge. The Wizard must know that the toads will be very unhappy about that. Should we perhaps warn the toads to place a watch on the far end of their toad tunnel and be prepared to stop the Wizard's men from blocking the tunnel? After all, toads are bigger than the goblins, much bigger. However, I wonder whether even the toads can stop the Wizard's magic if that's what he uses. In any case, he can't close it until his goblin army is back in Gyminge. He'll want them there to defend the castle. Equally, it's in our interest to keep them here when we go fight for the castle. There seem to be few fighting goblins left in Gyminge at present.

"How does he plan to block it? Do we know or have any ideas? It could be with a curtain, but perhaps a curtain doesn't work in that one spot. It could be with a great door or a wall or even with a torrent of water or a huge fire. Do we understand why he's doing it? Do we want him to do that while we have no other way to get in except through the toad tunnel? Does he already know our plans and see your Return coming? Is he abandoning attempts to get the Book of Lore?

"He already blocked the bird opening in the curtain. Is he pulling back into Gyminge and closing all ways in? Is that the real reason all his goblins were going back? Were the Chinese invaders just a face-saving excuse for him? Last evening the goblins were turned back to Squidgy's against the Wizard's own plans. What is he going to do now? Will he try it again or find some other way? He won't take it lying down. You can be certain of that.

"We don't have all the answers to Dayko's Rime yet. There are still unanswered questions. There's little doubt that by ourselves our chances of success against the Wizard are not good. Only the strong feeling that things are moving together to bring about the end we seek reassures us. I would like to work with Gerald and perhaps one or two others to look carefully at each single line of the Rime again to see if perhaps there's some hidden meaning we haven't yet discovered. It may mean the difference between success and failure."

Gumpa nods assent. "Specs is right. Things have gone well for us recently. We're lulled into a sense that the trend will continue. It may not. Then where are we? The warning is clear about what our first priority must be. If we can't find a way in to Gyminge because all paths are blocked, the Return can't take place. It's in the toad's own interest as well as ours to keep the toad tunnel open. We don't know what means the Wizard plans to use to close it, but we need to warn the toads. If they need help, we'll have to help them."

Jock sees gran'ma fidgeting. She's been shifting uncomfortably in her chair for some time. She's anxious to get back to planning what is now a double wedding.

"It's time to break up. I'll talk to Buffo about the toad tunnel as soon as I'm able. I'll have to try and persuade the old toad away from directing his choir long enough to talk though. We'll stop for now."

Gran'ma springs from her chair and heads for the stairs. The nine girls aren't far behind. Rachael, Jenn, and Titch take the three Shadow girls with them.

The Wizard at the Castle

When the Wizard and Rasputin left Colonel Tyfuss at the border, they wasted no time as they headed north. Even so, the cormorant and the raven arrive at the castle after dark. There, they find complete silence. The Wizard is confused. "Have the troops already surrendered to the Chinese? There's no smell of Chinese food in the air, no sound of tinkling temple bells or gongs. I don't see firecrackers going off or long crooked lines of dancing soldiers shaking tambourines or wearing huge dragon heads. What exactly is going on... or isn't going on?"

The Wizard thinks that the troops from the construction site at the border, and the 750 men from the Brook are even now battling their way towards the castle. What he doesn't know is that the Southern Zone construction crews, sent off by Colonel Tyfuss as ordered, are waiting for dawn before they battle their way through Blindhouse Wood fighting off an invisible Chinese enemy. A little thought would have told them they would be better off going against invisible enemies in the dark rather than the daylight. That way, both sides would be invisible, and the odds would be more even, but they don't have any officers with them who can tell them so. The officers are still on the Brook, together with all of their men.

The two birds wait for daylight to help them understand what's going on, and where, if anywhere, the fighting is most intense. It's frequently wise in wartime to wait until the reinforcements arrive. The Wizard floats silently on the lake water until dawn, nursing an awful headache and trying to get some rest. The raven sleeps in a tree near the guardhouse, occasionally flying to the edge of Blindhouse Wood to check in vain for any signs of the arrival of the goblin troops.

The first faint rays of daylight come and the troops do not. The cormorant, leading the raven, flies over the lake circling the castle. The Wizard tries to absorb what he sees. He can see the trestle for the double-drawbridge that Corporal Pimples is constructing. "There have been changes since I was here last. I need to understand more about what happened and what's being planned."

For hundreds of years, this has been his home. Most of the changes he caused to take place. It was he who turned the castle site into an island. He set up the pontoon bridge and the guardhouse on the shore. He doubled the size of the castle and put the wall between the courtyard to keep the northern section private and secure for himself and the goblin king. The alterations and extensions were all done by his command.

"I see signs of fires inside the castle. There's no activity in the great courtyard. Why are there no troops on guard? Where are the Chinese? Ominously, the flagpole is bare of any flag. Where is King Haymun? Rasputin's nest beside the chimney is missing. There's no pontoon bridge in position. I can see it's still there, but it's under water at the bottom of the lake. How did that happen? Did the Chinese sink it in their attack? I wonder if it's salvageable."

He dives to take a closer look. That isn't easy for a cormorant. "I can see that the task will be difficult, but given time, it's not impossible. A curtain bubble, perhaps even a pair of bubbles, under each pontoon slowly filling with air will lift it up."

Now that daylight has fully come, there's plenty of activity, and it's all on the land side of the lake south of the castle. There's a drawbridge under construction and the Wizard wonders, 'Are the Chinese building a new bridge?' But the shouts of command chasing away the silence are goblin commands, not Chinese. The cormorant comes in to land, its webbed feet catching and spreading water to each side in cascading rainbows. In other, happier times, the Wizard might have been a barefoot water skier towed behind a speedboat with his two heels sending up a great fan of spray either side of him on some calm, glistening lake surface. The Wizard reminds himself, "I should do that again someday, though today isn't the right time."

He taxis to the shore, paddling steadily, and steps onto the narrow beach. In only a moment, he's transformed from a cormorant back into the Wizard. He's bareheaded and thinks, 'I need to get a hat before I get sunstroke.' He immediately tells Rasputin, "Go fetch my tall hat from my closet."

The two castle gate guards suddenly realize this morning is going to be different than yesterday. "Where on earth did the Wizard come from?" They stand stiffly at attention.

The raven returns with the hat and the Wizard steps into the small boat tied to the shore. The Chinese had sunk all the boats, but the countryside has been scoured to find one small rowboat.

As he's spotted, trumpets and bugles sound. The bugler, who was dismissed back to Gyminge castle on permanent posting after he sounded the *Retreat* during the attack on the farmhouse, makes a quick selection from the tunes he knows. They are only three. *Three Blind Mice* is unlikely to go down well with the Wizard even though the novice musician recently introduced some whirling, twiddly bits that lighten it up a bit.

The Retreat seems unwise in view of the recent past. That leaves him with *Reveille* — the most hated of all bugle calls. The get-up-early-in-the-morning bugle call wakens soldiers from one end of the world to the other. From their camps in the woods, the tents, and the temporary barracks, men pull on their clothes, rub the sleep out of their eyes, and come running.

The sergeant major is the first to report to the Wizard. He wasn't expecting the Commander-in-Chief back so soon. Sam calls everyone on parade with huge volumes of sound. His tonsils vibrate like bell clappers; they have rarely worked so hard. In addition to the soldiers roused by the bugler, soldiers pour forth from the guardhouse, the mess hall, and the stable to report to the parade ground. Since the loss of the goblin king yesterday morning to the Chinese attackers on horseback, Sam resumed command of the castle. He released the quartermaster sergeant from the dungeon and rehearsed with Quartz the heroic story they will give when they hand over their duties to a superior officer. All the troops present have been told the same story of what happened so that there will be no confusion and no suspicion they might be lying.

Sam has one concern. 'Rasputin may be a problem. The bird will know, and will have told his boss, exactly what happened up until this time yesterday morning. Hopefully, the raven knows nothing of what happened afterwards. That gives some allowance that should prove helpful.'

Sam notices a large bump on the back of the Wizard's head and calls for a chair and a glass of water. While they wait, he salutes smartly. "Presenting myself and the castle garrison ready for inspection. Sir!"

Wearily, the Wizard settles his thin frame on the welcome chair. He lifts a bony finger up to feel his bump. "Ouch!" It's still very tender. He asks, "Where are the Chinese at present?"

The sergeant major reports proudly, "They have been evicted from the castle after fierce hand-to-hand fighting. They fled north into the Dark Forest taking the king with them as a hostage. Other Chinese seized and galloped off with the cavalry horses, but they didn't get anything valuable from the castle. The treasures are all intact. The north apartments were stoutly defended. There aren't sufficient words to describe the courage of the goblin guards who were outnumbered and caught by surprise in the night attack. They had no means to pursue the Chinese invaders, but the garrison of the castle in the Dark Forest has a squadron of cavalry. It can be presumed they are heavily engaged with the enemy. We have had no news from that battle site, although we expect a messenger at any time."

The Wizard moves his hat around trying to find a position on his head that doesn't cause pain. He takes it off and rests it in his lap while he tries to think. The sun is warm on his head. Surprisingly for him, he finds it difficult to think. 'I need to give orders concerning the bridge under construction and what to do about the pontoon bridge. I also need to pursue the Chinese and rescue their hostage.' He reaches at least one conclusion. "Rasputin, I'll deal with matters here. I want you to go to the castle in the Dark Forest and inquire how things are there. Before you do that, though, take a swing around Blindhouse Wood and see where the reinforcements from the south are. Off you go, lad. Hurry back, my good fellow. We need to organize the rescue of King Haymun before it's too late."

The Wizard sighs. 'I'm beginning to feel a little like Wellington making deployments before Waterloo and trying to find out where Blucher got to. Great minds think alike! I need to speak with Corporal Pimples, but before that, I'm having a bath and some breakfast. Life is hard for a leader.'

Searching for King Haymun

Rasputin has made his sweep of Blindhouse Wood and checked on things at Fyrdwald's Castle in the Dark Forest. He comes back to the Wizard as fast as he can fly. The raven skids to a halt after a steep landing.

The Wizard is having breakfast on the patio outside the dining room of his apartments. He wipes his lips with his napkin and raises his bushy eyebrows in an unspoken question.

"Boss, the news is not good. The castle in the Dark Forest no longer has a cavalry. Well, it has cavalrymen and lancers, but they don't have any horses. The Chinese took all their horses. At least seventeen of the invaders are invisible. Their horses had no riders that could be seen so the lancers didn't know who they were fighting. Fortunately, there were no casualties. But the cavalrymen are trapped inside the castle. The portcullis of the castle was jammed shut yesterday and can't be raised. If you agree, they will light a fire and burn down the gate so they can get out.

"The Chinese went towards Lyminge Castle about noon yesterday with King Haymun as their prisoner. He was seated in front of the Chinese commander who has ginger hair, long drooping mustaches, and a violent temper. He probably came from Manchuria and has already shown he will stop at nothing. There is little hope in the Dark Forest garrison that the king can be recovered alive.

"Furthermore, the Southern Zone construction troops are just now working their way through Blindhouse Wood. They haven't run into the Chinese ambush yet which they expect to be at the same place they left two days ago. They're moving slowly and with great caution. Most worrisome though, is that there's absolutely no sign of the 750 fighting men from the Brook. I circled as high as possible and could see almost to the fort at the border. But there's no sign of any troops on the road like you expected, boss."

This is where the Wizard excels while lesser commanders crumble. Outnumbered, surrounded by incompetence, entrance to his castle hampered by a destroyed bridge, his troops without officers, the king a captive, and an invisible enemy all around him is bad news from all sides. But the Wizard is unperturbed.

He calmly taps his second boiled egg six times in a circle and taps twice more in the middle. Using the end of his egg spoon, he skillfully removes the brown shell with a spiral motion. Tapping his egg spoon into the little mound of salt and pepper beside his eggcup, he slides the condiments off onto the top of the egg. He then scoops the first bite onto his spoon and into his mouth. He smacks his lips, and a crooked smile crosses his face. 'The taste is perfect! There's only one way to cook a boiled egg right, and Mrs. Squidge hasn't yet learned it.'

The cook, hovering in the doorway, sees the smile of satisfaction. He heaves a sigh of relief and mops his brow. The waiter brings more marmalade and buttered toast. Rasputin waits for orders.

"Rasputin, I think we may have lost King Haymun, possibly for good. However, we must make every attempt to save him. He has been a loyal ally." The Wizard places little value on any loyalty the king may have to him. 'Loyalty is a sign of weakness, but it sounds good to subordinates.' "We have at least one advantage, my good fellow. Perhaps we can't see the Chinese, but I doubt very much whether they can fly. Let's be on our way. The castle in the Dark Forest had better be our first stop. They seem to need some instruction."

The Wizard considers what kind of bird he should be. 'I rather enjoyed being a cormorant. However, my previous thought that cormorants have the capacity to understand Chinese from long association with fishermen doesn't seem to be the case. However, I do like the long straight beak with the curved bird-of-prey hook at the end. That seems to offer the best of both worlds to a hungry bird.' Without further thought, he becomes a cormorant once again.

After a period of steady flying, the cormorant and the raven reach the Dark Forest castle. They approach the well-groomed green lawn of the inner courtyard. It's kept closely cut, manicured to the same level of perfection as that on Plymouth Hoe where Sir Francis Drake casually played bowls while the Spanish Armada approached. The castle commander and his officers play bowls on the castle lawn in their leisure time and sometimes even when they're on duty. The two birds drift down into the courtyard. No game is being played today, so no time is wasted in awkward questioning and explanations.

The Wizard is at once himself again. He was unable to find a suitable location on his sore head for his hat to rest, so he left it behind. His grey hair, singed by the parsnip lamp, was trimmed by the court barber and is shorter than usual by quite a bit. Other than that, he is as crisp, as cutting, and as sure of himself as ever. 'My bump obviously doesn't affect the thinking part of my brain. I'm relieved about that.'

The officers come running. The commandant isn't a man of action. He doesn't need to be. He's a distant cousin of King Haymun and bears an unfortunate resemblance to him.

The Wizard doesn't waste time on formalities. He gets right to the point. "There will be no fire set to burn down the gate. You fools! Fires get out of control. Bring all the sawyers and carpenters, and have them break down the gate doors. Get the lancers fully armed. They must be ready to move off on foot to rescue the king the moment I return. If the portcullis gateway hasn't opened up, they will be dropped by ropes over the castle walls. There is to be no delay once I return with news of the whereabouts of the kidnap party and their captive. They will be moving out in double-quick time."

The Wizard collects all the information about what happened yesterday. 'Now I know what I'm looking for — four visible horsemen, one of them the goblin king, and seventeen invisible Chinese riding horses bareback. I must be off at once.' The commander is caught by surprise as he repeats a series of saluting and "Yes Sir" when the Wizard suddenly disappears. He stares in amazement at the ugly looking, duck-like creature with a vicious hooked beak now sitting in the spot where the Wizard was standing.

The birds search in vain. They fly over the estate at Up-Horton and then swing down to ask a few questions. "Did you see a group of Chinese horsemen holding your king captive?"

The occupants haven't seen anything out of the ordinary. "No, we haven't seen any Chinese. No strangers at all have passed through here. They must have taken a different path." The resident commandant doesn't mention the seven stray horses that were rounded up, stabled, and groomed during the past twenty-four hours. He's always been short of horses while the castle in the Dark Forest has always had more horses than it needs.

It's after lunchtime as they fly on to Lyminge Castle. That's the Wizard's old home. These days it's only used when the Wizard or King Haymun is on tour in the northern provinces.

"Rasputin, my lad, we're going to stop for a bite to eat. The meager staff at the castle doesn't know how to prepare a proper meal. I'll feast on the fish in the stream instead."

At the castle, the commander is unhappy that the glory days of Lyminge Castle have passed south to Gyminge. He certainly has no intention of mentioning that ten of the horses in his stable were rounded up yesterday as strays. He can tell from their harnesses that they had once been stabled elsewhere in the kingdom. He is always short of good horses too.

The Wizard reaches a conclusion that is totally inaccurate. "Rasputin, my lad, it's obvious the Chinese captors escaped across the border. They had to use the same magic they used to enter the kingdom in the first place. It means that they have taken their hostage with them. Ah, well! I'll order two, no, three days of state mourning for the monarch."

He searches his mind for adjectives to describe the dead or ex-king without being too extravagant. 'Loyal, devoted, diligent, painstaking, intelligent, curious, capable. Yes, a few of those words thrown in to any speech would do nicely. It will be like raisins in porridge or Yorkshire pudding. Who would be the most suitable man to appoint as a replacement? Or should I leave the post unfilled and assume that role myself?' A slow smile, almost a sneer, creeps across his face.

Rasputin notices and wonders what the Wizard is thinking now. 'It's probably big trouble for someone.' The Wizard makes a decision. "Rasputin, my lad, we'll not bother to fly back by the Dark Forest. Let them remain on continual alert waiting for my return. It will serve them right for lowering the portcullis in the first place and getting it jammed. They need to be more careful. Instead, we'll fly straight back to Goblin Castle."

As soon as the lake comes into sight, the cormorant swoops low over its surface. Sticking his legs out straight in front, he turns his webbed feet at right angles. As he hits the water, there are dazzling rainbows in the sheets of water. He comes to a halt by the walls of his castle. For him, it is Joy, pure joy!

Rasputin swerves up sharply to avoid a collision with the castle wall and lands where his nest used to be before the Chinese kicked it into the lake.

The Castle Bridge

The sergeant major and Corporal Pimples are busy on the bridge trestle.

The job of the quartermaster sergeant is to take care of the castle and its various occupants. Just now, Quartz is supervising the reconstruction of Rasputin's home on the slab next to the chimney.

The Wizard doesn't stop to ask about progress. It's been a long day, so it's well into dinner time, and he goes straight to his apartment. Having relaxed with a second cup of tea after a generous helping of glorious Butterscotch and Banana Trifle with Madeira, the Wizard goes out to see Rasputin. "Go check events at Blindhouse Wood again. Before you come back, fly really high once more and see if there's any sign yet of the goblins from the Brook."

The raven is getting tired; he's done a lot of flying recently, but he will do as his master wishes.

The Wizard reassures himself. "I have restored calm to the kingdom. The situation just required some clear leadership, and I have provided it. It now remains to issue some clear instructions. As yet there's no news of the Chinese enemy. Provided there's been no encounter in Blindhouse Wood, it would appear they have fled for their lives. In face of the resolute defense by the forces I left behind, whoever they were and however many, they have turned tail and run."

There are a couple of things that puzzle him, however. "I still need to determine the reason why they invaded my kingdom. Has there been a revolution in China? They seem to keep having revolutions there. Were they searching for a king to lead them and think that Haymun will fill the bill? Well, if so, they've made a bad mistake! The man is a fool!"

He lets out a sigh. "There are still some possible problems to resolve. Why have the Brook troops failed to show up? Has there been a mutiny? It will be wise to return there as soon as possible and show them that behind the offered lollipop of a gentle leader is a mailed fist. I'll change the rebels into cockroaches and teach them a lesson they won't forget!"

The Wizard turns his attention to matters that need to be dealt with before he goes back to the Brook. "I need to think about the cavalry. It appears they have no horses." He calls for the sergeant stable master. "How many horses does the cavalry need, allowing for spares?"

The stable master thinks of the number of horses he can comfortably stable and guesses forty. He says, "Eighty."

"Then take a squad of men and requisition eighty stallions from the local population. Pay well for them. Otherwise, there'll be unrest. In the future, the cavalry will breed its own horses. Forty breeding mares should see to the future, one foal per mare each year. Pay well for them also. Be on your way."

One more thing requires his attention. "What type of bridge do we need? Pontoon or drawbridge? I have enjoyed the pontoon bridge in the past. After all, it was my idea. Generally, it has worked well. However, problems with pontoons are always possible. They tend to sink when they get leaks. It's what eventually happens to most heavy things that float."

The Wizard is meeting Corporal Pimples for the first time. The young man with the thick spectacles is keen and persuasive. He lays his drawings out on the table and reports, "I have a working model prepared by the cook. Permission requested to demonstrate it, sir. It's in the next room."

The Wizard nods and follows the bridge designer who points proudly to the model. It was his daring idea to demonstrate the drawbridge by using cake, marzipan and icing sugar. It has to be handled with great care.

The cook is also present in case repairs happen to be needed. He sneaks in a quick word or two of apology. "I only had the morning to work on it, so it isn't up to my usual high standards. The icing wasn't quite firm enough yet. To add to its setting power, I added some plaster of Paris. That will completely spoil its taste, so it won't be wise to nibble any of the icing that may happen to break off. I prepared a side dish of mint chocolate fudge to snack on."

The pastry cook is a master chef who specializes in decorating cakes for special occasions such as weddings and funerals. Fortunately, he had a lemon and walnut cake already prepared. It was waiting for decoration to celebrate the funeral of the milkman's mother-in-law. He plans to use a flag of farewell or a broken heart dripping blood-red drops that's pierced by a golden arrow. He expects a large, sympathetic gathering for the funeral. They will have to put off that sad occasion until he can get another cake made. Or, until after the demonstration is over and he's scraped the base cake clean of plaster of Paris. He imagines his double-drawbridge in icing sugar as a design that could, with suitable words added, be used for all occasions — birthdays, funerals, births, or weddings.

The four ropes of the drawbridge are twisted white thread glued and dipped in icing. Beyond the fastening staples that hold them in position, the coils hang loose from the towers. These will demonstrate how the bridge is lifted. Each of the two supporting towers is wood coated with the hardened sugary goo. One of the towers rests on the top of the castle wall above the gate. The tower outside the guardhouse stands free.

While the master chef concentrated on creating his masterpiece, an apprentice cook was given the task of the wall and gates. He has done his best, but he'll never make master baker. The lake is also sugar icing in the proper shade of blue. The first choice of mirrored glass was rejected by Pimples as giving the wrong kind of reflection. The free ends of the drawbridge rest on a single moored pontoon at the center of the bridge. This will relieve the load on the cables when it's lowered to take foot and cart traffic.

The hinges on which each drawbridge rotates are simple, flat hinges painted white. They are glued to the thin, flat wooden bridge boards that the carpenters provided in a hurry. They are also coated with the quick drying icing. Any cracks that occurred in the icing were painted over, and now there are no signs of them.

Pimples is very intent. "Sir, will you slowly pull up the drawbridge at the castle gate while the chef pulls it up on the guardhouse side?" The sergeant major would like to be pulling up something too, but there are no more bridges. Corporal Pimples bends at the knees, and at eye level, ensures the two little boards are rising together. Slowly, the boards lift from horizontal to vertical. The pontoon floats in the lake free and clear.

"Now, lower the guardhouse drawbridge," orders Pimples. The chef slowly lowers his bridge until it rests on the pontoon once again.

"You can see, sir, that archers, spearmen, and stone throwers in the castle can easily deal with any enemy on the bridge. Your own bridge, sir, blocks any attack on the portcullis or the gate."

The Wizard is convinced, but doesn't let on. "Suppose the cable snaps or jams. What then?"

"The ropes, sir, will be especially woven and twisted. They will be capable of carrying three times any weight they are likely to encounter. There will be spare ropes available in storage at both ends of the bridge. They can be more easily replaced than a pontoon that might be sunk."

"Very well, you may proceed, Sergeant Pimples." The Wizard has just promoted the young corporal and is smiling. 'At last I have found someone else besides myself who thinks. This young man can go a long way, if his eyesight holds out.'

Back to the Brook

On his visit to Blindhouse Wood Rasputin discovers that the goblins are on their hands and knees crawling north along the main trail. It isn't a rapid crawl that an athlete might use, but a slow crawl at the speed of a baby on the first or second day he learned to move on all fours. The men have little concern about making rapid progress. Somehow, they feel that they may avoid being seen by the Chinese if they crawl on their hands and knees. At this point they would like Dr. Tyfuss to come see to their assorted bumps and bruises and torn flesh.

The watching bird realizes, "At this speed, it's going to take weeks for them to reach the castle! Although progress is slow, I'll let the

Wizard make any changes and give the orders necessary to speed things up."

As he flies high, he still sees no sign in the distant south of the goblins from the Brook. When Rasputin informs his master, the Wizard realizes he needs to take immediate action both in Blindhouse Wood and back on the Brook as well.

He tells the sergeant major, "I expect to see both trestles erected and ready for load testing when I return. I will personally arrange the refloating of the middle pontoon at that time." He doesn't explain when that will be or how the refloating will be done. He smiles his twisted smile. 'A little uncertainty is good for the souls of sergeants and sergeants major. Besides, I don't know or have any idea when I might return. There's still a good chance of obtaining the Book of Lore when I return to the Brook. I'm not anxious to give up the search while that chance remains.'

The Wizard has another thought. 'I wonder whether the number of Chinese invaders may have been somewhat exaggerated? If I ignore the invisible Chinamen who may or may not exist, I am only dealing with three or four men who were actually seen. The only evidence they left behind was four chopsticks found in the dungeons, and I can't understand the quartermaster's explanation of how they got there. Using just one chopstick each only accounts for four men. However, perhaps the Chinese are accustomed to sharing chopsticks or even using both ends at the same time.

'I need to find out where the Brook goblins are. I'm beginning to wonder, given these unclear circumstances, where I really want my men to be. Do I want them in Gyminge defending the castle and the border entrance to Gyminge against hordes of invisible Chinamen who may or may not exist? Or do I want them back on the Brook? If I'm going to block the toad tunnel, why have a checkpoint there to intercept toads who won't be able to get through anyway? But next February, the toads will start coming again. I'll need to have things sorted out well before then, come-what-may.'

"Come, Rasputin. It's time for the pair of us to be on our way back. This time, I'll be a raven too, and we can fly together. We'll call in at

Blindhouse Wood on the way. It may take some time to sort out what's going on there.

The weary, knee-sore goblins are surprised to look up and see their leader blocking their path. They stand up at attention.

The Wizard is exasperated. "What do you men think you're doing? Who's in charge here?"

There's no one in charge. All eyes are downcast, and heads shake from side to side in despair.

Griswold wastes no more time on them. "Well, be on your way. On the double! No more dillydallying. The way to the castle is clear. Get moving!"

He turns to Rasputin. "Before I leave for another experience of Mrs. Squidge's hospitality, I'll have a last conference with Dr. Tyfuss."

Arriving at the border fort, both the Wizard and Rasputin are surprised to see the goblin king. "How did you get here? We looked for you all over northern Gyminge and into Lyminge. Is this the way the Chinese escaped?"

Haymun is reluctant to admit he was captured by only three Twith. Dr. Tyfuss has told him the Wizard asked earlier about hordes of invisible Chinese. The goblin king fabricates a king-size lie. "Scores of Chinamen captured me in my bedroom. They forced a toe ring over my toe and banged my toe with a hammer to make it swell. They threw me face down on a horse. Most of the invaders did head north to escape the way they got in. Three of them dropped me here and then swung back and took off again going north."

Griswold is satisfied he'll have no more trouble from the Chinese. "What have you heard from the Brook goblins, Dr. Tyfuss?"

The doctor shakes his head. "They never showed up. I don't know what happened to them."

"Well, I've decided you should not block the tunnel just yet. Hold off on that until I tell you otherwise. Rasputin, my lad, because I'm taking the king back to the Brook with me, we'll have to go through the toad tunnel. I could make an opening for you to fly through, but we'll just go together. Come along, it's late, and Mrs. Squidge will already be in bed."

Squidgy's Boarding House

All the toads on the Brook are gathered on the bog rehearsing for the forthcoming weddings. Though the lyrics are incomplete, the composers have developed a ragtime rhythm. As the rhythm slowly builds, the simultaneous downbeat of toad feet in their hundreds causes the bog to develop movement. The slow sucking sounds of squelching bog and the loud, constant burping of the toads assist each other like echoes.

Mrs. Squidge is unaware of the reason for the noise, but it disturbs her sleep. Vaguely, she wonders, 'Don't toads ever sleep? What is all the racket about? It's enough disturbance to turn the bog into hard coal before it has a chance to even become peat!'

The commotion causes Mrs. Squidge to dream of the late Mr. Squidge. Mr. Squidge isn't really dead, but for Squidgy, he might as well be. She grudgingly admits to herself that he's most likely happy and contented, enjoying working in his new garden full of parsnips and turnips with the girl from the sweetshop. 'Now that he helps run a sweetshop rather than his butcher shop, I suppose that snacks from a box of chocolates must be more satisfying than sausage fried in oil drippings.' It reminds Squidgy that his favorite meal was Toad-in-the-Hole served with roast potatoes, beetroot, and boiled cabbage. She wonders what made him leave.

When Mrs. Squidge dreams about him, they are always bad dreams. In this one, she thinks the heavy beat she hears is him banging nails into an oak log. The nails are bending in the middle because the oak is so hard. 'Serves him right,' Squidgy thinks in her dream. 'I hope he hits his thumb!' Bang-Bang-Bang. Bang-Bang-Bang. As his hammer rings against the metal nails, one by one, each and every nail bends. 'Can't the man see what's happening? Why doesn't he stop? He's not doing any good just bending nails. He must have bent hundreds already. Is he never going to run out of nails?'

Squidgy stirs in her sleep and then slowly opens her eyes. The banging continues. "Where am I?" She realizes she is in her bed.

"Alright, alright, I'm coming, I'm coming!" She struggles out from under the bedclothes and stands up. As she pulls her dressing gown around her, she slides her feet into her slippers. After putting on her sleeping cap to cover her curlers, she lights the candle sitting on her nightstand. Although she has electricity, it's a habit she brought with her from Cornwall. She likes to take a candle when she goes up to bed and light another when she gets up. She goes to see who on earth is banging on her door at this time of night.

Just now she finds herself wishing that the person knocking would be Signor Antonio Raymondo. "He has such charming manners and loves his mother very much. That's such a good trait in a man. Maybe he's come for some more yeast buns. He seemed to enjoy the last ones so much." An uneasy thought crosses her mind as she goes downstairs. "Oh, dear. Those were from the same batch that changed Moley. Perhaps the signor was also changed in some way. He could be a different person altogether than the one I remember."

She opens the door and sees that it's the Wizard. He is alone. She's surprised. "There's no one with you?"

Griswold is annoyed. 'Finally! She was a long time coming. I've been banging forever trying to wake her up. She must sleep like a log. Even harder, like two logs!' However, he merely replies, "Yes. My tiny friend, King Haymun, has gone directly to Mole Hall. He fears he might be trodden underfoot in your busy household. Besides, I have instructed him to consult with his garrison officers and find out why they didn't follow my orders to come to Gyminge. I arranged all the details of the operation myself, so nothing should have gone wrong. I'll visit there in the morning and will be looking for explanations.

"Rasputin is in the ash tree, trying to catch up on his sleep. He's avoiding the titchy teros on the ridge of the cottage roof who are awake and restless."

Squidgy gushes, even though she's a little disappointed. "Oh, what a delightful surprise, my dear Griswold. You're back earlier than I expected. Oh, do come in. Would you like something to eat?"

"Well, a cup of hot cocoa would go down well, my dear. Thank you."

Although it's midsummer, there's a slight chill in the air. Squidgy kindles a fire on the hearth. As the wood crackles and blazes, she heads into the kitchen to make cocoa and arrange cookies on a plate. To please the Wizard, she loads it with shortbread and Jaffa cakes.

The Wizard sets aside recent reverses as a good general should and thinks positively about the future. He sits in the larger rocking chair by the fire drinking his cocoa. Slipping off his shoes, he warms his toes before the fire. He wiggles his toes and reflects, 'There are benefits to having holes in your socks. And since I would prefer any darns in my socks to match the original color rather than contrast, I'll not allow Mrs. Squidge to darn the holes in these. She seems to think that using bright yellow yarn to darn a black sock is somehow acceptable.'

The fire not only warms the Wizard, but creates a burning enthusiasm to share his thoughts. He likes to have a silent listener, no interruptions, just a listener, as he outlines his schemes. Squidgy is a good listener. She knows what the Wizard needs and supplies it. Mostly, it's silence with an occasional exclamation of awe and surprise.

The Wizard explains his brilliant new idea to Mrs. Squidge. "I've decided to have a huge sports festival called "Games on the Brook". There will be both team competitions and individual competitions — high jumps, races, tug-of-war, vaulting, steeple-chasing, long-distance runs, relays, weightlifting, the discus, and the javelin. The whole lot. I may even compete myself. I was quite a runner in my youth, you know. No Beyonders will be invited. They are too big, and they leave litter everywhere, filthy creatures. We can invite the animals, toads and frogs, maybe a few rabbits and so on. We could even have foxes and badgers if we could arrange a truce between them, but nothing bigger. No bird races either. They won't cooperate with us, so we won't invite them. We'll have a ceasefire for the day. You know, my dear lady, all sweetness and light." He leers wickedly at the woman, then winks, and Squidgy snickers in agreement.

"We'll throw down a challenge to the Twith. Seven of our goblins, I'll be their captain, of course, against the Twith. Get them into a tug-of-war, and hey, presto! We'll have them all. We'll have to make sure the judges are on our side, of course. The starters will need to be with us too. That won't be difficult. Everyone has his price. There'll need to be an organizing committee. Perhaps you could help on that committee, my dear lady. I doubt if they would consider me a resident of the Brook, although I've been here often enough to be counted as an old timer.

"With my organizing abilities behind the scenes, this could be a memorable occasion for the whole community. It would," the Wizard chuckles at the thought, "it would cement the relationships between our two countries. The idea will need some polishing of course, but I, that is, we, could put up some prizes to encourage success. It could also be an occasion for celebrating the completion of the work on your home although I don't think it will be wise to let strangers in to see the extent of the alterations."

The Wizard feels happier as the moments pass. Ideas, ideas, and more ideas pour into his fertile mind. 'Ideas are essential to progress. This is one of my particularly fruitful days of inspired thought. A leader needs that to go along with the humdrum days of detailed planning.'

"You know the saying, 'May the best man win?' Nonsense, that's child's talk, my good lady. There's no fun in that. There has to be room for ingenuity, originality, cunning, and deception. If that fails, there's always bribery and corruption and deliberately maiming the opposition. Good, healthy competition? Foolishness! Success is when the best man doesn't win. What's the point of being a Wizard if my talents aren't used to steer things the way I want them to go?

"To totally succeed though, it will be wise to persuade the Twith that the games are their idea. That way there'll be one hundred percent participation from their side. I'll hide my goblin army behind the paddock hedge. The moment the games start, they will be ready to move against the farmhouse at a moment's notice. Well, what do you think, my dear Mrs. Squidge?"

Mrs. Squidge thinks, 'I'd like to go back to bed and finish my night's rest.'

Over at the farmhouse, gran'ma's dreams are of beautiful brides, handsome grooms, bridesmaids, groomsmen, flower girls, and ring bearers. Visions of sugarplums dance through her head. Well, maybe not sugarplums, but butter mints, cashews, and wedding cakes. Now that she has a double wedding to plan for, the bowls of mints and nuts are overflowing. The punch bowl, too, is foaming over the edge. She stirs restlessly as she envisions the days being marked off the calendar. There are more red checkmarks than days left in her dream. Unexpectedly, cows float across the screen of her mind. It must be the hot cocoa she drank at bedtime.

Cymbeline and Elisheba are dreaming of processing to the byre holding beautiful bouquets of flowers. There are no cows in their dreams though.

Stormy's dreams are filled with organizing events for the Farewell Festival. Many are the same as what the Wizard just outlined to Mrs. Squidge for his "Games on the Brook". Will the Twith end up helping the Wizard fulfill his evil scheme? The Twith are alert and watching for any sign of attack by the Wizard. But will they succumb to his trickery? The clock is ticking for the Return and time is not in their favor.

CPSIA information can be obtained
at www.ICGtesting.com
Printed in the USA
FSHW02n0901210718
50764FS